FUNNY
STORIES

for Geraldine, Joe, Naomi, Eddie, Laura and Issac

KINGFISHER
An imprint of Kingfisher Publications Plc
New Penderel House, 283-288 High Holborn
London WC1V 7HZ
www.kingfisherpub.com

First published by Kingfisher 1988
This edition published by Kingfisher 2005
2 4 6 8 10 9 7 5 3 1

The acknowledgements on page 254 constitute
an extension of this copyright page.

A CIP catalogue record for this book is available from the British Library

ISBN-13: 978 0 7534 1152 0
ISBN-10: 0 7534 1152 0
1TR/THOM/MAR/90NS/F

Printed in India

FUNNY STORIES

CHOSEN BY
MICHAEL ROSEN

ILLUSTRATED BY
TONY BLUNDELL

CONTENTS

NOTHING TO BE AFRAID OF 7
Jan Mark

THE GUEST WHO RAN AWAY 15
Tunisian folktale

STUPID MARCO 17
Jay Williams

THE SQUIRE'S BRIDE 28
Norwegian folktale

THE BARON RIDES OUT 32
Adrian Mitchell (from *The Adventures of Baron Munchausen*)

THE MAULVI AND THE DONKEY 39
Pakistani folktale

ELEPHANT MILK, HIPPOPOTAMUS CHEESE 43
Margaret Mahy

THE TORTOISES' PICNIC 53
English folktale

THE FIRST SCHLEMIEL 55
Isaac Bashevis Singer

SING-SONG TIME 59
Joyce Grenfell

THE STOWAWAYS 64
Roger McGough

THE PUDDING LIKE A NIGHT ON THE SEA 69
Ann Cameron

A FISH OF THE WORLD 75
Terry Jones

THE RAJAH'S EARS 78
Indian folktale retold by Michael Rosen

A GOOD SIXPENN'ORTH 83
Bill Naughton

HAROLD AND BELLA, JAMMY AND ME 92
Robert Leeson

THE JESTER AND THE KING 99
Polish story retold by Michael Rosen

TIMES AREN'T WHAT THEY WERE 103
Karel Čapek

THE ENCHANTED POLLY 109
Catherine Storr

HUDDEN AND DUDDEN AND DONALD O'NEARY 119
Irish folktale

THE GREAT SEA SERPENT
Hans Christian Andersen 127

THE LIZARD LETDOWN
Christine McDonnell 138

HANDSEL AND GRISTLE
Michael Rosen 151

BURGLARS!
Norman Hunter 157

NO MULES
William Papas 165

THE MUSICIANS OF BREMEN
Janosch 169

THE GIRL WHO DIDN'T BELIEVE IN GHOSTS
David Henry Wilson 174

THE STORY-TELLER 180
Saki (H. H. Munro)

THE HOLIDAY 187
George Layton

THE ENCHANTED TOAD 200
Judy Corbalis

THE LITTLE HATCHET STORY 215
Anon *(USA)*

THE PRIVATE LIFE OF MR BIDWELL 219
James Thurber

CRICK, CROCK AND CROOKHANDLE 224
Italo Calvino

BRER RABBIT TRICKS BRER BEAR 227
Julius Lester

BRER WOLF, BRER FOX, AND THE LITTLE RABBITS 229
Julius Lester

THE LOADED DOG 233
Henry Lawson

SNOW-WHITE AND THE SEVEN DWARFS 240
Roald Dahl

THE WORLD IN A WALL 244
Gerald Durrell

THE HOLE 250
Eric Partridge

Acknowledgements 254

NOTHING TO BE AFRAID OF

JAN MARK

"ROBIN WON'T give you any trouble," said Auntie Lynn. "He's very quiet."

Anthea knew how quiet Robin was. At present he was sitting under the table and, until Auntie Lynn mentioned his name, she had forgotten that he was there.

Auntie Lynn put a carrier bag on the armchair.

"There's plenty of clothes, so you won't need to do any washing, and there's a spare pair of pyjamas in case – well, you know. In case . . ."

"Yes," said Mum, firmly. "He'll be all right. I'll ring you tonight and let you know how he's getting along." She looked at the clock. "Now, hadn't *you* better be getting along?"

She saw Auntie Lynn to the front door and Anthea heard them saying good-bye to each other. Mum almost told Auntie Lynn to stop worrying and have a good time, which would have been a mistake because Auntie Lynn was going up North to a funeral.

Auntie Lynn was not really an Aunt, but she had once been at school with Anthea's mum, and she was the kind of person who couldn't manage without a handle to her name; so Robin was not Anthea's cousin. Robin was not anything much, except four years old, and he looked a lot younger; probably because nothing ever happened to him. Auntie

Lynn kept no pets that might give Robin germs, and never bought him toys that had sharp corners to dent him or wheels that could be swallowed. He wore balaclava helmets and bobble hats in winter to protect his tender ears, and a knitted vest under his shirt in summer in case he overheated himself and caught a chill from his own sweat.

"Perspiration," said Auntie Lynn.

His face was as pale and flat as a saucer of milk, and his eyes floated in it like drops of cod-liver oil. This was not so surprising as he was full to the back teeth with cod-liver oil; also with extract of malt, concentrated orange juice and calves-foot jelly. When you picked him up you expected him to squelch, like a hot-water bottle full of half-set custard.

Anthea lifted the tablecloth and looked at him.

"Hello, Robin."

Robin stared at her with his flat eyes and went back to sucking his woolly doggy that had flat eyes also, of sewn-on felt, because glass ones might find their way into Robin's appendix and cause damage. Anthea wondered how long it would be before he noticed that his mother had gone. Probably he wouldn't, any more than he would notice when she came back.

Mum closed the front door and joined Anthea in looking under the table at Robin. Robin's mouth turned down at the corners, and Anthea hoped he would cry so that they could cuddle him. It seemed impolite to cuddle him before he needed it. Anthea was afraid to go any closer.

"What a little troll," said Mum, sadly, lowering the tablecloth. "I suppose he'll come out when he's hungry."

Anthea doubted it.

Robin didn't want any lunch or any tea.

"Do you think he's pining?" said Mum. Anthea did not. Anthea had a nasty suspicion that he was like this all the time. He went to bed without making a fuss and fell asleep before the light was out, as if he were too bored to stay awake. Anthea left her bedroom door open, hoping that he would have a nightmare so that she could go in and comfort him, but Robin slept all night without a squeak, and woke in the morning as flat-faced as before. Wall-eyed Doggy looked more excitable than Robin did.

"If only we had a proper garden," said Mum, as Robin went under the table again, leaving his breakfast eggs scattered round the plate. "He might run about."

Anthea thought that this was unlikely, and in any case they didn't have a proper garden, only a yard at the back and a stony strip in front, without a fence.

"Can I take him to the park?" said Anthea.

Mum looked doubtful. "Do you think he wants to go?"

"No," said Anthea, peering under the tablecloth. "I don't think he wants to do anything, but he can't sit there all day."

"I bet he can," said Mum. "Still, I don't think he should. All right, take him to the park, but keep quiet about it. I don't suppose Lynn thinks you're safe in traffic."

"He might tell her."

"Can he talk?"

Robin, still clutching wall-eyed Doggy, plodded beside her all the way to the park, without once trying to jam his head between the library railings or get run over by a bus.

"Hold my hand, Robin," Anthea said as they left the house, and he clung to her like a lamprey.

The park was not really a park at all; it was a garden. It did not even pretend to be a park and the notice by the gate said KING STREET GARDENS, in case anyone tried to use it as a park. The grass was as green and as flat as the front-room carpet, but the front-room carpet had a path worn across it from the door to the fireplace, and here there were more notices that said KEEP OFF THE GRASS, so that the gritty white paths went obediently round the edge, under the orderly trees that stood in a row like the queue outside a fish shop. There were bushes in each corner and one shelter with a bench in it. Here and there brown holes in the grass, full of raked earth, waited for next year's flowers, but there were no flowers now, and the bench had been taken out of the shelter because the shelter was supposed to be a summer-house, and you couldn't have people using a summer-house in winter.

Robin stood by the gates and gaped, with Doggy depending limply from his mouth where he held it by one ear, between his teeth. Anthea decided that if they met anyone she knew, she would explain that Robin was only two, but very big for his age.

"Do you want to run, Robin?"

Robin shook his head.

"There's nothing to be afraid of. You can go all the way round, if you like, but you mustn't walk on the grass or pick things."

Robin nodded. It was the kind of place that he understood.

Anthea sighed. "Well, let's walk round, then."

They set off. At each corner, where the bushes were, the path diverged. One part went in front of the bushes, one part round the back of them. On the first circuit Robin stumped glumly beside Anthea in front of the bushes. The second time round she felt a very faint tug at her hand. Robin wanted to go his own way.

This called for a celebration. Robin could think. Anthea crouched down on the path until they were at the same level.

"You want to walk round the back of the bushes, Robin?"

"Yiss," said Robin.

Robin could *talk*.

"All right, but listen." She lowered her voice to a whisper. "You must be very careful. That path is called Leopard Walk. Do you know what a leopard is?"

"Yiss."

"There are two leopards down there. They live in the bushes. One is a good leopard and the other's a bad leopard. The good leopard has black spots. The bad leopard has red spots. If you see the bad leopard you must say, 'Die leopard die or I'll kick you in the eye,' and run like anything. Do you understand?"

Robin tugged again.

"Oh no," said Anthea. "I'm going *this* way. If you want to go down Leopard Walk, you'll have to go on your own. I'll meet you at the other end. Remember, if it's got red spots, run like mad."

Robin trotted away. The bushes were just high enough to hide him, but Anthea could see the bobble on his hat doddering along. Suddenly the bobble gathered speed and Anthea had to run to reach the end of the bushes first.

"Did you see the bad leopard?"

"No," said Robin, but he didn't look too sure.

"Why were you running, then?"

"I just wanted to."

"You've dropped Doggy," said Anthea. Doggy lay on the path with his legs in the air, halfway down Leopard Walk.

"You get him," said Robin.

"No, *you* get him," said Anthea. "I'll wait here." Robin moved off, reluctantly. She waited until he had recovered Doggy and then shouted, "I can see the bad leopard in the bushes!" Robin raced back to safety. "Did you say, 'Die leopard die or I'll kick you in the eye'?" Anthea demanded.

"No," Robin said, guiltily.

"Then he'll *kill* us," said Anthea. "Come on, run. We've got to get to that tree. He can't hurt us once we're under that tree."

They stopped running under the twisted boughs of a weeping ash. "This is a python tree," said Anthea. "Look, you can see the python wound round the trunk."

"What's a python?" said Robin, backing off.

"Oh, it's just a big snake that squeezes people to death," said Anthea. "A python could easily eat a leopard. That's why leopards won't walk under this tree, you see, Robin."

Robin looked up. "Could it eat us?"

"Yes, but it won't if we walk on our heels." They walked on their heels to the next corner.

"Are there leopards down there?"

"No, but we must never go down there anyway. That's Poison Alley. All the trees are poisonous. They drip poison. If one bit of poison fell on your head, you'd die."

"I've got my hat on," said Robin, touching the bobble to make sure.

"It would burn right through your hat," Anthea assured him. "Right into your brains. *Fzzzzzzz.*"

They by-passed Poison Alley and walked on over the manhole cover that clanked.

"What's that?"

"That's the Fever Pit. If anyone lifts that manhole cover, they get a terrible disease. There's this terrible disease down there, Robin, and if the lid comes off, the disease will get out and people will die. I should think there's enough disease down there to kill everybody in this town. It's ever so loose, look."

"Don't lift it! Don't lift it!" Robin screamed, and ran to the shelter for safety.

"Don't go in there," yelled Anthea. "That's where the Greasy Witch lives." Robin bounced out of the shelter as though he were on elastic.

"Where's the Greasy Witch?"

"Oh, you can't see her," said Anthea, "but you can tell where she is because she smells so horrible. I think she must be somewhere about. Can't you smell her now?"

Robin sniffed the air and clasped Doggy more tightly.

"And she leaves oily marks wherever she goes. Look, you can see them on the wall."

Robin looked at the wall. Someone had been very busy, if not the Greasy Witch. Anthea was glad on the whole that Robin could not read.

"The smell's getting worse, isn't it, Robin? I think we'd better go down here and then she won't find us."

"She'll see us."

"No, she won't. She can't see with her eyes because they're full of grease. She sees with her ears, but I expect they're all waxy. She's a filthy old witch, really."

They slipped down a secret-looking path that went round the back of the shelter.

"Is the Greasy Witch down here?" said Robin, fearfully.

"I don't know," said Anthea. "Let's investigate." They tiptoed round the side of the shelter. The path was damp and slippery. "Filthy old witch. She's certainly *been* here," said Anthea. "I think she's gone now. I'll just have a look."

She craned her neck round the corner of the shelter. There was a sort of glade in the bushes, and in the middle was a stand-pipe, with a tap on top. The pipe was lagged with canvas, like a scaly skin.

"Frightful Corner," said Anthea. Robin put his cautious head round the edge of the shelter.

"What's that?"

Anthea wondered if it could be a dragon, up on the tip of its tail and ready to strike, but on the other side of the bushes was the brick back wall of the King Street Public Conveniences, and at that moment she heard the unmistakable sound of a cistern flushing.

"It's a Lavatory Demon," she said. "Quick! We've got to get away before the water stops, or he'll have us."

They ran all the way to the gates, where they could see the church clock, and it was almost time for lunch.

Auntie Lynn fetched Robin home next morning, and three days later she was back again, striding up the path like a warrior queen going into battle, with Robin dangling from her hand, and Doggy dangling from Robin's hand.

Mum took her into the front room, closing the door. Anthea sat on the stairs and listened. Auntie Lynn was in full throat and furious, so it was easy enough to hear what she had to say.

"I want a word with that young lady," said Auntie Lynn. "And I want to know what she's been telling him." Her voice dropped, and Anthea could hear only certain fateful words: "Leopards . . . poison trees . . . snakes . . . diseases!"

Mum said something very quietly that Anthea did not hear, and then Auntie Lynn turned up the volume once more.

"Won't go to bed unless I leave the door open . . . wants the light on . . . up and down to him all night . . . won't go to the bathroom on his own. He says the – the –," she hesitated, "the *toilet* demons will get him. He nearly broke his neck running downstairs this morning."

Mum spoke again, but Auntie Lynn cut in like a band-saw.

"Frightened out of his wits! He follows me everywhere."

The door opened slightly, and Anthea got ready to bolt, but it was Robin who came out, with his thumb in his mouth and circles round his eyes. Under his arm was soggy Doggy, ears chewed to nervous rags.

Robin looked up at Anthea through the bannisters.

"Let's go to the park," he said.

THE GUEST WHO RAN AWAY

TUNISIAN FOLKTALE

A WEARY TRAVELLER stopped at a Bedouin's tent and asked for shelter for the night. Without delay the man killed a couple of chickens and handed them to his wife to stew for their guest's supper.

As the woman stirred the meat in her copper cooking pot, she smelled the rich steam and could not resist tasting a piece to see if it was soft. But mouthful followed mouthful, and soon nothing was left of the two birds but one neck. This she gave to her little son to nibble. The boy found it so tasty that he whined, "Give me some, Mother, give me some!" The woman slapped the little boy and scolded him: "It's a shameful habit your father taught you; enough of it, I tell you!"

On the other side of the woven hanging which screened the women's part of the tent from the rest, the traveller overheard this. "What habit has his father taught your child?" he asked curiously. "Oh," said the woman, "whenever a guest arrives at our tent, he cuts off his ears and roasts them over the fire for my son to eat." Making not a sound, the traveller picked up his shoes and fled.

"What's the matter with our guest? Why has he left in such a hurry?" asked the Bedouin, entering the tent soon after. "A fine guest indeed!" exclaimed his wife. "He snatched the chickens out of my pot and ran away!" Hitching up his robes, the Bedouin gave chase, shouting, "Let me have one, at least; you may keep the other!" But his guest only ran faster.

STUPID MARCO

JAY WILLIAMS

THE YOUNGEST SON of the King of Lirripipe was called Marco. That is, he was called Marco – or Your Highness – in public. But among themselves, people spoke of him as 'Poor dear Marco', or 'Alas, poor Marco', or just sighed and rolled their eyes. This was because, although he was cheerful and good-hearted and handsome, he was not bright enough to tell his right hand from his left.

He was not exactly stupid. But then, neither was he exactly as brilliant as a prince ought to be. His two older brothers quickly passed all their classes in government, politics, courtly bowing, economics, arithmetic, and science. But Marco looked out the window and smiled and hummed and made up poetry. It wasn't bad poetry, but on every one of his classroom papers his instructor sadly wrote, *Failed*.

However, Marco had three great accomplishments. In the first place, he was so charming and pleasant a person that no one could help liking him and wanting to help him. Secondly, he could whistle very loudly between his fingers. And thirdly, he knew an infallible cure for hiccups.

In consequence, people found excuses for him. Nobody minded very much his being a little slow-witted, and he was popular everywhere in the kingdom.

One day, his father called Marco into the throne room.

"My dear boy," he said, "the time has come for you to

undertake your Quest. As you know, it is the custom in Lirripipe for every young prince, when he has finished his schooling, to go forth and rescue a princess for his bride. Your two older brothers have successfully done so. Now it is your turn."

"Yes, Father," said Marco. "My turn for what?"

The king sighed and patiently repeated what he had said. "I am going to make it easy for you," he went on.

"There is a very nice princess named Aurelia, who is being held prisoner in a tower not far from here. I have written instructions for rescuing her on this piece of paper. You will set out tomorrow morning early and go three miles to the south. When you come to the fork in the road, turn left and continue until you come to the tower. Then follow the instructions."

"Certainly, Father," said Marco. "But how will I know which way is left?"

"I have thought of that, too," said the king, taking up the golden pen and inkwell which stood beside his throne.

The following morning, Marco set out. Mounted on his fine black steed with his sword by his side he looked handsomer than ever. And on the backs of his hands were written the words *right* and *left*.

His mother kissed him good-bye and then stood back to wave. "Oh, dear, I hope he can stay out of trouble," she murmured to the king.

"Well, my love," said the king, "he does have certain accomplishments. He is so amiable and attractive that I am sure he will find people to help him wherever he goes. And as a last resort, he can cure someone's hiccups, or whistle."

Off went Marco. For the first mile, he rode merrily enough. Then it began to rain. Down it came, until the feather on his hat was bent, and his clothes were drenched. Of course, he had forgotten his raincoat. He kept up his spirits, however, by singing songs to himself, and at last he came to the fork in the road.

He looked down at his hands. But on the back of each

hand there was only a blue smear. The rain had washed away the ink.

"I'll just have to make a guess," said Marco. And he took the road to the right.

He travelled on and on. The rain stopped, the sun came out and warmed and dried him. Mile after mile he travelled, for many days. At last, one day after he had ridden to the top of a hill, he saw spread out below him a glittering city. He rode down to it and entered the gates.

In the centre of the city was an elegant castle. In the downstairs window of one of its towers a maiden sat with her chin on her hand, staring into space. Her smooth brown hair hung in long braids tied with golden bows, and her eyes were the colour of forget-me-nots.

Marco took off his hat. "Good morning!" he said. "Are you the Princess Aurelia?"

The girl yawned. "Never heard of her," she said.

Marco shook his head. "Ah, well, I've done it again," said he. "You see, I have to rescue Princess Aurelia. My father said she was in a tower not far from our kingdom, but I've travelled for miles and miles. I must have taken the wrong road. I *thought* it seemed rather a long way. I'm afraid," he finished with an engaging grin, "I'm not very smart. I can't even tell my right hand from my left."

The girl stopped yawning and looked at him more closely. Then she smiled in return, "My dear," she said, "you aren't fit to be out alone. You need someone to look after you. I'd better go along with you and help you find this princess."

"That would be marvellous," said Marco. "But I haven't the faintest idea where she is."

"Well," said the girl, "my father has a magical parrot which can answer any question put to it. If you'll wait a moment, I'll get the bird, and we'll see if we can locate her."

She helped Marco climb in through the window. "My name," she said, "is Sylvia."

Marco introduced himself. Then Sylvia went off and

fetched the parrot. It was made all of ivory, with emerald eyes, and it sat on a perch of gold.

Sylvia asked, "Where is the Princess Aurelia?"

The parrot whirred and ticked. Then it said, "She is shut up in the Green Glass Tower among the hills of Gargovir."

"Ah," said Sylvia. "And how do we get there from here?"

Again, the parrot ticked and whirred. "Only one person can tell you how to reach the Green Glass Tower," it croaked. "A maiden named Roseanne who lives in the village of Dwindle."

"Good," said Sylvia. "I know where Dwindle is, at any rate. We'll leave at once."

They set out together, Sylvia on a milk-white horse. The way was shortened by Marco, who told stories and sang songs and recited his verses. By the time they got to Dwindle, Sylvia remarked thoughtfully, "I'm not sure it matters all that much, knowing your right hand from your left."

A friendly innkeeper showed them the house where the maiden, Roseanne, lived. "Don't bother knocking," he said, "because she never answers. Just go right in – if you can get the door open," he added, rather mysteriously.

They tied up their horses outside the cottage. It was a pretty place, thatched with straw and covered with honeysuckle which perfumed the air. They pushed at the door and after a struggle got it open. Then they saw why it had been so difficult. The floor was covered with gold pieces which had piled up against the door like a drift of yellow snow.

A girl was washing dishes with her back to the door. She was humming and making such a clatter in the sink that she hadn't heard Marco and Sylvia enter.

Marco cleared his throat and said, "I beg your pardon."

The girl turned round. "Oh! You startled me," she exclaimed.

Four bright gold pieces fell from her mouth and clinked to the floor.

The girl clapped her hand to her forehead and said, "Drat!"

Another gold piece dropped from her lips. She took down a large pad that hung on the wall and began writing busily on it. Marco and Sylvia came and looked curiously over her shoulders.

"I am Roseanne. Welcome," the girl wrote. "As you see, I have something of a problem. Some time ago, I saved the life of the good fairy, Melynda. As a reward, she said to me, 'My child, since you are poor but kind, a gold piece shall fall from your mouth with every word you speak.' "

"Heavens!" said Sylvia. "Can't you make her change her mind?"

"I don't know how to find her," Roseanne wrote, mournfully. Then she added, as an afterthought, "I'm sorry about the floor. I had some friends in for a party last night, and I haven't had a chance to sweep up yet."

"I do wish I could help you somehow," Marco said, earnestly. "I don't know any magic, but I do know an infallible cure for hiccups. Would you say that what you have is a kind of hiccups?"

"It wouldn't hurt to try," Roseanne said, clasping her hands. Five more gold pieces went jingling down to join the rest.

"Very well," said Marco. "You must put your head in a

large paper bag. Hold your breath while I count ten, and then breathe in and out through your mouth ten times."

Roseanne got out a paper bag and did as he ordered. When at last she took it off her head, they gazed at her in suspense. "Speak!" said Sylvia.

"I'm afraid to," Roseanne replied. But nothing happened – not a gold piece appeared. With a look of joy, she touched her lips. "It worked!" she said. "I'm cured."

She burst into laughter and, throwing her arms around Marco, gave him a kiss.

"What can I do to show my gratitude?" she said.

"You can tell us how to get to the Green Glass Tower," said Marco. "I have to rescue a princess there."

Roseanne nodded. "I can tell you how to get to the Green Glass Tower," she said, "but alas, my telling you won't do you much good. The tower is a hundred and ninety miles from here, beyond deep ravines, high mountains, pits full of flame, the Direful Mud, the Bottomless Bog, and the River of Knives."

"Dear me," said Marco.

"The only way to get there," Roseanne continued, "is to use the seven-league boots belonging to Fylfot the Necromancer, who lives at the other end of this village."

"Do you think he would lend them to me?" Marco asked, worriedly.

"He will lend them to you," Roseanne replied, "if you give him something he needs, which he doesn't know he wants and which he won't know he has when he gets it."

Poor Marco looked at her in bewilderment. "I can't even remember the beginning of that sentence," he said. "What does it mean?"

"I don't know," said Roseanne, "but I know that it is so."

"Never mind," Sylvia put in. "We'll go and see this Necromancer. Perhaps he'll help Marco anyway."

Bidding Roseanne farewell, they went to the other end of the village. A tall, narrow dark house stood alone in a garden of toadstools. At an open window high under the eaves sat the Necromancer. He had his back to the window and was reading.

"Good afternoon, sir," called Marco.

The Necromancer did not stir.

"Good afternoon," Marco repeated, more loudly. "Hey! *Yoo-hoo!* SIR!"

"He must be deaf as a post," remarked Sylvia.

Now in fact, the Necromancer was not usually deaf. But some days before, while engaged in magic, he had dropped a heavy spell on the foot of a small but bad-tempered imp. In revenge, the imp had settled invisibly on the Necromancer's head and plugged up his ears with its fingers.

Sylvia said to Marco, "Give him a whistle, and maybe that will attract his attention."

Marco put his fingers between his lips and whistled. It was so loud and shrill a whistle that chimneys in the village shook. Birds fell out of the sky covering their ears with their wings. And the invisible imp with a squeak of fright left the Necromancer's head and flew off into the next kingdom.

The Necromancer, of course, did not know what had

happened. He had not heard Marco's whistle, nor had he known that the imp was plugging up his ears.

All he knew was that suddenly he could hear again. The clock was ticking. The wind was rustling the leaves. He turned and glanced out of the window and saw a handsome young man and a pretty girl standing in the street staring up at him.

"Good afternoon," he said. "Were you waiting to see me?"

"We need your help," Marco answered, "but I hope we haven't disturbed you."

"Disturbed me? Certainly not," said the Necromancer. He found that he was suddenly feeling very fit and he thought to himself that this fine young man deserved his attention.

He hurried downstairs and let Marco and Sylvia in. "What can I do for you?" he said.

"Please lend me your seven-league boots," said Marco. "I have to go to the Green Glass Tower to rescue Princess Aurelia."

The Necromancer looked grave. "My friend," he said, "I will lend you the boots with pleasure. But I am sorry to say that if you go to that tower you will be going to your death. For there is a two-headed giant on guard, and he is under orders to slay any young man who comes to the gate."

"I shall just have to take a chance," said Marco. "Please let me have the boots."

The Necromancer got them out of a closet and blew the dust off them. "I don't travel much at my age," he explained. "Now, there is one small difficulty. With each step you take in these boots, you will go seven leagues.

"Since a league is three miles, seven leagues is twenty-one miles. However, the Green Glass Tower is exactly one hundred and ninety miles away, and twenty-one does not go into a hundred and ninety. If you can wait a little while, I will figure out for you how you can go a hundred and ninety miles in strides of twenty-one miles each."

"How long will it take you?" demanded Sylvia.

"About three days, I should think," said the Necromancer.

"Never mind," Sylvia said, briskly. "I know what to do. Put on the boots, Marco."

Marco slipped them on over his own boots, like galoshes. "What now?" he said.

"Now, you may take nine giant strides," Sylvia replied.

He seized her around the waist and off he went. With every stride they sailed high in the air. Far below, they could see jagged cliffs, deep holes darting out fire, a smoking sea of mud, a black quaking bog, and the glitter of a river of sharp steel blades. But with each stride, Marco managed to touch clear ground and then he was off again, soaring over all the obstacles.

With the ninth stride, they stood in safety among grassy hills. Marco looked about. "I don't see any tower," he said.

"We have come 189 miles," said Sylvia. "We shall have to walk the last mile."

Marco slipped off the boots and tucked them under his arm. He and Sylvia began walking, and to pass the time, Marco sang songs and told jokes.

Before long, they saw rising up before them a shining round tower of dark green glass, as smooth and as cold as ice.

They stopped a short distance away and stared at it. No one could possibly climb the walls. There were no windows, for of course in a glass tower one wouldn't need any. Before the front gate stood a giant with two heads. Both his faces were hideous and frowning. He bore a club twice as long as a man, bristling with iron spikes.

Suddenly Marco snapped his fingers. "My father gave me instructions for rescuing the princess," he said. "I have them right here." He looked in his wallet. He searched through his pockets. "No I haven't," he said, glumly. "I must have lost them on the road, in the rainstorm."

"Oh, Marco!" said Sylvia. And she almost added, "What an idiot!" But she liked him far too much for that, so instead she said, "I have an idea. Wait right here, and don't move."

"All right," said Marco. Then he said, "Wait for what? What are you going to do?"

"I'm going into the tower," said Sylvia, calmly.

"But –"

"Don't worry. The monster has instructions to bash any young man who comes to the gate. But I'm a girl."

She marched to the gateway. Sure enough, although the giant glared at her with all four of his eyes, he didn't move. Sylvia entered the tower.

In the great hall, she found an old man mopping the floor.

"Is there a princess named Aurelia here?" she asked.

The caretaker leaned on his mop and eyed her. "Why, my dearie," he cackled, "if you've come to visit her, you're just too late. She was rescued yesterday by as nice a young man as ever I did see."

"What?" cried Sylvia. "How did he manage?"

"Had a bit of paper, he had, that told him what to do," said the caretaker. "He said he found it by the roadside. He came in by the back door, you see. No giants there."

"Bother," said Sylvia. "Thank you very much."

She went back to join Marco, and broke the news to him.

"What a shame," said Marco, looking very downcast. "Of course, I don't mean it's a shame about Aurelia; I'm glad she was rescued. But I just can't seem to do anything right. What on earth am I going to say to the king, my father?"

"I suppose," said Sylvia, thoughtfully, "no other princess will do? It *had* to be Aurelia?"

Marco brightened. "Why, no. All I have to do is rescue a princess," he said. "Any princess – it doesn't really matter which one."

"In that case, everything is all right," said Sylvia. "I am a princess."

"You are? How splendid!" Marco said. "What shall I rescue you from?"

"You've already rescued me," Sylvia answered. "You rescued me from boredom. Until you came along, I was ready to scream with weariness and dullness. But with you, I've never known a dull moment."

Marco laughed with delight and took her in his arms. Then his face fell again. "No, it won't do," he said. "Why, I can't even tell my right hand from my left."

"That doesn't matter in the slightest," said Sylvia. "You'll have me, and I can always tell you which is which."

They kissed each other and turned about, and set out hand in hand for home.

THE SQUIRE'S BRIDE

NORWEGIAN FOLKTALE

THERE WAS ONCE a rich squire with a mint of silver in the barn and gold aplenty in the bank. He farmed over hill and dale, was ruddy and stout, yet he lacked a wife. So he had a mind to wed.

After all, since I am rich, he thought, I can pick and choose whatever maid I wish.

One afternoon the squire was wandering down the lane when he spotted a sturdy lass toiling in the hayfield. And he rubbed his grizzled chins, muttering to himself, "Oh aye, I fancy she'd do all right, and save me a packet on wages too. Since she's poor and humble she'll take my offer, right enough."

So he had her brought to the manor house where he sat her down, all hot and flustered.

"Now then, gal," he began, "I've a mind to take a wife."

"Mind on then," she said. "One may mind of much and more."

She wondered whether the old buffer had his sights set on her; why else should she be summoned?

"Aye, lass, I've picked thee out. Tha'll make a decent wife, sure enough."

"No thank you," said she, "though much obliged, I'm sure."

The squire's ruddy face turned ruby red; he was not used

to people talking back. The more he blathered, the more she turned him down, and none too politely either. Yet the more she refused, the more he wanted what he could not have. With a final sigh, he dismissed the lass and sent for her father; perhaps the man would talk some sense into his daughter's head.

"Go to it, man," the squire roared. "I'll overlook the money you owe me and give you a meadow into the bargain. What d'ye say to that?"

"Oh, aye, Squire. Be sure I'll bring her round," the father said. "Pardon her plain speaking; she's young yet and don't know what's best."

All the same, in spite of all his coaxing and bawling, the girl was adamant – she would not have the old miser even if he were made of gold! And that was that.

When the poor farmer did not return to the manor house with the girl's consent, the squire stormed and stamped impatiently. And next day he went to call on the man.

"Settle this matter right away," he ranted on, "or it'll be the worse for you. I won't bide a day longer for my bride."

There was nothing for it. Together the master and the farmer hatched a plan: the squire was to see to all the wedding chores – parson, guests, wedding feast – and the farmer would send his daughter at the appointed hour. He would say nothing of the wedding to her, but just let her think that work awaited her up at the big house.

Of course, when she arrived she would be so dazzled by the wedding dress, afeared of the parson and awed by the guests that she would readily give her consent. How could a farm girl refuse the squire? And so it was arranged.

When all the guests had assembled at the manor and the white wedding gown laid out and the parson, in black hat and cloak, settled down, the master sent for a stable lad. "Go to the farmer," he ordered, "and bring back what I'm promised. And be back here in two ticks or I'll tan your hide!"

The lad rushed off, wondering what the promise was. In no time at all he was knocking on the farmer's door.

"My master's sent me to fetch what you promised him," panted the lad.

"Oh, aye, dare say he has," the farmer said. "She's down in the meadow; you'd better take her then."

Off ran the lad to the meadow and found the daughter raking hay.

"I've come to fetch what your father promised the squire," he said all out of breath.

It did not take the girl long to figure out the plot.

So that's their game, she thought, a twinkle in her eye. "Right, then, lad, you'd better take her then. It's the old grey mare grazing over there."

With a leap and a bound the lad was on the grey mare's back and riding home at full gallop. Once there he leapt down at the door, dashed inside and called up to the squire.

"She's at the door now, Squire."

"Well done," called down the master. "Take her up to my old mother's room."

"But, master –"

"Don't but me, you scoundrel," the old codger roared. "If you can't manage her on your own, get someone else to help."

On glimpsing the squire's angry face he knew it was no use arguing. So he called some farmhands and they set to work. Some pulled the old mare's ears, others pushed her rump; they heaved and shoved until finally they got her up the stairs and into the empty room. There they tied the reins to a bedpost and let her be.

Wiping the sweat from his brow, the lad now reported to the squire.

"That's the darndest job I've ever done," he complained.

"Now send the wenches up to dress her in the wedding gown," said the squire.

The stable lad stared.

"Get on with it, dung-head. And tell them not to forget the veil and crown. Jump to it!"

Forthwith the lad burst into the pantry to tell the news.

"Hey, listen here, go upstairs and dress the old mare in wedding clothes. That's what the master says. He must be playing a joke on his guests."

The cooks and chambermaids all but split their sides with laughter. But in the end they scrambled up the stairs and dressed the poor grey mare as if she were a bride. That done, the lad went off once more to the squire.

"Right, lad, now bring her downstairs. I'll be in the drawing room with my guests. Just throw open the door and announce the bride."

There came a noisy clatter and thumping on the stairs as the old grey mare was prodded down; at last she stood impatiently in the hallway before the door. Then, all at once, the door burst open and all the guests looked round in expectation.

What a shock they got!

In trotted the old grey mare dressed up as bride, with a crown sprawling on one ear, veil draped over her eyes, and gown covering her rump. Seeing the crowd, she let out a fierce neigh, turned tail and fled out of the house.

The parson spilled his glass of port all down his purple front; the squire gaped in amazement, the guests let out a roar of laughter that could be heard for miles around.

And the squire, they say, never went courting again.

As for the girl, some say she married, some say not. It matters little. What is certain is that she lived happily ever after.

THE BARON RIDES OUT

ADRIAN MITCHELL

I WAS LESS THAN a man but more than a boy when I decided to leave home and see the world.

My father shouted, my mother swore and my 48 younger brothers and sisters begged me to stay. But I was as firm as a fortress.

"If you must go, you must go," said my parents. They often said the same thing at the same time.

My 48 younger brothers and sisters used their pocket money to buy me a farewell present. They gave me a large parcel. I unwrapped it on the lawn.

Out stepped a fine horse. "But it's wild!" shouted my mother and father, "wild as a windmill!"

For the horse was standing on its hind legs. It gnashed its teeth and lashed out with its front hooves. It chased my parents and my 48 brothers and sisters three times around our castle (about 33 miles).

Then it came up to me, rolling its crazy eyes. I returned its stare. Then I somersaulted onto its back, grabbed its mane and whispered three words into its left ear.

The brute calmed down at once. My parents and brothers and sisters had retired to the tea-room upstairs.

Luckily the window was open, so I urged my horse to jump through it. The beast landed delicately in the centre of the tea-table.

There he walked, trotted, cantered and galloped without breaking one cup or saucer. My family were delighted with this performance.

"Please leave home now and see the world," said my dear mother and father as one parent. With a wave and a leap my horse and I were on the lawn. Within seconds we had disappeared over the horizon. And that's as true as trumpeters.

What were the three words I whispered in my horse's ear? "Never you mind."

And that is the name I called my new horse – Never You Mind. So I rode out on Never You Mind, up the valleys and down the mountains until we came to the great port of Birmingham.

There we set sail in a twenty-masted sailing ship. Two days from home the wind dropped. It was so calm that I wrote my name on the water with my finger. The next day my signature could still be clearly read.

But the ship would not move. So I whistled and warbled as best I could. Soon I attracted a crowd of seagulls as well as a few albatrosses. I spoke to them in their own feathery language and explained our plight.

The birds donned a harness which I had designed. They flew ahead and drew our ship across the seas so speedily that the water below us began to boil and steam.

By now we were in a windy zone, so, after rewarding the birds with orange-crumbs and bread-pips, we set our sails.

Soon we dropped anchor at the island of Ceylon. We took on board wood, water and toffee. It was a humdrum visit, except for the storm.

A mighty wind tore up the island's trees by the roots. Some of them weighed many tons. But the wind carried them so high that, from the ground, they looked like the feathers of little birds.

At dawn the storm stopped suddenly. All the trees fell about five miles straight downwards into their proper places and took root again. All except one.

This was the largest tree of all. When it was blown up into the air a man and woman, a very honest old couple, were gathering cucumbers on its branches.

As the tree fell, their weight overbalanced it. It landed on the King of the island, who was killed at once.

He had left his house to go shopping for a new crown when this lucky accident happened. I say lucky, for the King was a very greedy and cruel man. All his subjects were as happy as hippos to see him squashed.

They chose the old cucumber couple to rule over them and built them a yellow seven-storey palace made entirely from banana skins.

And that's as true as tragedy.

As for me, I rode off into the centre of Ceylon upon Never You Mind. As we paused at a river to drink, I thought I heard a rustling noise. Turning round I was interested to see an enormous lion.

He was striding towards me. His tongue lolled from his mouth. It was obvious that he wanted to eat me for lunch and Never You Mind for pudding.

What was to be done? My rifle was only loaded with swan-shot. This would kill nothing bigger than a small wombat.

I am well-known as a lover of animals. I decided to frighten the lion. I fired into the air. But the bang only angered him. He ran towards me at full speed.

I tried to run away. But the moment I turned from the lion I found myself face to face with a large crocodile.

Its mouth was open wide. I could have walked inside without bending my head.

So, the crocodile was in front of me. The lion was behind me. On my left was a foaming river. On my right was a precipice. At the bottom of the precipice I could see a nest of green and yellow snakes.

I gave myself up for lost. The lion rose up onto his back legs. He was ready to pounce. At that second I tripped and fell to the ground. So the lion sprang over me.

For a long moment I lay still. I expected to feel the claws of the lion in my hair and the jaws of the crocodile around my heels. Then there was an awful noise. I sat up and looked around.

Imagine my joy when I saw that the lion had jumped so far that he had jammed his head into the open mouth of the crocodile. They were struggling together, each of them trying to escape.

I drew my sword and cut off the lion's head with one stroke. Then, with the butt of my rifle, I drove the lion's head down the crocodile's throat. The crocodile died of suffocation – a brief, merciful death, I am pleased to say.

Some absurd versions of this story have been spread. In one of these, the lion jumps right down the crocodile's throat and is emerging at the other end when I cut off his head. This, of course, is impossible. I think it shameful that the truth should be treated so lightly.

I looked about me for my trusty steed, but could spy no trace of Never You Mind. Finally I found him cowering in a rabbit hole.

My timid horse had sweated with fear. He had sweated away so much of himself that he was by now no bigger than a badger.

I am a great lover of animals, and fed him upon cream buns and fried potatoes. By the time we reached Poland, one month later, I had built him up to his usual size.

Riding through the endless snows, I saw a poor beggar lying by the wayside, shivering in his rags. Although cold myself, I threw my velvet cloak over him.

At once I heard a voice from the heavens saying: "My son, you will be rewarded for this noble act."

I rode on. Darkness fell. No village was to be seen. Snow was everywhere.

Tired out, I dismounted. I tied Never You Mind's reins to what I took to be the pointed stump of a tree. I lay down and slept.

I dreamt that I was back in the tropical heat of Ceylon. When I woke up it was daylight. I was astonished to find myself in a village, lying in a churchyard. I heard Never You Mind neighing, but when I looked around he was not to be seen.

Then I looked up. My good horse was hanging by his bridle from the weathercock on the church's steeple.

I understood at once. When I arrived the village had been covered by a snowdrift which reached to the church tower's top. During the night the weather changed for the warmer. The snow had melted.

I had sunk down to the churchyard in my sleep, gently, as the snow melted away. What I thought to be a tree stump was the top of the steeple.

Without thinking twice I took my pistol, shot the bridle in two, caught Never You Mind in my arms, mounted him and rode off in the direction of Russia.

The first Russian I met embraced me.

"Baron Munchausen!" he cried.

"And by whom do I have the honour of being hugged?" I asked.

"Pardon me," he said. "I am the Czar of Russia. They call me Peter the Great."

"I am glad to meet you, Peter," I said.

"Oh, Baron, will you please lead my armies against the Turks?"

"Certainly not," I replied.

But then the poor Czar argued, pleaded and finally begged – so I gave in.

It would be boastful to list the victories which followed. Let Peter the Great take the glory.

But there was an amusing incident when we took Constantinople. I had galloped, on Never You Mind, far ahead of my armies.

The Turkish Army was fleeing before me. I thundered after them through the West Gate of the city and chased them out of the East Gate.

I stopped in the market-place and watched them vanish. But when I looked around I was surprised to see that my armies had still not arrived in the city.

Never You Mind was panting. I rode him to a horse trough and he began to drink. I had never known him to drink so many gallons. But I understood his thirst when I looked behind me.

The hind quarters and back legs of the poor creature were missing. He had been cut in half. The water was running out of him as fast as he could drink it.

How had this happened? I found out when I rode his front half back, very gently, to the West Gate. When we had ridden through the gate, the enemy had dropped the portcullis – a heavy falling iron door with spikes at the bottom. This had cut off Never You Mind's back parts. His belly, buttocks, tail and hind legs were waiting anxiously for me outside the gate.

And so were my armies.

This might have been the end of my good horse. But I managed to bring together the front and back halves of Never You Mind while they were still hot.

I sewed them up with young shoots of laurel. These bound Never You Mind together neatly. He was, within hours, as fit as a fireplace.

The laurel sprigs grew and formed a curving, leafy arch over my head when I rode. This proved to be a great benefit in hot countries, where I was protected from the sun by the shade of my laurels.

And how did I travel home to my parents and my 48 sisters and brothers? Never You Mind. And that's as true as treacle.

THE MAULVI AND THE DONKEY

PAKISTANI FOLKTALE

In places like Pakistan or India, we call a teacher of muslim religion a maulvi. Well, once there was a maulvi who lived in a village. He had many young boys to teach. Some of them were clever and some were stupid. The maulvi used to think they were as stupid as asses, you know, donkeys. One day he shouted at these stupid ones:

"I've made men out of asses before and I can do it again."

Now as it happens, just as he was shouting this, a 'dhobi' or washerman was passing by the schoolroom and he heard what the maulvi said. The dhobi thought: "That's wonderful. He can make donkeys into men," and he rushed home and told his wife all about it.

Now, the dhobi and his wife didn't have any children. "At last we can have a son," they said. "We can take our favourite donkey to the maulvi sahib and get him changed into a man." Together they went to see the maulvi.

"Excuse me," they said, "could you use your powers to change our donkey into a man?"

The maulvi was amazed. "It's impossible," he said.

"No no no," said the dhobi. "*I* know you can do it. I know you can."

"But it's impossible," said the maulvi.

But the dhobi kept on and on at the maulvi and so the maulvi began to think that this was some kind of madman here.

"I'll play along with him," he thought.

"Very well," he said, "I'll do it. It'll be very, very hard so it'll cost four hundred rupees and it'll take four whole months to do."

"All right," said the dhobi, "it's a deal." And he went home and fetched the money and the donkey and came back to the maulvi. "That's a very fine donkey," said the maulvi. "He will make a great man."

When the dhobi had gone, the maulvi turned to one of his boys. "Take the donkey away. Take him deep into the jungle, tie him up and leave him there."

Four months later the dhobi came back.

"Well," he says, "is it done?" And the maulvi said "Where have you been my friend? Your donkey has become a very important government man, he is a Kazi, the Kazi of Karachi. You'd better go there and see him."

"Will he recognize me now that he is a famous man?" said the dhobi.

"Certainly," said the maulvi, "but just so that he can recognize you easily take the gunny bag you used to put his feed in. He'll certainly remember that." The dhobi was delighted. His donkey had become an important man. The Kazi of Karachi. He left straight away for the city. When he got there the Kazi's court was in session.

"Oh Allah be praised," said the dhobi, "the maulvi sahib has changed our donkey into such an important man, a judge of a big city."

After that the dhobi tried to catch the Kazi's eye. He moved into places where the Kazi could see him easily. He waved at the Kazi – "Cooee cooee" – but the Kazi was very busy with his work and took no notice of him. When this didn't seem to be working, the dhobi remembered what the maulvi had said: "Ah-hah – the feeding bag!"

and he started waving the feeding bag about at this very important man.

The Kazi stopped writing and looked up from his desk. The dhobi held up the feeding bag and smiled at him. The Kazi saw this and wondered what the funny man was up to.

"Bring me this man," he said to one of his guards.

The dhobi was very pleased at this. "At last he has recognized me."

The Kazi said to him, "What is all this nonsense?"

The dhobi felt hurt and shouted at the Kazi. "You don't recognize your owner you stupid donkey?" Then he waved the feeding bag under the Kazi's nose and said, "Didn't you eat corn from this every morning? Just because the maulvi has made a human being out of you, you shouldn't forget you are really a donkey." And then he said to the Kazi, "Come, let's go home."

The Kazi thought the man was some kind of lunatic so he tried to be nice to him but the dhobi didn't listen. At last the Kazi had to have him thrown out by his guards. The dhobi shouted as he was pushed out by the guards. "You used to be a donkey and I paid money to make a man out of you. This is how I'm repaid for my troubles. Better a donkey than an ungrateful man." From there the dhobi went straight to the maulvi and offered him another four hundred rupees to change the Kazi back into a donkey.

"All right," said the maulvi. "Come back with the money tomorrow." And all the time the dhobi was thinking of how he was going to get his own back on the Kazi.

Meanwhile the maulvi had the donkey brought back from the jungle. When he returned, the dhobi recognized his donkey straightaway. So he says to the donkey, "Do you recognize me now? Do you? You didn't when you were a Kazi did you? Oh no. I don't suppose I was good enough for you, was that it? Well now you'll know who I am."

At that the dhobi climbed up on to the poor donkey and thrashed him all the way home.

ELEPHANT MILK, HIPPOPOTAMUS CHEESE

MARGARET MAHY

THERE WAS ONCE AN orphan called Deedee who had the biggest feet in the world. They were so big she had grown extra strong ankles and knees in order to pick them up and put them down again. These enormous feet were a great embarrassment to her, and to the matron of the orphanage, as well. She didn't like having such a big-footed orphan clumping around her. She thought it spoiled the look of the orphanage.

Now, just down the road, there lived a man and a woman who were so lazy they had not washed the dishes for three years. Dirty dishes were piled up to the kitchen ceiling, down the hall, and along the garden path. It was lucky for them they had been given so many cups, saucers and plates when they were married. However, one morning they got up and looked around and found they had run out of clean dishes.

"What *shall* we do?" cried the man. "We positively can't wash all these, and yet there isn't a clean dish in the house."

"Ring up the orphanage," suggested his wife, "and we'll adopt a daughter to wash our dishes for us. Then, when she's done, we'll eat clean again."

"What a good idea!" cried the man, and he rang up the orphanage at once.

"Have you got a girl orphan who can cook and clean all day, and half the night as well?" he asked. "I don't want one that needs a lot of food or sleep, but I want one that's a good, strong, steady girl, because there's a lot to do around here and my wife and I are very delicate."

"Yes, yes," said the orphanage matron. "We have just the orphan for you. Her name is Weedy Deedee. She won't eat much. She's little and thin, but she's got such big feet she's as steady as a rock. I'll send her round in a brace of shakes." Then she went to the window and called, "Deedee! Deedee! Weedy Deedee! Pack your bag and sign the book. You've been adopted by the people down the road."

Weedy Deedee came clumping down the road from the orphanage, her big feet looking particularly enormous in their blue sneakers. She was about as tall as a rosebush, thin as string, with hair like bootlaces and feet like rowboats, but she had gentle, hopeful eyes and a lovely smile.

When she saw the dishes all the way down the garden path she sighed and set to work. She washed cups and saucers, bread and butter plates, dinner plates, soup bowls, pudding bowls, mugs, glasses and tankards. She rinsed knives and forks and spoons, and then scoured saucepans, soup-pots and frying pans. She washed dishes all the way up the garden path, all the way down the hall and all the way through the kitchen from floor to ceiling. Finally, every dish was clean and every spoon sparkling.

"What next?" asked Weedy Deedee for she knew there was more to come.

"Dear adopted daughter Deedee," said the man. "You may do the washing."

"And then the ironing!" said his wife.

"Make the beds!" commanded the man.

"Polish the furniture!" cried the woman.

"Chase the spiders!"

"Swat the flies!"

"Sweep!"

"Dust!"

"And then when you've done that, you may weed the garden," the man concluded.

It looks like a full morning, thought Weedy Deedee. So she set to work. Though she was little and stringy she was strong at heart. She washed and ironed, made and polished, chased and swatted, and swept, dusted and weeded. The house shone like a treasure as much to be looked at as lived in.

"That's that!" said Weedy Deedee. "And now, dear adopted parents, may I please have something to eat because I'm very hungry, and it's a long way past my dinner time."

The man and the woman looked at each other in dismay. They hadn't reckoned on feeding her.

"She's very small," said the man doubtfully.

"Except for her feet!" the woman muttered. "I've heard that those with extra large feet eat extra large dinners in order to maintain them."

"And she's worked very hard, too. She must be tremendously hungry by now," the man said. "Never mind! I have an idea. Leave this to me." Then he turned to Deedee. "Dear adopted daughter," he said, "we have a delicious meal of roast turkey and cranberry sauce, not to mention three colours of jelly and ice cream for pudding.

But your dear adopted mother and I have one more job for you. We want you to paint the ceiling."

"It certainly needs it," said Deedee. "Where's the ladder?"

"That's the problem. We don't have a ladder," said the man with a horrid smile.

"Then I'll stand on the table," Deedee said.

"What!" cried the woman. "Stand on my beautiful, polished, mahogany table with your whopping great feet? Never!"

"But I can't reach the ceiling!" exclaimed Deedee. "I'm too small."

"Oh dear," the man said, shaking his head. "So you are. How tragic. You'd better go back to the orphanage until you've grown taller. How sad. It breaks our hearts. And you've done so well too, up until now."

"That's it," cried the woman. "Come back when you're taller."

"You're still our dear adopted daughter and we'll think of you fondly, and pray for the day that you grow about three feet further towards the ceiling."

Weedy Deedee hadn't unpacked yet. She clumped all the way back to the orphanage with her change of clothes and her toothbrush in a small case. But when she got there the gate was closed tight.

"Off you go!" said the matron, popping her head out of the window. "We got another orphan in the moment you left, and there isn't any room now for you."

"What shall I do?" asked Weedy Deedee.

"Anything you like!" said the matron. "You're as free as a bird. Ah, freedom . . . freedom . . . would that I were as free and as happy-go-lucky as you!" and she popped her head back in again and locked the window . . . just to make sure.

So Weedy Deedee was turned loose on the world to wander and wonder. The roads of the world were very dusty and long, but luckily at that time of the year they were very pretty, all tangled along the sides with buttercups, daisies and foxgloves. She wandered and she wondered for quite a long time, until even *her* feet became sore and tired, in spite of being big. So when she came to a clear stream, its banks all tall with foxgloves, Weedy Deedee sat down on the bank, took off her blue sneakers, and put her feet into the water where they floated like two great white fish among the cresses.

"Oh, I'm so *hungry*," sighed Weedy Deedee. "I could eat a whole fried elephant, and still have room for a hippopotamus in chocolate sauce for pudding."

Funnily enough, just as she said this, an elephant came round the corner of the road and then another and another until there was a whole herd of elephants eating up the buttercups and daisies. Then a hippopotamus came round the corner, and another and another, until a whole herd of hippos was waddling by, all smiling and beguiling in the afternoon sunshine.

Then came a different sound of feet, really big feet this time, feet that were certainly even bigger than Weedy Deedee's. She could hear them coming down the road and around the corner, and the thought of bigger feet than hers so terrified her that she jumped up and tried to hide in a clump of foxgloves. She was so weedy she fitted in among the foxgloves easily . . . all except her feet, of course. They, poor lonely things that they were, had to stay sticking out into the world where everyone could see them.

Suddenly the herdsman – owner of the herds of elephants and hippos – came around the corner. He was definitely a giant, young and probably very handsome, except he was so big it was difficult to take him in all at once. By the time you got to his nose you had forgotten what his eyebrows were like. He had a lion bounding beside him, a kind of working dog. He saw Weedy Deedee's sneakers looking like blue canoes, moored among the buttercups and daisies on the bank of the stream.

"What beautiful shoes!" he cried wistfully. "Oh, if I were to find the feet that fitted this footwear I know I would love them." Weedy Deedee couldn't help wiggling her toes through sheer nervousness and the movement caught the giant's blue eyes.

"What beautiful feet sticking out of the foxgloves," he exclaimed in amazement. "What rounded rosy heels, what wonderful wiggling toes! If I could meet the maiden attached to these adorable extremities, I would make her mine. These must be the most beautiful feet in the whole world."

Weedy Deedee couldn't help laughing.

"They're the biggest, anyway!" she cried, looking out through the foxgloves.

The giant stared at her in astonishment. Then he began to

laugh, too. The lion licked Weedy Deedee's feet and made them tickle, so that the laughing went on for some time.

"Well, that's life!" said the giant at last. "I find a pair of feet to love and they're attached to Deedee, who is no bigger than a rose bush. Never mind! Come out of the foxgloves, for there's no need to hide. The lion's tame and so am I. The elephants and the hippos can wallow and graze, and you can sit down and share my lunch with me."

"That would be wonderful," said Weedy Deedee, "because I've had a really full day so far. I was adopted first thing this morning, then I washed three years of dirty dishes, and tidied a very untidy house. Then it turned out I wasn't tall enough to paint the ceiling, and I had to go back to the orphanage until I grew three feet taller. But, meanwhile, the orphanage had got another orphan in my place so I was set free as a bird, and I wandered and wondered my way here. I'm as hungry as a hippopotamus, for I haven't had a bite or sup all day."

"It doesn't bear thinking of," said the giant, and passed a slice of cheese as big as a tea tray, and a cup of milk as large as a bucket, while his elephants grazed around eating the buttercups and daisies, and the hippos had a nice wet wallow under the willow trees.

A strange thing happened. As Weedy Deedee ate the cheese and drank the milk she thought that her feet had suddenly grown smaller.

"Look at that!" she cried. "My feet have suddenly gone all little. What a pity! Up till now my feet were the only bit of me that anyone has ever admired."

"They haven't got smaller," said the giant. "It's you who've grown taller. It must be from drinking elephant milk and eating hippopotamus cheese. After all, that's what I've eaten all my life, and look at me. You've actually grown about three feet taller."

"What?" cried Weedy Deedee. "Do you mean that I've grown tall enough to paint the ceiling . . . just when I was enjoying myself?"

"Oh, forget about that!" said the giant. "Stay here and grow even taller and marry me. I've got a castle up on the hill with a garden full of sunflowers. Be mine and we will herd elephants and hippos together and garden, and have forty-nine children – seven times seven – and live happily ever after."

Now she was a bit bigger, and could take in rather more of the giant's enormous face, Weedy Deedee could see he had a nose she liked and trusted.

"That sounds like a wonderful life," she said. "But I'd better paint the ceiling first, and tell my parents that I'm getting married. After all they did adopt me this morning, and my mother might like to help me make my wedding dress. I've read that that's what mothers do. I'll go home, paint the ceiling and get the wedding dress, and then I'll come back to you."

"Take some milk and cheese to eat on the way," said the giant. "I've plenty left."

So Deedee put some milk and cheese into a bundle, put on her blue sneakers, and set off over the roads of the world, golden in the evening sunlight.

The man and the woman who had adopted her were eating a dinner of roast turkey and cranberry sauce. Three colours of jelly, as well as ice cream, stood waiting for their attention. Dirty breakfast and lunch dishes were piled on the clean bench. Deedee looked at them sternly.

"It's our darling adopted daughter back again so soon," said the man uneasily.

"And she's grown!" remarked the woman sourly. "She *has* grown. She's grown enough to paint the ceiling, after all. It shows what you can do if you put your mind to it."

"The paint pots are in the wash house," the man said. Deedee mixed the paint and cleaned the brushes. Without any trouble at all she painted the ceiling, while the man and the woman watched her, throwing the turkey bones over their shoulders.

"Dear adopted mother," said Deedee while she painted.

"I am going to be married, and I thought you might help me make my wedding-dress."

"Me!" screeched the woman. "Me make a wedding dress for a weedy, not-so-little Deedee who I've only just met today. Think again!"

Deedee did think again, and looked very seriously at her darling adopted mother.

The man smiled at her weakly. "Have a wing of turkey!" he said "Only a wing! There isn't a lot of meat on a turkey and my wife and I – we're very delicate, you know, and the doctor said . . ."

"Thank you! I've brought my own supper," Deedee replied, and she poured her elephant milk into a tall vase and put her hippopotamus cheese on a platter before her.

"What's that?" asked her adopted parents greedily.

"Elephant milk and hippopotamus cheese," Deedee told them, and she drank every drop and ate every crumb.

Suddenly her feet looked a lot smaller and the ceiling a lot closer. Weedy Deedee was weedy no more. She grew up through the house. Her arms went out through the windows, her head burst through the ceiling. Stretching towards the sky she felt the whole house lift off its floor and fold around her a wedding dress of wood and tin, shining with polish and paint.

Down below on the floor the man and the woman sat among their great set of dishes, dirty and clean, staring at her with terror. Weedy Deedee had grown, at last, to match her feet.

"Get your great feet out of here!" shouted the man, sounding as whining as a spiteful gnat. "Get out, get out, you diabolical Deedee!"

"I'm going! I'm taking my feet where they will be well and truly appreciated," Deedee replied calmly. "And don't call me Deedee anymore. Call me . . . Désirée!"

Back up the road went Deedee-Désirée wearing the wedding-dress house, until the roads of the world led her to the giant's castle. The giant came down through the sunflowers to meet her, his faithful lion bounding at his side.

"I was waiting for you," he said. "What took you so long?"

"Painting the ceiling!" said Deedee-Désirée with a laugh. "This is the only wedding dress in the world with a painted ceiling."

So they were married, and together they washed dishes and weeded gardens, herded hippos and milked elephants. They had seven times seven (forty-nine) children who played among the sunflowers. And these children grew to be the most beautiful and happy giants in the land, with bright eyes and the nicest feet in the world – and so they should have been, for they lived on elephant milk, hippopotamus cheese, and a handful of sunflower seeds whenever they felt like a change.

THE TORTOISES' PICNIC

ENGLISH FOLKTALE

THERE WERE ONCE three tortoises – a father, a mother, and a baby. And one fine spring day they decided that they would like to go for a picnic. They picked the place they would go to, a nice wood at some distance off, and they began to get their stuff together. They got tins of salmon and tins of tongue, and sandwiches, and orange squash, and everything they could think of. In about three months they were ready, and they set out, carrying their baskets.

They walked and walked and walked, and time went on, and after about eighteen months they sat down and had a rest. But they knew just where they wanted to go and they were about halfway to it, so they set out again. And in three years they reached the picnic place. They unpacked their baskets and spread out the cloth, and arranged the food on it and it looked lovely.

Then Mother Tortoise began to look into the picnic baskets. She turned them all upside down, and shook them, but they were all empty, and at last she said, "We've forgotten the tin-opener!" They looked at each other, and at last Father and Mother said, "Baby, you'll have to go back for it." "What!" said the baby, "me! Go back all that long way!" "Nothing for it," said Father Tortoise, "we can't start without a tin-opener. We'll wait for you." "Well, do you swear, do you promise faithfully," said the baby, "that you won't touch a thing till I come back?" "Yes, we promise faithfully," they said, and Baby plodded away, and after a while he was lost to sight among the bushes.

And Father and Mother waited. They waited and waited and waited, and a whole year went by, and they began to get rather hungry. But they'd promised, so they waited. And another year went by, and another, and they got really hungry. "Don't you think we could have just one sandwich each?" said Mother Tortoise. "He'd never know the difference." "No," said Father Tortoise, "we promised. We must wait till he comes back."

So they waited, and another year passed, and another, and they got ravenous.

"It's six years now," said Mother Tortoise. "He ought to be back by now."

"Yes, I suppose he ought," said Father Tortoise. "Let's just have one sandwich while we're waiting."

They picked up the sandwiches, but just as they were going to eat them, a little voice said, "Aha! I knew you'd cheat." And Baby Tortoise popped his head out of a bush. "It's a good thing I didn't start for that tin-opener," he said.

THE FIRST SCHLEMIEL

ISAAC BASHEVIS SINGER

A long time ago a lot of Jewish people used to speak a language called Yiddish.

Nowadays not so many people speak it – You know what 'nosh' is? Food. That's a Yiddish word.

Another one – not so well known – is 'Schlemiel'. It means a fool, a silly person.

THERE ARE MANY Schlemiels in the world but the very first one came from the village of Chelm. He had a wife, Mrs Schlemiel, and a Little Schlemiel.

Schlemiel's wife used to get up early in the morning to sell vegetables at the market. Mr Schlemiel stayed at home and rocked the baby to sleep. He also looked after the cockerel which lived in the room with them, feeding it corn and water.

One day before she left for market, she said, "Schlemiel, I'm going to the market and I will be back in the evening. There are three things that I want to tell you. Each one is important – listen –"

"What are they?" asked Schlemiel.

"First, make sure that the baby does not fall out of his cradle."

"Good. I will take care of the baby."

"Second, don't let the cockerel get out of the house."

"Good, the cockerel won't get out of the house."

"Third, there is a pot of poison on the shelf. Be careful not to eat it, or you will die," said Mrs Schlemiel pointing to the pot of jam she had put high up in the cupboard.

She had decided to fool him, because she knew that once he tasted the delicious jam, he would not stop eating until the pot was empty. He was like that.

It was just before Hannukkah, when Jewish people give presents and have nice things to eat.

As soon as his wife left, Schlemiel began to rock the baby and to sing him to sleep.

"I'm a big Schlemiel

You're a little Schlemiel . . ."

The baby soon fell asleep and Schlemiel dozed too, still rocking the cradle with his foot.

Suddenly the cockerel started crowing. It had a very strong voice. When it came out with its "Cock a doodle-doo", it sounded like a bell. Now, when a bell rang in Chelm, it usually meant there was a fire. Schlemiel woke up from his dream, jumped up and knocked over the cradle. The baby fell out and hurt his head. Schlemiel ran to the window and opened it to see where the fire was. The moment he opened the window, the cockerel flew out and hopped away.

Schlemiel called after it, "Cockerel, you come back. If Mrs Schlemiel finds you gone, she will rant and rave and I will never hear the end of it."

But the cockerel paid no attention to Schlemiel. It didn't even look back, and soon it had gone.

When Schlemiel realized there was no fire, he closed the window and went back to the baby, lying there, crying. By this time he had a big bump on his head. Schlemiel comforted the baby, put the cradle right, and put him back in it.

And he began to rock the cradle and sing a song,

"I'm a big Schlemiel,
You're a little Schlemiel . . ."

and so he sung the baby to sleep.

Now, Schlemiel began to worry about his troubles. He knew that when his wife came back and found the cockerel gone and the baby with a bump on his head, she would be so angry. Mrs Schlemiel had a very loud voice and when she scolded and screamed, poor Schlemiel trembled with fear. Schlemiel could see, that night when she got home, his wife would be even more angry, and call him names.

Suddenly Schlemiel said to himself,

"What is the sense of such a life? I'd rather be dead."

And he decided to end his life. But how to do it?

He then remembered what his wife told him in the morning about the pot of poison that stood on the shelf. "That's what I'll do. I will poison myself. When I'm dead she can tell me what she likes."

Schlemiel was a short man and he could not reach the shelf. He got a stool, climbed up on it, took down the pot, and began to eat.

"Oh, the poison tastes sweet," he said to himself.

"Oh well, sweet poison is better than bitter," and so he finished up the jam. It tasted so good, he licked the pot clean.

"So," he said, "it's not really so bad to die. With such poison, I wouldn't mind dying every day," and then he lay down on the bed.

He was sure that the poison would soon begin to burn his insides and that he would die. Instead he dozed off.

Schlemiel was woken up by the sound of the door creaking open. The room was dark and he heard his wife's voice.

"Schlemiel, why didn't you light the lamp?"

"It sounds like my wife, Mrs Schlemiel. But how is it possible that I hear her voice? I happen to be dead. Or can it be that the poison hasn't worked yet and I am still alive?" He got up, legs shaking, and saw his wife.

Suddenly she began to scream at the top of her voice.

"Just look at the baby! He has a lump on his head.

"Schlemiel, where is the cockerel? Oy veh. He's lost the cockerel and he's let the baby get a bump on his head.

"Schlemiel, what have you done?"

"Don't scream, dear wife. I'm about to die. You'll soon be a widow."

"Die? Widow? What are you talking about? You look as healthy as a horse."

"I've poisoned myself," Schlemiel replied.

"Poisoned? What do you mean?" asked Mrs Schlemiel.

"I've eaten your pot of poison."

And Schlemiel pointed to the empty pot of jam.

"Poison?" said Mrs Schlemiel. "That's my pot of jam for Hannukkah."

"But you told me it was poison," Schlemiel insisted.

"You fool," she said, "I did that to keep you from eating it before the holiday, now you've swallowed the whole pot." And Mrs Schlemiel burst out crying.

Schlemiel too began to cry, but not from sorrow. He wept tears of joy that he would stay alive. The wailing of the parents woke the baby and he too began to bawl. When the neighbours heard the crying, they came running and soon all Chelm knew the story. The good neighbours took pity on the Schlemiels and brought them a fresh pot of jam.

The cockerel which had got cold and hungry from wandering around outside, returned by itself, and the Schlemiels had a happy holiday after all.

SING-SONG TIME

JOYCE GRENFELL

CHILDREN, WE'VE HAD our run around the classroom, and now it's time to start our day's work. We're going to have a sing-song together, and Miss Boulting is going to play for us, so come and settle down over here, please.

Kenny, why haven't you taken your coat off?

No, it isn't time to go home yet, Kenny! You've only just come.

You'd rather go home? Bad luck.

No, you can't go, not quite yet.

Kenny, you've only been here about ten minutes. Come and sit on the floor next to Susan. You like Susan.

No, Susan, I don't think he wants to sit on your lap.

No, I thought he didn't.

Kenny! We don't want to see your tongue, thank you.

No, not even a little bit of it. Put it back, please.

All of it.

And give your jacket to Caroline, I'm sure she'll hang it up for you.

Thank you, Caroline.

Who is that whistling?

Sidney, you know we never whistle indoors. You can whistle in the garden, but we never whistle indoors.

Yes, I know you have just whistled indoors, but don't do it any more.

And don't punch Jacqueline.

I'm sure she didn't say she liked you punching her, did you Jacqueline?

Well, I don't think it's a good idea, so we won't have any more punching.

He is rather a disruptive element in our midst, Miss Boulting, but he does try to belong more than he used to, so we are encouraged, bless his heart.

Let's be *kind* to each other today, shall we? We are going to learn some more of the Drum Marching Song we began yesterday.

Who remembers how it starts?

No, David, it doesn't begin "Twinkle, Twinkle Little Star". That's another song.

Yes, I know you know it, but we aren't going to sing it now.

No. Not today.

And not tomorrow.

I don't know when.

We are going to sing our Drum Marching Song now.

Edgar and Neville, why are you standing on those chairs?

You can see into the fish tank perfectly well from the floor. Get down, please.

No, Neville, you can't hold a fish in your hand.

Because fishes don't like being held in people's hands.

They don't like coming out of the water, you see. Their home is in the water.

Well they do have to come out of the water when we eat them, but these aren't *eating* fishes. These are *friend* fishes. It's Phyllis and Fred. We wouldn't want to eat Phyllis and Fred.

No, Sidney, you wouldn't.

I don't think they'd be better than sausages.

Come back, please. You don't have to go and see Phyllis and Fred. You know them perfectly well.

I don't know what they are doing behind the weeds, Sidney. Just having a nice friendly game, I expect.

Neville, you tell us how the Drum Marching Song begins.

Yes! That's right.

"Rum tum tum, says the big bass drum". Well remembered, Neville.

When we know the song well we're going to march to the Drum Song. But today we'll just stand and sing it; so, everybody *ready*?

"Rum tum tum, says the big bass drum."

Just a minute, Miss Boulting.

Where is your drum, Kenny? No, not on your head. It's in front, isn't it, on a make-believe string round your neck.

Sidney, I heard what you said. You know it isn't "Rum tum tummy".

It may be funnier, but it isn't right.

Yes, it is a funny joke. Let's get the laughter over, please.

Finished?

Now then. Ready?

Thank you, Miss Boulting.

"Rum tum tummy . . ."

Yes, I made a mistake. It was silly, of me, wasn't it? Yes, very silly.

Sh – sh –. It wasn't as silly as all that.

I think we'll go on to the next bit perhaps . . .

Miss Boulting . . .

"Rooti-toot-toot, says the . . ."

Who says 'Rooti-toot-toot', David?
No, David, not 'Twinkle Twinkle'.
Yes, Lavinia, the '*Cheerful* Flute'.
And what is a flute?
No, Dicky, it isn't an orange.
It isn't a banana.
It isn't an apple.
It isn't FRUIT, it's FLUTE.
FLUTE.
And what is a flute?
Yes, Lavinia, it's in a band. It's a musical instrument in a band. And how do we play it?
No, we don't kick it and bash it about, Sidney.
Now think.
We *blow* it.
Yes, Edgar, we *blow* it, and the music comes out of it. It's a musical instrument, and we *blow* down it.
Rachel, don't blow at Timmy.
And Timmy, don't blow back.
I'm sorry she blew you a very wet one. But don't blow a wet one back.
Now use your hankies, and wipe each other down, both of you. I'm sure you're both sorry.
No, Kenny, it isn't time to go home yet.
Shirleen, why are you taking your skirt off?
I'm sure Mummy wants you to keep it nice and clean, but you won't get it dirty from singing, you know.
Yes, it is very pretty.
Yes, and it's got little doggies all over it. Little blue and little pink doggies. Put it on again, please. Yes, your panties are pretty; *and* your vest.
But pull down your skirt now.
George. Remember what I asked you not to do? Well, then . . .
"Rooti-toot-toot, says the cheerful flute."
Rest.
Sidney, you're whistling again. And if you are going to

whistle you must learn to do it properly. You don't just draw in your breath like that, you have to blow in and out.

It's no good saying you bet I can't whistle, because I can. I've been able to whistle for a very long time, but I'm not going to do it now. But I can.

I don't know why I compete with him, Miss Boulting. I really shouldn't.

Let's start our Drum Marching Song from the very beginning, shall we?

One, two . . .

What did you say, Miss Boulting?

Already! So it is. Oh, good. And here is Mrs Western with our milk and biscuits.

Get into a nice straight line by the trolley, please.

No, Kenny, it isn't time to go home yet. There is still an hour and a half to go . . .

THE STOWAWAYS

ROGER MCGOUGH

WHEN I LIVED IN Liverpool, my best friend was a boy called Midge. Kevin Midgeley was his real name, but we called him Midge for short. And he was short, only about three cornflake packets high (empty ones at that). No three ways about it. Midge was my best friend and we had lots of things in common. Things we enjoyed doing like . . . climbing trees, playing footy, going to the pictures, hitting each other really hard. And there were things we didn't enjoy doing like . . . sums, washing behind our ears, eating cabbage.

But there was one thing that really bound us together, one thing we had in common – a love of the sea.

In the old days (but not so long ago) the River Mersey was far busier than it is today. Those were the days of the great passenger liners and cargo boats. Large ships sailed out of Liverpool for Canada, the United States, South Africa, the West Indies, all over the world. My father had been to sea and so had all my uncles, and my grandfather. Six foot six, muscles rippling in the wind, huge hands grappling with the helm, rum-soaked and fierce as a wounded shark (and that was only my grandmother!) By the time they were twenty, most young men in this city had visited parts of the globe I can't even spell.

In my bedroom each night, I used to lie in bed (best place

to lie really), I used to lie there, especially in winter, and listen to the foghorns being sounded all down the river. I could picture the ship nosing its way out of the docks into the channel and out into the Irish Sea. It was exciting. All those exotic places. All those exciting adventures.

Midge and I knew what we wanted to do when we left school . . . become sailors. A captain, an admiral, perhaps one day even a steward. Of course we were only about seven or eight at the time so we thought we'd have a long time to wait. But oddly enough, the call of the sea came sooner than we'd expected.

It was a Wednesday if I remember rightly. I never liked Wednesdays for some reason. I could never spell it for a start and it always seemed to be raining, and there were still two days to go before the weekend. Anyway, Midge and I got into trouble at school. I don't remember what for (something trivial I suppose like chewing gum in class, forgetting how to read, setting fire to the music teacher), I forget now. But we were picked on, nagged, told off and all those boring things that grown-ups get up to sometimes.

And, of course, to make matters worse, my mum and dad were in a right mood when I got home. Nothing to do with me, of course, because as you have no doubt gathered by now, I was the perfect child: clean, well-mannered, obedient . . . soft in the head. But for some reason I was clipped round the ear and sent to bed early for being childish. Childish! I ask you. I *was* a child. A child acts his age, what does he get? Wallop!

So that night in bed, I decided . . . Yes, you've guessed it. I could hear the big ships calling out to each other as they sidled out of the Mersey into the oceans beyond. The tugs leading the way like proud little guide dogs. That's it. We'd run away to sea, Midge and I. I'd tell him the good news in the morning.

The next two days just couldn't pass quickly enough for us. We had decided to begin our amazing around-the-world voyage on Saturday morning so that in case we didn't like it we would be back in time for school on Monday. As you can imagine there was a lot to think about – what clothes to take, how much food and drink. We decided on two sweaters each and wellies in case we ran into storms around Cape Horn. I read somewhere that sailors lived off rum and dry biscuits, so I poured some of my dad's into an empty pop bottle, and borrowed a handful of half-coated chocolate digestives. I also packed my lonestar cap gun and Midge settled on a magnifying glass.

On Friday night we met round at his house to make the final plans. He lived with his granny and his sister, so there were no nosy parents to discover what we were up to. We hid all the stuff in the shed in the yard and arranged to meet outside his back door next morning at the crack of dawn, or sunrise – whichever came first.

Sure enough, Saturday morning, when the big finger was on twelve and the little one was on six, Midge and I met with our little bundles under our arms and ran up the street as fast as our tiptoes could carry us.

Hardly anyone was about, and the streets were so quiet and deserted except for a few pigeons straddling home after all-night parties. It was a very strange feeling, as if we were the only people alive and the city belonged entirely to us. And soon the world would be ours as well – once we'd stowed away on a ship bound for somewhere far off and exciting.

By the time we'd got down to the Pier Head, though, a lot more people were up and about, including a policeman who eyed us suspiciously. "Ello, Ello, Ello," he said, "and where are you two going so early in the morning?"

"Fishing," I said.

"Train spotting," said Midge and we looked at each other.

"Just so long as you're not running away to sea."

"Oh no," we chorused. "Just as if."

He winked at us. "Off you go then, and remember to look both ways before crossing your eyes."

We ran off and straight down on to the landing stage where

a lot of ships were tied up. There was no time to lose because already quite a few were putting out to sea, their sirens blowing, the hundreds of seagulls squeaking excitedly, all tossed into the air like giant handfuls of confetti.

Then I noticed a small ship just to the left where the crew were getting ready to cast off. They were so busy doing their work that it was easy for Midge and me to slip on board unnoticed. Up the gang-plank we went and straight up on to the top deck where there was nobody around. The sailors were all busy down below, hauling in the heavy ropes and revving up the engine that turned the great propellers.

We looked around for somewhere to hide. "I know, let's climb down the funnel," said Midge.

"Great idea," I said, taking the mickey. "Or, better still, let's disguise ourselves as a pair of seagulls and perch up there on the mast."

Then I spotted them. The lifeboats. "Quick, let's climb into one of those, they'll never look in there – not unless we run into icebergs anyway." So in we climbed, and no sooner had we covered ourselves with the tarpaulin than there was a great shuddering and the whole ship seemed to turn round on itself. We were off! Soon we'd be digging for diamonds in the Brazilian jungle or building sandcastles on a tropical island. But we had to be patient, we knew that. Those places are a long way away, it could takes days, even months.

So we were patient. Very patient. Until after what seemed like hours and hours we decided to eat our rations, which I divided up equally. I gave Midge all the rum and I had all the biscuits. Looking back on it now, that probably wasn't a good idea, especially for Midge.

What with the rolling of the ship and not having had any breakfast, and the excitement, and a couple of swigs of rum – well you can guess what happened – woooorrppp! All over the place. We pulled back the sheet and decided to give ourselves up. We were too far away at sea now for the captain to turn back. The worst he could do was to clap us in irons or shiver our timbers.

We climbed down on to the deck and as Midge staggered to the nearest rail to feed the fishes, I looked out to sea hoping to catch sight of a whale, a shoal of dolphins, perhaps see the coast of America coming in to view. And what did I see? The Liver Buildings.

Anyone can make a mistake can't they? I mean, we weren't to know we'd stowed away on a ferryboat.

One that goes from Liverpool to Birkenhead and back again, toing and froing across the Mersey. We'd done four trips hidden in the lifeboat and ended up back in Liverpool. And we'd only been away about an hour and a half. "Ah well, so much for running away to sea," we thought as we disembarked (although disembowelled might be a better word as far as Midge was concerned). Rum? Yuck.

We got the bus home. My mum and dad were having their breakfast. "Aye, aye," said my dad, "here comes the early bird. And what have you been up to then?"

"I ran away to sea," I said.

"Mm, that's nice," said my mum, shaking out the cornflakes. "That's nice."

THE PUDDING LIKE A NIGHT ON THE SEA

ANN CAMERON

"I'M GOING TO MAKE something special for your mother," my father said.

My mother was out shopping. My father was in the kitchen looking at the pots and the pans and the jars of this and that.

"What are you going to make?" I said.

"A pudding," he said.

My father is a big man with wild black hair. When he laughs, the sun laughs in the window-panes. When he thinks, you can almost see his thoughts sitting on all the tables and chairs. When he is angry, me and my little brother Huey shiver to the bottom of our shoes.

"What kind of pudding will you make?" Huey said.

"A wonderful pudding," my father said. "It will taste like a whole raft of lemons. It will taste like a night on the sea."

Then he took down a knife and sliced five lemons in half. He squeezed the first one. Juice squirted in my eye.

"Stand back!" he said, and squeezed again. The seeds flew out on the floor. "Pick up those seeds, Huey!" he said.

Huey took the broom and swept them up.

My father cracked some eggs and put the yolks in a pan and the whites in a bowl. He rolled up his sleeves and pushed back his hair and beat up the yolks. "Sugar, Julian!" he said, and I poured in the sugar.

He went on beating. Then he put in lemon juice and cream and set the pan on the stove. The pudding bubbled and he stirred it fast. Cream splashed on the stove.

"Wipe that up, Huey!" he said.

Huey did.

It was hot by the stove. My father loosened his collar and pushed at his sleeves. The stuff in the pan was getting thicker and thicker. He held the beater up high in the air. "Just right!" he said, and sniffed in the smell of the pudding.

He whipped the egg whites and mixed them into the pudding. The pudding looked softer and lighter than air.

"Done!" he said. He washed all the pots, splashing water on the floor, and wiped the counter so fast his hair made circles around his head.

"Perfect!" he said. "Now I'm going to take a nap. If something important happens, bother me. If nothing important happens, don't bother me. And – the pudding is for your mother. Leave the pudding alone!"

He went to the living room and was asleep in a minute, sitting straight up in his chair.

Huey and I guarded the pudding.

"Oh, it's a wonderful pudding," Huey said.

"With waves on the top like the ocean," I said.

"I wonder how it tastes," Huey said.

"Leave the pudding alone," I said.

"If I just put my finger in – there – I'll know how it tastes," Huey said.

And he did it.

"You did it!" I said. "How does it taste?"

"It tastes like a whole raft of lemons," he said. "It tastes like a night on the sea."

"You've made a hole in the pudding!" I said. "But since

you did it, I'll have a taste." And it tasted like a whole night of lemons. It tasted like floating at sea.

"It's such a big pudding," Huey said. "It can't hurt to have a little more."

"Since you took more, I'll have more," I said.

"That was a bigger lick than I took!" Huey said. "I'm going to have more again."

"Whoops!" I said.

"You put in your whole hand!" Huey said. "Look at the pudding you spilled on the floor!"

"I am going to clean it up," I said. And I took the rag from the sink.

"That's not really clean," Huey said.

"It's the best I can do," I said.

"Look at the pudding!" Huey said.

It looked like craters on the moon. "We have to smooth this over," I said. "So it looks the way it did before! Let's get spoons."

And we evened the top of the pudding with spoons, and while we evened it, we ate some more.

"There isn't much left," I said.

"We were supposed to leave the pudding alone," Huey said.

"We'd better get away from here," I said. We ran into our bedroom and crawled under the bed. After a long time we heard my father's voice.

"Come into the kitchen, dear," he said. "I have something for you."

"Why, what is it?" my mother said, out in the kitchen.

Under the bed, Huey and I pressed ourselves to the wall.

"Look," said my father, out in the kitchen. "A wonderful pudding."

"Where is the pudding?" my mother said.

"WHERE ARE YOU BOYS?" my father said. His voice went through every crack and corner of the house.

We felt like two leaves in a storm.

"WHERE ARE YOU? I SAID!" My father's voice was booming.

Huey whispered to me, "I'm scared."

We heard my father walking slowly through the rooms.

"Huey!" he called. "Julian!"

We could see his feet. He was coming into our room.

He lifted the bedspread. There was his face, and his eyes like black lightning. He grabbed us by the legs and pulled. "STAND UP!" he said.

We stood.

"What do you have to tell me?" he said.

"We went outside," Huey said, "and when we came back, the pudding was gone!"

"Then why were you hiding under the bed?" my father said.

We didn't say anything. We looked at the floor.

"I can tell you one thing," he said. "There is going to be some beating here now! There is going to be some whipping!"

The curtains at the window were shaking. Huey was holding my hand.

"Go into the kitchen!" my father said. "Right now!"

We went into the kitchen.

"Come here, Huey!" my father said.

Huey walked towards him, his hands behind his back.

"See these eggs?" my father said. He cracked them and put the yolks in a pan and set the pan on the counter. He stood a chair by the counter. "Stand up here," he said to Huey.

Huey stood on the chair by the counter.

"Now it's time for your beating!" my father said.

Huey started to cry. His tears fell in with the egg yolks.

"Take this!" my father said. My father handed him the egg beater. "Now beat those eggs," he said. "I want this to be a good beating!"

"Oh!" Huey said. He stopped crying. And he beat the egg yolks.

"Now you, Julian, stand here!" my father said.

I stood on a chair by the table.

"I hope you're ready for your whipping!"

I didn't answer. I was afraid to say yes or no.

"Here!" he said, and he set the egg whites in front of me. "I want these whipped and whipped well!"

"Yes, sir!" I said, and started whipping.

My father watched us. My mother came into the kitchen and watched us.

After a while Huey said, "This is hard work."

"That's too bad," my father said. "Your beating's not

done!" And he added sugar and cream and lemon juice to Huey's pan and put the pan on the stove. And Huey went on beating.

"My arm hurts from whipping," I said.

"That's too bad," my father said. "Your whipping's not done."

So I whipped and whipped, and Huey beat and beat.

"Hold that beater in the air, Huey!" my father said.

Huey held it in the air.

"See!" my father said. "A good pudding stays on the beater. It's thick enough now. Your beating's done." Then he turned to me. "Let's see those egg whites, Julian!" he said. They were puffed up and fluffy. "Congratulations, Julian!" he said. "Your whipping's done."

He mixed the egg whites into the pudding himself. Then he passed the pudding to my mother.

"A wonderful pudding," she said. "Would you like some, boys?"

"No thank you," we said.

She picked up a spoon. "Why, this tastes like a whole raft of lemons," she said. "This tastes like a night on the sea."

A FISH OF THE WORLD

TERRY JONES

A HERRING ONCE DECIDED to swim right round the world. "I'm tired of the North Sea," he said. "I want to find out what else there is in the world."

So he swam off south into the deep Atlantic. He swam and he swam far far away from the seas he knew, through the warm waters of the equator and on down into the South Atlantic. And all the time he saw many strange and wonderful fish that he had never seen before. Once he was nearly eaten by a shark, and once he was nearly electrocuted by an electric eel, and once he was nearly stung by a sting-ray. But he swam on and on, round the tip of Africa and into the Indian Ocean. And he passed by devilfish and sailfish and sawfish and swordfish and bluefish and blackfish and mudfish and sunfish, and he was amazed by the different shapes and sizes and colours.

On he swam, into the Java Sea, and he saw fish that leapt out of the water and fish that lived on the bottom of the sea and fish that could walk on their fins. And on he swam, through the Coral Sea, where the shells of millions and millions of tiny creatures had turned to rock and stood as big as mountains. But still he swam on, into the wide Pacific. He swam over the deepest parts of the ocean, where the water is so deep that it is inky black at the bottom, and the fish carry lanterns over their heads, and some have lights on their tails.

And through the Pacific he swam, and then he turned north and headed up to the cold Siberian Sea, where huge white icebergs sailed past him like mighty ships. And still he swam on and on and into the frozen Arctic Ocean, where the sea is forever covered in ice. And on he went, past Greenland and Iceland, and finally he swam home into his own North Sea.

All his friends and relations gathered round and made a great fuss of him. They had a big feast and offered him the very best food they could find. But the herring just yawned and said: "I've swum round the entire world. I have seen everything there is to see, and I have eaten more exotic and wonderful dishes than you could possibly imagine." And he refused to eat anything.

Then his friends and relations begged him to come home and live with them, but he refused. "I've been everywhere there is, and that old rock is too dull and small for me." And he went off and lived on his own.

And when the breeding season came, he refused to join in the spawning, saying: "I've swum around the entire world, and now I know how many fish there are in the world, I can't be interested in herrings any more."

Eventually, one of the oldest of the herrings swam up to him, and said: "Listen. If you don't spawn with us, some herrings' eggs will go unfertilized and will not turn into healthy young herring. If you don't live with your family, you'll make them sad. And if you don't eat, you'll die."

But the herring said: "I don't mind. I've been everywhere there is to go, I've seen everything there is to see, and now I know everything there is to know."

The old fish shook his head. "No one has ever seen everything there is to see," he said, "nor known everything there is to know."

"Look," said the herring, "I've swum through the North Sea, the Atlantic Ocean, the Indian Ocean, the Java Sea, the Coral Sea, the great Pacific Ocean, the Siberian Sea and the frozen Arctic. Tell me, what else is there for me to see or know?"

"I don't know," said the herring, "but there may be something."

Well, just then, a fishing-boat came by, and all the herrings were caught in a net and taken to market that very day. And a man bought the herring, and ate it for his supper.

And he never knew that it had swum right round the world, and had seen everything there was to see, and knew everything there was to know.

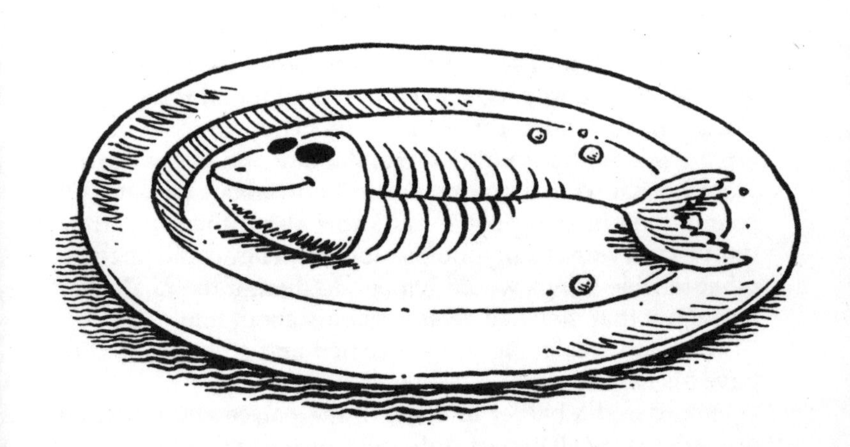

THE RAJAH'S EARS

INDIAN FOLKTALE

ONCE, LONG AGO in India when there were kings called rajahs and people lived in fear of them, there was a rajah who had very big ears. They were so big he wore a special hat to hide them. All day and every day he wore his hat so that no one would know about his ears. Of course, one or two people did know about them but they didn't say a word to anyone else about it. They could imagine what terrible things would happen to them if the rajah ever found out that they had been gossiping about him.

The rajah was going to get married and so he wanted to have his hair cut.

He ordered a barber to come to the palace and when he arrived he sent all his servants and courtiers outside.

Then he said to the barber,

"Now listen here, young man, in a moment I am going to take my hat off. Then you will see that I have ears that are not small. No one in the whole country knows about my ears. If ever I hear that you have been talking about my ears, gossiping or telling tales, then I shall cut your head off. If I ever hear that anyone knows about my ears, I will know that you told them, and I will do as I say, I will cut your head off. Do you understand?"

"Yes, your majesty," said the barber.

The rajah took his hat off and the barber cut his hair. All

the time he was cutting away with his scissors, he was trying not to look at the rajah's ears. But they were right in front of him all the time, just where he was looking.

So he said over and over again to himself,

"I must not tell anyone about the rajah's ears,

I must not tell anyone about the rajah's ears."

When he had finished, the rajah put his hat on and sent the barber off saying, "Remember what I said, young man."

"Yes, your majesty, not a word to anyone."

And that's the way it was, for the rest of the day; he didn't breathe a word about it to anyone at all. But all the time, the barber was thinking about it. At work, the next day, when he was cutting other people's hair, and chatting with a customer, he was thinking about it. The customer says, "I don't suppose much happens to you here, does it? Day in, day out, cutting people's hair?"

Straightaway, the thought of the rajah's big ears leapt into his mind. "Well,sir," he says, "the other day I was cutting the rajah's hair and you won't believe it but you know he's got enormous –"

And he stopped himself. What am I saying? he thought, I'll get my head cut off.

"What's he got?" said the customer.

"Enormous jewels on his rings," said the barber.

Phew, that was a close one, he said to himself.

At home that night, his wife was changing her earrings and he found himself saying, "Those earrings look very nice on you, my dear."

"Thank you," says his wife, "you don't think they're too small?"

"They don't look too small on you dear, but I tell you who they *would* look funny on – that's the rajah because he's got really big ear –"

What am I saying? he said to himself. I'll get my head cut off.

"What's he got?" said the wife.

"He's got really big earrings. Small ones would look funny on him."

Phew, that was another close one, he thought.

Outside in the yard, his children were playing and he went out to call them in for bedtime.

Two of them were pulling faces at each other, sticking their tongues out and pulling their ears.

"Don't do that," says the barber, "you look like the rajah."

"Why do we look like the rajah?" says one.

"Because he's got big –"

What am I saying? the barber thought, I'll get my head cut off.

"He's got big children," said the barber, "and they look like the rajah. You look like his children . . . so you look like the rajah."

Phew, that was another close one.

And so it went on all the next day. He was dying to tell someone. In the end he had a plan. The next morning, instead of going straight to work, he went off to the woods.

I know what I'll do, he thought, I'll tell a tree. I'll tell a tree that the rajah's got big ears and that'll be that. It won't bother me anymore. I'll have told someone who can't tell anyone else. The rajah will never find out, and I'll feel a lot better.

So the barber crept up to a great big tree in the woods. He looked behind him and to either side. He looked behind the tree and all round it and then he stood up in front of it and said,

"The rajah's got big ears."

Oooh, that felt so much better. It felt like a great load had been taken off his back and off he went to work happier than he had been for days.

Later that day, a woodcutter came to the woods and chopped down the very same tree that the barber had talked to. The woodcutter sold the wood from the tree to a musical instrument maker and the instrument maker made some drums called tabla and a stringed instrument called a sitar.

The instrument maker sold the tabla and sitar to a band that was one of the best in the country. In fact, so good was this band, that they were asked to play at the rajah's wedding.

Everyone was there, all the rajah's relations, all his servants, all his servants' servants, even the rajah's barber.

What a day it was. There was a wonderful ceremony, followed by a great feast and then came the dance.

The musicians made ready, there was a hush and then the music began.

But of all surprising and awful things to happen, the sound coming out of the musical instruments wasn't a wedding dance but a song, and the words of the song were:

"The rajah's got big ears,
oh yes the rajah's got big ears,
do you know what
I know what
The rajah's got big ears."

"Stop, stop, stop," shouted the rajah.

"I heard that," he roared, "I heard every word of that."

The hundreds of wedding guests stood in silence.

The thought of his barber sprang into the rajah's mind. Only the barber knew about his ears, only the barber could have told anyone.

"BARBER!" bellowed the rajah, "barber, where are you?"

The barber stepped forward.

"Yes, your majesty?"

"I heard that song. You heard that song. You have disobeyed me. I told you not to tell a single person and now everyone knows."

"But your majesty, I didn't tell a single person."

"Oh yes you did, and tonight you lose your head."

"But, your majesty, I didn't tell a single person. I told a tree. That's not a person, is it?"

The rajah stopped. A smile crept on to his face.

He muttered to himself.

" 'I didn't tell a person. I told a tree.' The man's right, he didn't tell a single person. Oh, what am I making a fuss about? It's only ears. So what if I have got big ears? Some people have got big feet, some people have got little noses. We're all different and we always will be."

At that, he pulled off his hat and said,

"Friends and relations, the rajah's got big ears. Let the band play."

The band played and everyone sang,

"The rajah's got big ears,
oh yes the rajah's got big ears
do you know what
I know what
The rajah's got big ears."

A GOOD SIXPENN'ORTH

BILL NAUGHTON

THREE OF US were on our way home from school one January afternoon when a man with a cigarette-end in his mouth asked us would we like a job. "I want you to cart this loose load of coal into that coalshed. It'll be worth a bob," he added.

"Apiece?" I asked.

"Between you," he said.

It was an enormous heap of large coal gleaming in the grey light of the back street. We gazed at it for a minute, and then had a whisper among us. "Make it eighteen-pence mister," I suggested, "an' we'll take it on – for then we'll have a tanner each."

He agreed, and we set to work. Harry Finch filled the buckets, I ran in with them, and Basher stacked it inside the shed. The man leant on a broom and flicked an occasional piece of coal from my path. He kept blowing on his hands to keep warm. Two hours saw the job done, by which time the sweat was pouring out of us, and I was feeling weak in the legs. Then the man knocked on the back door, and a woman came out and gave him half a crown. He turned and gave us sixpence each.

"Not much," I said, looking at the little coin in my blistered hand, "considering you got a bob."

"I'm the contractor," he said. "And don't forget, you'd have had nothing but for me."

"He's right," agreed Harry and Basher. "And besides," went on Harry, "just think of the fun we can have with a tanner at the Fair. The New Year rush is over, and all the prices are down, because it travels tomorrow."

"Good idea," I said. "I'll meet you at seven o'clock, an' we'll go to the Fair and have a right good tanner's worth."

Scrubbed and excited, the three of us met on time and made off for the Fair. Once clear of the narrow streets and high black factories, we spotted from the main road the strange pale glow like a halo over the Fair. We walked faster, and as we neared the fairground we were caught by the exciting smells, fragments of blaring music and voices, and by the sense of movement: of roundabouts, big swings, cakewalks, helter-skelters, and whatnot, so that we broke into a trot.

The ground under our feet was slushy, and the glaring lights illuminated an almost deserted Fair. We liked it that way. Our heads stopped reeling, and we were able to stroll about the place and savour the atmosphere without being overcome and spending our money rashly.

"Take it easy," I warned my mates, "and let's keep scouting round till we've found the top value for money."

We watched the Flying Pigs, Big Boats, Bumper Cars, all going cheap, but we clung to our sixpences. We inspected every game of chance and skill: Hoopla, All Press, Dartboards, Ringboards, Roll-a-Penny, Skittles, Bagatelle, Rifle Range, and Coconut Shies.

"Look at that hairy 'un," whispered Harry. "I've allus wanted to knock off a coconut – and I reckon that 'ud drop with a touch."

"That's what you think," I said.

"I vote we have a good feed of them hot peas," said Basher. "Just smell 'um. What you spend on your guts, my Mum reckons, is never lost."

"Don't rush it, Basher," I said.

"A coconut's the best bet," said Harry. "You might even knock *two* off – and they'd last for days."

"We didn't come by our money so easy," I cautioned them, "so let's use our discretion afore we part with it."

At that moment my eye caught sight of the figure of a man in silk shirt and riding-breeches, a silver-handled whip in his hand, poised on a platform beneath the brightest lights on the fairground.

"Ladies and gentlemen," called out a beautiful blonde lady. "Introducing Waldo – the greatest lion-tamer of all time. Any moment now he will enter the cage of Nero! Nero the Untamable! The African jungle lion that has killed four trainers – the largest lion in Europe – the fiercest in captivity. Waldo will positively enter his cage! Will he come out alive?"

I felt hands tugging me back by the jacket. "Hy, where are you off?" asked Basher.

"Quick," I said, "let's get in afore the crowd."

"What crowd?" asked Harry.

"One small coin, ladies and gentlemen, sixpence only, brings you the greatest thrill of all time!"

"Keep still," hissed Basher.

"Get your tanners ready," I said, "we can't afford to miss it."

"No, you don't," said Basher. "Black peas, a whacking great plateful for tuppence, an' finish off with roasted spuds."

"Big hairy coconuts," whispered Harry.

I couldn't take my eyes off Waldo, unsmiling and unafraid. He bowed to us, stepped from the platform, and disappeared. Before Basher and Harry could hold me I was at the paybox.

"Half, please."

"*Half?* Why, you're going in for a *quarter* tonight. Two bob's the proper price. . . . You don't expect to see a chap eaten by a lion for threepence?"

I handed over the sixpence. I waved to my mates, but they wouldn't come. So I quickly went inside the tent, so as to get near the front. Inside were four people, and they looked at me pityingly. There was a well-dressed couple, an old man, and a woman who looked like a Sunday school teacher. It was very cold, and after the bright lights outside one could only see dimly. I went and stood near the stage.

There was no sign of Waldo. After a long time I heard the beating of a drum and the woman announcer. I felt like going out again and listening.

"We can't wait much longer," I heard the man say to the woman. "Is he never going to go in to that wretched beast?"

Only five more people came in during the next twenty minutes. I felt chilled, and I was aware of an empty spot of skin in the palm of my hand, where I had clutched the sixpence. Then there was a final beating of the drum, and Waldo appeared on the stage before me.

His face was all powdered, and there was a smell of stale beer off him. He looked at us with disgust. And then the announcer bustled in. The curtain was pulled open, and there was a cage. Lying in the nearest corner was a big lion. It was less than a yard away from me, and it blinked its eyes and gave a good-tempered yawn.

"During the act, ladies and gentlemen, there must be complete silence. One sound, and Waldo may never come out alive. His life is in your hands. Since no insurance company will insure Waldo's life, I ask any of you who can afford it to place an extra coin in the hat. Thank you!"

Waldo cracked his whip outside the cage, and Nero slowly got to his feet. The woman took a revolver out of her pocket. Waldo went to the door of the cage, and sprang back when the lion came. This seemed to disturb the lion. As it moved away Waldo quickly opened the cage and darted inside. He cracked the whip, and Nero loped wearily round the cage. He went after it, cracking the whip over his head. "*Silence!*" called the announcer. Nero skipped round the cage for about two minutes, then sank down to rest in the same corner. Waldo leapt to the door, opened it, and got out. Nero never moved. It looked at me again, blinked, sighed, and rested.

"Ladies and gentlemen," called the blonde announcer, putting away the revolver, "that concludes the performance."

I couldn't believe it.

I exchanged one last look with the lion as the curtain was drawn across the stage. I even clapped feebly with the others. And the next thing I was outside.

"Look!" shouted Harry Finch. "That shaggy 'un – I knocked it off." He dangled an enormous coconut before my eyes.

"Black peas an' roasted spuds," sighed Basher. "Here" – he grabbed my head and pressed my ear against his fat, warm stomach – "can you hear 'em churning about inside? Luv'ly."

Harry shook the coconut against my ear. "Fair loaded with milk. I knocked it clean off with the last ball. A right good tanner's worth."

"Not as good as mine," said Basher. "First I had a plate of hot peas, then a bag of roasted spuds, an' then another plate of hot peas."

The image of old Nero seemed fastened before my eyes; the smell of the lion, the sleepy old head, and gentle blinking eyes. *The fiercest lion in captivity*. We went walking along the streets homeward.

"How was the lion-taming show?" they asked at last.

"Champion," I said. "Worth anybody's money."

"You've not had much to say about it," remarked Harry, suspiciously.

"Yes, you've kept your trap shut," accused Basher.

"It were that exciting," I said, "as it took my breath away."

"Something did," they said.

I longed to tell them, to unload the misery of my heart, but I dared not. I'd never have lived it down if I had.

"Sorry, lads," I said, "but I've got to be in early." And I ran off home.

I slept badly that night. Next morning when I was on my way to school Harry Finch called out, "He's here, Mum!"

"What's up?" I asked.

"Haven't you heard?" he said.

"Heard what?" I said.

"Waldo the Lion-tamer has been badly mauled by that wild lion. It's on the front page of the *Dispatch*. I told me mum an' she wants to ask you about it."

Out came Mrs Finch with her spectacles on and the *Dispatch* in her hand. "Ee luv, they say he's in a critical condition –"

"Let's have a look, please," I said to Mrs Finch. It was true. The lion had mauled him! I gave her the paper back. "I'm not surprised," I said, "the way that lion went at him. It clawed the blinking shirt off his back. He could hardly hold it at bay with his whip, an' a woman with a revolver was about to shoot it."

"Ee, suffering Simon! An' did you see all that?"

"'Course I did. Your Harry had a coconut instead."

By this time a few neighbours were at their doors, and when I went off there was a crowd of lads all wanting to hear about Waldo and Nero. I described the powerful physique of Waldo, and the beauty of the woman with the revolver, and told of the wild roaring lion that tried to claw at me through the bars. The school whistle made us run, but in the classroom they began to whisper questions to me. Teacher told me to stop talking.

"Please, miss," said Harry, "it isn't his fault. He was telling me about seeing Waldo the Lion-tamer all but torn to bits last night."

"Is that the person who was so severely mauled?" she asked. "Then you'd better come in front and tell us all."

I went to the front of the classroom and began. "The lion was making furious deep-throated roars even before Waldo attempted to get into the cage. And when it caught sight of him in his blue silk shirt it went into a fury. I was very close to the cage, and when its huge body hit the bars it made the whole tent shudder. The roars were bloodcurdling."

Suddenly the class door opened and in came Mr Victor, the headmaster. I was going back to my place, but he called me out again. "Oh, I must hear this – please continue."

I began all over again, adding any new bits that came to mind, when suddenly there was a knock on the door and a monitor ushered in Major Platt, the Inspector of Schools.

"I'm afraid I've interrupted something," he said.

"Not at all, Major," said Mr Victor hurriedly. "It just happens that this boy was present at the fairground performance last evening when the lion-tamer was so badly mauled."

"My goodness, I must hear this!" exclaimed Major Platt. All three of them sat down, and I stepped back a foot to stand on the teacher's platform. I felt in fine form.

"After three attempts to enter the cage the lady with the pearl-handled revolver tried to dissuade the Great Waldo, but he refused to give up, and I heard him say: 'The show must go on.' Then, by a ruse, he got Nero away from the door, and the next moment he was inside. The iron door slammed after him. He was alone in the cage with the African man-eating lion. A mighty roar rended the air at that moment, and the big crowd shuddered. Waldo attempted bravely to keep the lion down with his whip – but it gave one spring. The next moment I saw his silk shirt fall to shreds on the floor. But he was unhurt. He drove it into a corner – again it sprang. The woman darted to the bars with the revolver, but I heard Waldo shout, 'Don't shoot!' His eye never left that of the lion. For a long time it parried, trying to knock the whip from his hand. Then at last it succeeded, and again it sprang with an angry roar. Waldo fell to the floor. But in a trice he was clear. But he couldn't get to the door of the cage. And he had lost his whip. The lion seemed to be sizing him up. Then, just as it was about to spring, he snatched a piece of shirt from the floor and waved it in front of its face. When it sprang he was already at the door. The blonde lady unfastened it. Just in the nick of time he got out. Then I noticed a line of blood across his bare back. The entire place trembled as the lion hit the door. Waldo could scarcely stand up. I was right up in front of the crowd. He gave a bow to the audience, and then the lady helped him away. The audience clapped like mad. The lion snarled with fury. Then I went out to meet my mates. One was eating hot peas. The other had knocked off a hairy coconut."

Major Platt, smiling solemnly, or so it seemed to me, patted me on the head. "One day, my boy," he said, "you will make a true journalist." And he slipped a thick, heavy coin into my fist.

Modestly I went back to my place between Harry and Basher. Their eyes were fastened enviously on me, and I couldn't resist opening my hand and letting them glimpse the half-crown. They let out a gasp. And Harry grunted, "The lion turned out the best sixpenn'orth after all."

As I sat down I felt the excitement drain away, and Harry's words brought up a picture of the real Nero before me. I saw the two old eyes of Nero, so weary and worn, and I wondered at the agony it must have suffered to provoke its old jungle temper. In fact, I had half a mind to go out and confess the truth before the entire class. I felt that was the right thing to do. And I would have done it – only, I was a bit scared Major Platt might have taken the half-crown back.

HAROLD AND BELLA, JAMMY AND ME

ROBERT LEESON

HAROLD WAS A SHOW OFF. Whatever you knew, he knew better. Whatever you had, he had better. And he could always win the argument by thumping you, because he was bigger. That was the main reason why we put up with him. Because the gang in the street round the corner from us would have slaughtered us if it hadn't been for Harold. With him around we could slog 'em any time. So, even when he gave you the pip, which was about ten times a day, you put up with him.

As I said, whatever was going new, his family had to have it first – sliced bread, gate-legged tables, copper fire irons, zip fasteners. They had rubber hot water bottles when the rest of us still had a hot brick in an old sock, a gas cooker when our Mams still cooked on the open range, an electric iron when Mam still heated her iron on the fire and spat on it to test the heat. They were first to have a five-shilling flip in a monoplane at Blackpool and they were first to have the telephone put in round our way. That was a dead loss because there was almost no one to ring up. It was sickening all round, they way they carried on. But worst of all was when they got the wireless.

Mr Marconi's invention was slow to arrive in Tarcroft.

That is if you didn't count the crystal sets owned by the doctor and the man who hired out the charabanc. Most people couldn't afford the wireless at first. But, of course, when Mr Marconi did arrive round our way, he came to Harold's house first.

We were sitting, the four of us, one day in the branches of the old oak tree that stands in the Meadows at the top of the Lane, when Harold spoke up:

"We're getting a wireless."

There was silence for a second or two. What could you say? Then, just as Harold was going to speak again, Jammy said:

"So are we."

"Get off. You're a little ligger, Jammy."

"Am not."

"Are."

"Want to bet?" asked Jammy, and he stretched himself out along his branch with hands behind his head, lying balanced. I don't know how he dared do it, twenty feet up.

"Want to bet?" he repeated.

Harold kept his mouth shut a minute, then burst out:

"All right, what make is it?"

"Cossor."

"They're no good. Ours is a Philips."

"Get off. Cossor are better than Philips any day."

"Not."

"Are."

Bella made a face at me. Harold went on.

"Our wireless pole's twenty-five foot high."

"Ours is thirty foot," said Jammy.

"It never."

"'Tis 'n' all."

"How d'you know?"

"Because our Dad climbed it when he fixed the aerial."

Harold laughed like a drain.

"I always knew you were a monkey – that proves it."

Jammy retorted: "I bet your Dad couldn't climb the clothes post."

"My Dad wouldn't mess about climbing a wireless pole like a chimpanzee. We had a man in to fix ours. I bet your Dad didn't buy a wireless. Bet he put it together with bits and pieces."

That was getting near the mark. Jammy's Dad was always fixing things.

"He never," said Jammy, but he looked a bit funny.

"OK," went on Harold. "Bet you can't get Radio Luxembourg."

"Can a duck swim? Course we can."

"All right. What do you listen in to?"

"Ovaltineys."

"They're no good. Joe the Sanpic Man's miles better."

"Him? He's barmy, like you."

"You're crackers."

"You two give me a headache," snapped Bella. But Harold wouldn't give up.

"How big's your wireless cabinet?" he asked craftily.

"How big's yours?" asked Jammy.

"Ya ha," sneered Harold. "You daren't say because ours is bigger and you know it."

"Want to bet?" said Jammy. But I had a feeling he was getting desperate.

"OK. How much?" Harold was sure of himself and I began to feel sorry for Jammy.

"Ten to one." Jammy was getting wild now.

"What in, conkers?"

"No, tanners."

"You never, that's a dollar if you lose."

Bella climbed down to a lower branch, hung on for a moment with her hands, then dropped to the ground.

"I'm off."

I jumped down after her and Jammy followed. He was mad. Harold was laughing at him and I knew Jammy was making it up. Next day, though, we all went down to the Clough and played sliding in the old sandpit. It was smashing. I thought the stupid bet had been forgotten. I hated quarrels and so did Bella. But Harold hadn't forgotten at all.

Next week, Bella came round after school. That Wednesday there was to be a wedding in the Royal Family. School was closed for a half day. Would we like to come round and listen to it on their wireless? I thought to myself, Harold's Mam's as bad as he is.

When we got round there on the day, there was quite a crowd in their front room. Jammy's mother was there and some other women from our street and even one from round the corner.

She wore a funny big hat and had a put-on accent.

"Oh, I see you've had your sofa covered in rexine."

"Oh, yes," said Harold's Mam, "it's the latest thing for *settees.*" She said the word 'settee' a bit louder, but the other woman didn't seem to notice.

"I'm not sure I fancy rexine, myself, it makes your drawers stick to your bottom."

"Would you care for a cup of tea?" Harold's Mam said quickly to our Mam, who was staring out of the window to hide a smile.

While all this was going on, Harold was nudging Jammy and pointing to the corner. There on a special table stood the wireless, a big brown walnut cabinet with ornamental carving over the loudspeaker part and a line of polished buttons along the bottom. I thought Jammy looked sick. That wireless was enormous. It must have been two feet high and a foot across. Harold's mother switched on. There was a lot of crackling and spitting.

"Just atmospherics," she said.

Jammy looked more cheerful. Perhaps it wouldn't work. But it did. Harold's mother gave the cabinet a very unladylike thump on the top and the crackling stopped. We could hear an organ playing and an old bloke droning on about something, then some singing, then a lot more crackling. Another hefty bang on the top and we heard a bloke with a posh voice telling us what we'd been listening to, in case we hadn't got it. I didn't think much to it all, but Mam and the other women said it was lovely. Then Jammy's mother piped up.

"On Saturday afternoon, I'd like you all round to our house for a cup of tea. There's a nice music programme we can listen in to."

Harold's mother looked a bit peeved but smiled and said: "Delighted." But Jammy looked green. Harold sniggered and whispered, "That'll cost you a dollar."

When we got outside I said: "Hey, Harold, this bet's daft. Jammy hasn't got a dollar. It'll take him months to save that up."

Bella nodded. But Harold smirked.

"Serve him right. He should keep his big mouth shut." He turned round and swung on the gate. "See you on Saturday, Jammy – have the money ready. I'll take two half dollars, or five bobs, ten tanners or twenty three-penny joeys. But not sixty pennies, 'cause it weighs your pockets down."

Jammy slouched off down the road by himself.

Saturday tea time came round all too soon and there we were in Jammy's kitchen. They didn't have a front room.

Jammy's mother had a good fire going, though it was the middle of July, and the kettle was boiling. The table was loaded with bread and butter, meat paste and corned beef sandwiches, and scones. We all sat down. Harold looked all round him, a fat grin on his face.

"Where's the wireless, Missis?"

"You speak when you're spoken to," said his Mam.

"That's quite all right," said Jammy's Mam. "Alan, just take the dust cloth off will you, love."

Jammy nipped sharply up from the table and whipped away a cloth that was hanging in the corner. I heard Harold choke on a mouthful of bread and butter. We all stared as Jammy switched on and the music came through with hardly any crackling.

But the cabinet! It must have been five foot high, not on a table, but standing on the floor. The loudspeaker part was decorated with cream-coloured scroll work. Below were two sets of knobs and switches, that seemed to go all the way down to the floor.

"Another butty, Harold?" Jammy said sweetly. Bella and I sniggered. Mam tapped me on the head and said "sh!"

As soon as tea was over, Harold made an excuse and dashed out first. By the time we got to the door, he was heading off up the road.

"Whatever did our Harold dash off like that for?" asked his mother.

"Gone to dig up his money box, I should think," chuckled Bella.

"I shall never understand what you have to giggle so much for, child. Come along," said Bella's Mam, and swept away down the path, followed by Bella.

I turned to Jammy, who was his normal cheerful self.

"You won that one, Jammy," I said. "What are you going to do with that five bob?"

He grinned. "Nowt. He can keep it. It was worth it just to see that look on his face. Besides," he added and whispered in my ear, "it wasn't a real wireless cabinet. It was an old second-hand kitchen cabinet. Dad did it up and fitted our wireless into the top part."

"But what about all those knobs?"

"Oh, he put them on for show. He uses the bottom part to keep his beer in."

I laughed all the way home.

Any time after that, when Jammy wanted to annoy Harold all he had to say was, "Same to you – with knobs on!"

THE JESTER AND THE KING

POLISH STORY

FOR MANY YEARS MATENKO had been the jester of King Jan of Poland, entertaining the king and his court with jokes, tricks and funny faces. But now Matenko was growing old, and people no longer laughed at his jokes. Rheumatism made it hard for him to turn somersaults, his face was so wrinkled that he could no longer make it look funny, and his memory was becoming so bad that he could no longer learn new jokes. Finally, King Jan decided that he must get a new court jester. He called Matenko and said, "The Queen and I are very sorry, Matenko, but you are getting old. It is time for you to retire. Take this purse of gold pieces and go and live in the little cottage which I have had built especially for you in your native village."

Matenko was heartbroken. Sadly he and his wife Wanda carried their belongings from the great court to the humble cottage which the king had given them. There were not many gold pieces in the king's purse, and soon they had almost no money left. "How can I earn a living?" wondered Matenko. "Telling jokes is the only trade I know." He looked for work in the village, but the only jobs to be had were sweeping floors, digging ditches or collecting potatoes, and his rheumatism was too bad to allow him to do any of these. Wanda also tried to find work, but there was no one in the village rich enough to pay someone else to do the cooking or washing for them. At last the two old people were starving. "There is nothing else to do but lie down and die," Matenko said in despair one day. Then suddenly he had an idea. "Wait, there is just one chance that we may not have to starve. Wanda, my good wife, trust me and do just as I tell you." Then Matenko explained his plan to her.

That very evening Wanda put on her best clothes and chopped a raw onion so that tears ran down her wrinkled cheeks, then she went to the palace to see the queen. "Your Majesty," Wanda sobbed, "my poor Matenko is dead." The queen felt very sorry indeed for the poor old woman, and gave her a purse full of gold coins to pay for the funeral and to buy food for herself. Still sobbing, Wanda thanked the good queen and came home.

"We have 50 gold pieces! Hoorah!" cried Matenko, and he danced about the little cottage as he counted the coins in the queen's purse.

First thing in the morning Matenko chopped a raw onion and went to the palace to see the king. "Your Majesty," he sobbed, "my poor old wife is dead!" The king felt very sorry for his old jester and gave him a purse before sending him home.

"Hoorah!" cried Matenko when he reached home and counted out 200 gold pieces from the king's purse. "Now we have a little fortune." Then he kissed his wife and set out to complete the rest of his plan.

On the sideboard in their little cottage he set two big, lighted funeral candles, and beside them he laid the two purses with all the gold pieces still in them. Then he told Wanda to lie down on the floor. "Cross your arms over your chest, and don't move. You must pretend to be dead," he told her. He covered her from head to foot with a white sheet. Then he lay down beside her, covered himself with another white sheet, and crossed his arms over his chest. And so they lay and waited.

In the meantime, as soon as Matenko had left the palace

with the purse of coins, the king hurried into his wife's chamber to tell her that the old jester's wife had died. "But my dear, you must be mistaken," said the queen. "It is the jester, not the jester's wife, who is dead." Then they began to quarrel as to which of them was right. "Let us go and see who is dead," suggested the queen at last. So they ordered their carriage and drove to the jester's cottage.

When they knocked and walked into the little cottage they found the candles lit, their purses on the sideboard, and the two old people covered with white sheets. Obviously Matenko and Wanda were both dead.

"But which of them died first?" asked the queen, "it must have been Matenko."

"No, it must have been Wanda," said the king. They began to quarrel again, when Matenko jumped up from under his sheet and said, "Your Majesty, my wife died first, but I was dead before her."

"You old rascal!" laughed the king and queen at the same time, too glad to find the old couple still alive to be really angry. When they tearfully explained that they had pretended to be dead because they had been starving, the king and queen felt very much ashamed. At once they promised to send money to Matenko and Wanda whenever they needed it.

The old jester and his wife lived comfortably for many years. Every now and then Matenko used to say happily to Wanda, "You see, my dear, even an old jester can sometimes play a clever trick."

TIMES AREN'T WHAT THEY WERE

KAREL ČAPEK

IT WAS QUIET in front of the cave. The men had gone off early in the morning, waving their spears, towards the hills, where a herd of deer had been sighted; meanwhile the women were picking berries in the forest and their shrill cries and chatter could only be heard now and then; the children were mostly splashing down in the stream – and besides, who would have taken any notice of the grubby and mischievous little ragamuffins? So Johnny, the old cave man, dozed in the unusual quiet, in the soft October sunshine. To tell the truth he was snoring and his breath whistled in his nose, but he pretended not to be asleep but to be watching over the cave of his tribe and ruling it, as befits an old chief.

Old Mrs Johnny spread out a fresh bear skin and set about scraping it with a sharp flint. It had to be done thoroughly, span by span – and not the way that girl did it, thought old Mrs Johnny suddenly; the lazybones only gave it a lick and a promise and ran off to cuddle the children and romp with them – a skin like this, she thought, won't last a bit! it's too bad, they either handle them roughly or let them rot! But I shan't interfere if my son doesn't tell her himself. The truth is that girl doesn't know how to take care of nice things.

And here's a hole pierced in the skin right in the middle of the back! My goodness me, thought the old lady in shocked astonishment, what butter-fingers stabbed this bear in the back? Why, it ruins the whole hide! My old man would never have done a thing like that. He always aimed at the neck and hit it –

"Ah ha," yawned old Johnny at that moment and rubbed his eyes. "Aren't they back yet?"

"Of course not," grunted the old lady. "You must wait."

"Tcha," sighed the old man and blinked sleepily. "Of course not yourself! Oh, all right. And where are the women?"

"Shall I go and look for them?" snapped the old lady. "You know they're lounging about somewhere –"

"Ahyaya," yawned Johnny. "They're lounging about somewhere. Instead of – instead of doing this or that – Well, well."

There was silence. Old Mrs Johnny swiftly scraped the raw hide with angry concentration.

"I tell you," said Johnny, scratching his back thoughtfully, "you'll see, they won't bring anything back this time either. It stands to reason: with those good-for-nothing bone-headed spears of theirs. And I'm always saying to our son: look here, no bone is hard and firm enough to make spears out of! Why, even a woman like you must know that neither bone nor horn has the – well, the striking force. You hit a bone with it and you don't cut through bone with bone, do you? That's only sense. A stone spearhead, now – of course it's more work, but then, what an instrument it is! And what do you think our son said?"

"Yes," said Mrs Johnny bitterly. "You can't tell them anything nowadays."

"I don't want to tell them anything," said the old man crossly. "But they won't even listen to advice! Yesterday I found such a lovely flat piece of flint under the rock over there. It only needed trimming a little round the edges to make it sharper and it would have been a spearhead, a beauty. So I brought it home and showed it to our son. 'Look, here's a stone for you, what?' 'So it is,' he answered, 'but what should I do with it, Dad?' 'Why, bless me, it could be worked up into a spearhead,' I said. 'Nonsense, Dad,' he said, 'who'd bother about chipping and sharpening that? Why, we've whole heaps of that old junk in the cave and it's no use for anything! It won't hold on to the shaft, lash it how you may, so what can you do with it?' A lazy lot they are!" shouted the old man angrily. "No one wants to trim a piece of flint properly these days, that's what it is! They just want to be comfortable! Of course a bone spearhead is made in the twinkling of an eye, but it breaks at once. That doesn't matter, our son says, you just make another and there you are. Well, perhaps, but where does that get you? A new spearhead every other minute! Who ever saw the like, tell me that! Why, a good flint spearhead used to last for ages and ages! But what I say is, just you wait! one day they'll be glad to return to our honest stone weapons! That's why I keep them whenever I find them: old arrows and hammers and flint knives. – And he calls it junk!"

The old man nearly choked with grief and rage.

"You know," said Mrs Johnny to make him think of something else, "it's just the same with these hides. 'Mother,' that girl says to me, 'why on earth do you do all that scraping, it's such a lot of trouble! You try dressing the hide with ash, at least that doesn't stink.' You'd teach me, would you?" the old lady burst out at her absent daughter-in-law. "I know what I know! People have always scraped hides, and what hides they used to be! Of course, if it's too much trouble for you – That's why they're always inventing and trying out something new. – Dressing hides with ash, indeed! Who's ever heard of such a thing?"

"There you are," yawned Johnny. "*Our* way of doing things isn't good enough for them. Oh no! And they say stone weapons are uncomfortable to the hand. Well, it's certainly true we didn't think very much about comfort! But nowadays – dear, dear, dear, mind you don't bruise your poor hands! I ask you, where's it all going to end? Take the present-day children. 'Just leave them alone, grandad,' our daughter-in-law says, 'let them romp.' Very well, but what are they going to grow up like?"

"If only it didn't make them so loutish," lamented the old lady. "They're ill bred, and that's the truth!"

"It's the fault of this modern education," declared Old Johnny. "And if just now and then I drop a word to our son he says: 'Dad, you don't understand, times have changed, this is a different epoch. Why,' he says, 'even these bone weapons aren't the last word! some day people will discover a better material –' Now, you know, that's really beyond everything! As though anyone had ever seen any resistant material but stone, wood or bone! Why, even a silly woman like you must admit that – that – that it's absolutely outrageous!"

Mrs Johnny let her hands fall into her lap. "Oh dear," she said. "Where can they get these absurd ideas from?"

"They say it's the lastest fashion," mumbled the toothless old man. "I tell you, over yonder, four days' journey from here, a new tribe has moved in, a pack of foreigners, and our boy says that's what they're doing. So you see, our youngsters have got all this nonsense from them. These bone-headed weapons and all. They even – they even buy the stuff from them," he shouted angrily, "for our good hides! As if anything good ever came from foreigners! Never have anything to do with foreign riff-raff. Why, that's the teaching handed down to us by our forefathers: when you see a foreigner, fall upon him and bash his head in without more ado. That's always been the rule: no palaver, just kill him. 'Not a bit of it, Dad,' says our son, 'times have changed, we're beginning to exchange goods with them.' Exchange goods! If I kill a man and take what he's got I get his goods and don't give him anything for them – so why exchange? 'No, no, Dad,' says our son, 'you pay in human lives and it's a pity to waste them.' So there you are: they say it's a waste of human lives. That's the modern view," growled the old man with distaste: "They're cowards, that's what they are! And how are so many people going to get enough to eat if they don't kill each other, tell me that? Why, elk are getting confoundedly scarce as it is! It's all very well not wanting to waste human lives; but they have no respect for tradition, they don't honour their forefathers and their parents. Everything's going to rack and ruin," old Johnny burst out violently. "The other day I saw one of these young whipper-snappers daubing clay on the wall of the cave in the likeness of a bison. I gave him a box on the ear, but our son said: 'Let him be, why, the bison looks absolutely alive!' Now, that really is beyond everything! Who ever heard of wasting time like that? If you've not enough to do, boy, then trim a piece of flint, but don't paint bison on the wall! What's the use of such nonsense?"

Mrs Johnny pursed up her lips severely. "If it were only bison," she let drop after a moment.

"What do you mean?" asked the old man.

"Oh nothing," said Mrs Johnny defensively, "I'm ashamed to talk about it . . . Well, if you must know," she said with sudden decision, "this morning I found . . . in the cave . . . a piece of mammoth tusk. It was carved like . . . like a naked woman. Breasts and all."

"You don't mean it!" said the old man, astonished. "And who carved it?"

Mrs Johnny shrugged her shoulders with a shocked expression on her face. "Who knows? One of the youngsters, I suppose. I threw it into the fire, but – Such breasts it had! Fi!"

"Things can't go on like this," said old Johnny, getting the words out with difficulty. "It's perverse! You know, it all comes of their carving all manner of things out of bone! We never thought of doing anything so shameless because you simply couldn't do it in flint. This is what it leads to! These are their vaunted discoveries! They must always be inventing something, always starting something new, till they bring everything to rack and ruin. And you mark my words," cried Johnny the cave man with prophetic illumination, "the whole thing won't last much longer!"

THE ENCHANTED POLLY

CATHERINE STORR

THE WOLF SAT GLOOMILY in his kitchen. Once, in happier days, he had actually had Polly there for a short time. Now all he had to comfort him was a nearly empty larder and his small library of well pawed-over books. It was one of these he was reading now.

He read about clever animals who caught beautiful little girls and kept them, sometimes as servants, sometimes as wives. Sometimes they meant to eat them. But it was disappointing that though all the tigers, lions, dragons, foxes, wolves and other animals seemed to have very little difficulty in catching their prey, most of them somehow or other failed to keep them. The beautiful little girls generally managed to escape at the last minute, often by tricks which the wolf considered very unsportsmanlike.

The story he was reading just now was about a dragon chasing a princess, who had once been in his cave, but had then run away. She couldn't run as fast as the dragon could move, but she turned herself first into a fly, then into an old woman, lastly into a bridge over a river. The dragon never managed to recognize her in any of her disguises, and in the end he was drowned in the river under the princess-bridge.

"Terrible the things these girls get up to! No wonder I've never been able to catch that Polly. Here am I, a simple wolf, while she can turn into almost anything she chooses. It's all so unfair!" the wolf exclaimed. Then he remembered that even if he couldn't take on different shapes, he at least had brains. "I'll show her! She shan't deceive me. Whatever she pretends to be, I shall know it's really her. I'm not stupid like that dragon. I am clever," the wolf thought. He had heard that fish was good for the brains, so he opened a tin of tuna and gobbled it down for supper. In case that didn't do the trick, he slept with another tin of tuna under his pillow that night. He very cleverly decided not to open it first, in case the oil made a mess on the bedclothes. "Wow! I am brilliant this evening," he said to himself.

The next day, Polly, coming home from school, saw the wolf standing outside a shop and staring fixedly in at the window. She had hoped that he wouldn't notice her, but just as she was behind him, he turned round. She was preparing to run, when he spoke.

"Little girl!"

Polly looked around. There were plenty of people walking up and down near by, but there was no other little girl in sight.

"Little girl! Little girl!" the wolf said again.

"Are you talking to me?" Polly asked.

"Of course I am talking to you. You don't think that when I talk to myself I call myself 'little girl', do you? I'm not little, for one thing, and I'm not a girl, for another. I don't make stupid mistakes like that," the wolf said irritably.

"If you mean me, why don't you say my name?" Polly asked.

"Because I don't know it, of course. You look remarkably like a girl called Polly, but I know you aren't her because she is somewhere else, in disguise. That's why I have to call you 'little girl'. Now stop asking silly questions and give me a sensible answer for a change," the wolf said.

"A sensible answer to what?"

The wolf pointed to the window he had been gazing at.

"Do you see those two flies inside the window?"

Polly looked. Sure enough, two flies were climbing up on

the other side of the glass. As soon as one reached nearly to the top, it buzzed angrily down to the bottom again. The wolf was following their movements with great interest, his long tongue lolling out and sometimes twitching slightly.

"Those flies. I daresay they look just the same to you, little girl? You can't tell which is which? Can you?"

Polly looked carefully and then said, "No, I can't."

"You see no difference between them?"

"Perhaps that one that's crawling up now is a little bigger," Polly said, pointing.

"Nonsense. They are exactly the same. But I'll tell you something that will surprise you. Although they look alike to you, I know which is which," the wolf said.

"Which is which, then? I mean, if they look exactly the same, what's the difference between them?"

"You're trying to muddle me. What I mean is, I know which of them really is a proper fly and which isn't."

"Which is the proper fly?" Polly asked.

The wolf looked closely at both flies. Then he pointed. "That one."

"If that's the real fly, what is the other one?" Polly asked.

"Aha! Now, little girl, you are going to be surprised. That other fly – is a girl."

"A girl fly?"

"Don't be so stupid. Not a girl fly. A real girl, like you. A human girl. Young, plump. Well, plumpish. Delicious."

Polly looked at the two flies again. The real fly was doing the angry buzzing act down from the top of the window to the bottom. The fly who was really a girl was skipping up the glass. At this moment she stopped and began twiddling her front pair of legs.

"You see? She knows that I know who she is. She is wringing her hands because she sees that I have penetrated her disguise and that in a moment I shall claim her as my own," the wolf said, triumphant.

"Flies often do that with their front legs. My mother says it looks like knitting," Polly said.

"Nonsense. Only flies that are really girls would do it. Look at the other fly. The real one."

As the wolf said this, the other fly also stopped on its path up the window and also knat with its front legs.

"You see?" Polly said.

"He's copying the Polly fly," the wolf said quickly.

"Polly?" said Polly.

"That . . . Fly . . . Is . . . Only . . . Pretending to be a fly. She . . . Is . . . Really . . . A . . . Girl," the wolf said in the loud slow tones used for speaking to fools or foreigners.

"Why?" Polly asked.

"I can't go back to the beginning. All I can tell you is that there is a maddening child who lives round here, the one who looks rather like you, called Polly. She thinks she is clever. She believes that if she disguises herself as a fly, I shan't know who she is, so she will escape from my clutches. But she's not all that clever. I don't suppose she's any cleverer than you are. And I am much too clever for her. It didn't take me any time to see that that was no ordinary fly."

"What happens next?" Polly asked, interested.

"I catch her and eat her all up," the wolf replied.

"I wouldn't think she'll taste very good. Not if she's still a fly."

"She won't remain a fly. Directly I lay my paw on her and say her real name, she will be compelled to resume her ordinary shape. She'll be a girl again, like you. And then . . . Yum!" the wolf said with gusto.

"How are you going to lay your paw on her? Both those flies are inside the window and we're outside," Polly said.

"I am now going into the shop to claim my prize," the wolf said. He disappeared. Polly took the opportunity to get herself safely home to tea.

A day or two later, Polly, walking down the High Street, caught sight of the wolf standing very close to a group of three stout elderly ladies, who were talking to each other as they waited for the bus. They were so busy gossiping that they didn't notice the wolf edging nearer and nearer, until he was within touching distance of the stoutest of the ladies. His paw was raised to touch the stoutest lady on the shoulder, when she turned her head and saw a very large, dark person standing uncomfortably close.

"Here! Move off, can't you? No one asked you to join the party," she said, taking a surprised step backwards.

"Aha!" the wolf said.

"Pardon? What's that supposed to mean?" the stoutest lady asked.

"I said, Aha. You can't deceive me . . ."

"Here! Who do you think you're talking to? You be careful, me lad, or I'll get the police on to you."

"It's no good. I know you," the wolf said.

"I don't know you. And I don't want to, so take yourself off," the stoutest lady said, raising her umbrella threateningly. The two women behind her pressed closer and one of them seized a handful of the wolf's fur.

"You are Polly, and I claim you as my own," the wolf said, trying to lay a paw on the stoutest lady's shoulder.

There was a scuffle. There were cries of "Keep your dirty paws off me!" and "Who do you think you are?" and "Never been so insulted in my life." Someone was calling for the police. Others were trying to beat the wolf with sticks or umbrellas. One of the stout ladies was having hysterics. The wolf was howling with rage and pain. It was lucky for him that just then the huge red bus lumbered up, and since it was already late and the next one probably wouldn't be there for nearly an hour, the stout ladies had to leave him on the pavement, and climb into the bus, murmuring angrily as they went.

Polly felt almost sorry for the wolf. This did not prevent her from keeping a safe distance the next day, when she saw him standing disconsolately on a bridge that ran over a motorway not far from her home. He looked bedraggled. One ear had been torn, and there were small bare patches on his neck as if handfuls of fur had been pulled out. He was peering down at the motorway beneath the bridge, and Polly was wondering whether to go home and hope that he hadn't seen her, when he called out to her.

"Little girl! Little girl!"

"If he doesn't recognize me, perhaps it's safe to stay," Polly thought, and she moved a little nearer.

"Little girl! Come and look at this bridge," the wolf said.

"I'm looking," Polly said.

"Have you noticed anything funny about it?" the wolf asked.

"No, I haven't. What's funny about it?" Polly called back.

"Ssssh. Don't shout like that. She might hear."

"Who might hear?"

"Polly."

"Where is Polly?" Polly asked. She wanted to see just how stupid the wolf could be.

"She has turned herself into a bridge this time," the wolf said.

"A bridge? Why?"

"You must be the same little girl who was so stupid last

time I tried to explain about Polly. She turns herself into different shapes so that I shan't recognize her. Don't you remember? Last time she was disguised as an old lady. The time before that she was a fly. This time it's a bridge. In the stories it's a bridge over a river, but there doesn't seem to be a river round here, so I suppose she thought a motorway would do instead. She's made one mistake, though."

"What's that?" Polly asked.

"This bridge hasn't got a road going over it. And it's got steps each end. That's stupid. How can cars climb up steps?"

"This bridge isn't meant for cars. It's meant for people," Polly said.

"Nonsense. Bridges are meant for cars. And horses and carts. Why should there be a bridge just for people? They can walk across a bridge for cars, but cars can't climb stairs and get across a silly bridge like this. That's how I know it isn't a real bridge. It's that stupid little Polly," the wolf said.

"So what are you going to do?" Polly asked.

"I shall seize her and tell her that I know that it's her. Then she has to go back to her real shape. Then I shall eat her," the wolf said.

"That's what you said before," Polly said.

"When? What did I say before? Something very intelligent, I'm sure."

"When you were watching those flies. What happened to them?"

"The flies. Oh, that," the wolf said.

"Yes, that. Wasn't one of the flies Polly after all?"

"Of course it was. I told you so at the time," the wolf said.

"Then why didn't you catch her and eat her up?" Polly asked.

"It was very confusing. They buzzed so. And rushed up and down the window. You saw for yourself. They were very much alike, you must agree."

"I couldn't tell which was which," Polly said.

"Exactly. That was the difficulty," the wolf said.

"So you got the wrong one?"

"I laid my paw on the Polly fly and said her name. Nothing happened. I had got the real fly by mistake. Meanwhile the other fly, the Polly fly, had gone. Flown. It was most disappointing."

"What went wrong with the old ladies?" Polly asked.

The wolf looked surprised and pained.

"It was a disgraceful affair. I should prefer not to talk about it. I was treated abominably."

"And now you've discovered that Polly is disguised as this bridge?" Polly asked.

"That's right."

"What are you waiting for? When are you going to lay your hand on this bridge and say that you know who it really is?" Polly asked. She was ready to run if she thought the wolf might come to his senses and make a grab for the real Polly.

"I'm just making sure in my mind that I remember how to swim," the wolf said.

"What has swimming got to do with it?" Polly asked, surprised.

The wolf groaned loudly.

"I must say that for sheer stupidity you beat even that stupid little Polly I was telling you about. Don't you ever read a good book? Don't you know that the princess turns herself into a bridge, and the dragon or the giant or the wolf who is after her stands on the bridge and says her real name and then she turns back into a princess again? And then the dragon, or whoever it is, falls into the river below and is drowned. That's because dragons are stupid. But I am not stupid. I have very cleverly had swimming lessons in the public baths. I just have to remember how to work my front and back legs, and I shan't drown. Instead I shall quickly swim to the river bank, climb out and eat up the princess. I mean, I shall eat up the Polly."

"But there isn't a river under this bridge," Polly pointed out.

The wolf looked down at the endless procession of lorries, cars and coaches passing beneath the bridge.

"No. I had forgotten. In that case there's no need to wait. I don't have to remember how to swim and I needn't get my fur wet. So much the better." He turned towards the middle of the bridge.

"Wolf!" Polly called after him.

"What is it now?"

"When you say Polly's name and the bridge disappears, you won't be in a river, but you will be down there," Polly said, pointing down to the motorway.

"What about it?" the wolf said.

"The traffic won't stop for you. All the cars and coaches

and things are going much too fast. Their brakes couldn't work quickly enough. You'll get run over. Squashed. Flat as a pancake," Polly said.

The wolf stopped. He looked over the railing to the stream of traffic below.

"Are you quite sure they won't stop?" he asked.

"Quite sure."

"You wouldn't like to do a small scientific experiment? You jump down there and we shall see how many cars stop and what happens to you?"

"No, thank you, Wolf. I wouldn't like to do that at all," said clever Polly.

The wolf returned from the middle of the bridge and stood carefully to one side.

"Do you think I should be safe if I fell from here?" he asked.

"It's still quite a long way to fall on to the ground," Polly said.

"What would you suggest then?"

"I think you should go over to the other side. Then you should go down the steps to the bottom, so that you don't fall anywhere. Then you can lay your paw on that end of the bridge and tell it that you know it's Polly," Polly said.

"You are really quite a kind little girl. And not as much stupider than Polly as I thought," the wolf said, preparing to do as Polly had advised. Half-way across the bridge he turned and looked back.

"Wait there and see the great transformation! See a bridge turn into a Polly and get snapped up by the clever wolf," he shouted.

But Polly knew better than that. Before the wolf had got down the steps on the further side of the motorway, Polly had run home. She didn't want to risk being chased and caught, when the wolf discovered that the bridge was only a bridge after all.

HUDDEN AND DUDDEN AND DONALD O'NEARY

IRISH FOLKTALE

ONCE UPON A TIME there were two farmers, and their names were Hudden and Dudden. They had poultry in their yards, sheep on the uplands, and scores of cattle in the meadow-land alongside the river. But for all that they were not happy. For just between their two farms there lived a poor man by the name of Donald O'Neary. He had a hovel over his head and a strip of grass that was barely enough to keep his one cow, Daisy, from starving; and, though she did her best, it was but seldom that Donald got a drink of milk or a roll of butter from Daisy. You would think that was little here to make Hudden and Dudden jealous, but so it is, the more one has the more one wants, and Donald's neighbours lay awake of nights scheming how they might get hold of his little strip of grass-land. Daisy, poor thing, they never thought of; she was just a bag of bones.

One day Hudden met Dudden, and they were soon grumbling as usual, and all to the tune of "If only we could get that vagabond Donald O'Neary out of the country."

"Let's kill Daisy," said Hudden at last; "if that doesn't make him clear out, nothing will."

No sooner said than agreed, and it wasn't dark before Hudden and Dudden crept up to the little shed where lay poor

Daisy trying her best to chew the cud, though she hadn't had as much grass in the day as would cover your hand. And when Donald came to see if Daisy was all snug for the night, the poor beast had only time to lick his hand once before she died.

Well, Donald was a shrewd fellow, and downhearted though he was, began to think if he could get any good out of Daisy's death. He thought and he thought, and the next day you could have seen him trudging off early to the fair, Daisy's hide over his shoulder, every penny he had jingling in his pockets. Just before he got to the fair, he made several slits in the hide and put a penny in each slit. Then he walked into the best inn of the town as bold as if it belonged to him, and, hanging the hide up on a nail in the wall, sat down.

"Some of your best whiskey," said he to the landlord. But the landlord didn't like his looks. "Is it fearing I won't pay you, you are?" said Donald; "Why I have a hide here that gives me all the money I want." And with that he hit it a whack with his stick and out hopped a penny. The landlord opened his eyes, as you may fancy.

"What'll you take for that hide?"

"It's not for sale, my good man."

"Will you take a gold piece?"

"It's not for sale I tell you. Hasn't it kept me and mine for years?" and with that Donald hit the hide another whack and out jumped a second penny.

Well, the long and short of it was that Donald let the hide go for a pile of gold; and, that very evening, who but he should walk up to Hudden's door?

"Good-evening, Hudden. Will you lend me your best pair of scales?"

Hudden stared and Hudden scratched his head, but he lent the scales.

When Donald was safe at home, he pulled out his pocketful of bright gold and began to weigh each piece in the scales. But Hudden had put a lump of butter at the bottom, and so the last piece of gold stuck fast to the scales when he took them back to Hudden.

If Hudden had stared before, he stared ten times more now, and no sooner was Donald's back turned, than he was off as hard as he could pelt to Dudden's.

"Good-evening to you, Dudden. That vagabond, bad luck to him . . ."

"You mean Donald O'Neary?"

"And who else should I mean? He's back here weighing out sackfuls of gold."

"How do you know that?"

"Here are my scales that he borrowed, and here's a gold piece still sticking to them."

Off they went together, and they came to Donald's door. Donald had finished making the last pile of ten gold pieces. And he couldn't finish because a piece had stuck to the scales.

In they walked without an "If you please" or "By your leave."

"Well, I never!" was all they could say.

"Good-evening, Hudden, good-evening Dudden. Ah! you thought you had played me a fine trick, but you never did me a better turn in all your lives. When I found poor Daisy dead, I thought to myself, 'Well, her hide may fetch something', and it did. Hides are worth their weight in gold in the market just now."

Hudden nudged Dudden, and Dudden winked at Hudden.

"Good-evening, Donald O'Neary."

"Good-evening, kind friends."

The next day there wasn't a cow or a calf that belonged to Hudden or Dudden but her hide was going to the fair in Hudden's biggest cart drawn by Dudden's strongest pair of horses.

When they came to the fair, each one took a hide over his arm, and there they were walking through the fair, bawling out at the top of their voices, "Hides to sell! hides to sell!"

Out came the tanner.

"How much for your hides, my good men?"

"Their weight in gold."

"It's early in the day to come out of the tavern." That was all the tanner said, and back he went to his yard.

"Hides to sell! Fine fresh hides to sell!"

Out came the cobbler.

"How much for your hides, my men?"

"Their weight in gold."

"Is it making game of me you are! Take that for your pains," and the cobbler dealt Hudden a blow that made him stagger.

Up the people came running from one end of the fair to the other. "What's the matter? What's the matter?" cried they.

"Here are a couple of vagabonds selling hides at their weight in gold," said the cobbler.

"Hold 'em fast, hold 'em fast!" bawled the innkeeper, who was the last to come up, he was so fat. "I'll wager it's one of the rogues who tricked me out of thirty gold pieces yesterday for a wretched hide."

It was more kicks than halfpence that Hudden and Dudden got before they were well on their way home again, and they didn't run the slower because all the dogs of the town were at their heels.

Well, as you may fancy, if they loved Donald little before, they loved him less now.

"What's the matter, friends?" said he as he saw them tearing along, their hats knocked in, and their coats torn off, and their faces black and blue. "Is it fighting you've been? Or mayhap you met the police, ill luck to them?"

"We'll police you, you vagabond. It's mighty smart you thought yourself to be, deluding us with your lying tales."

"Who deluded you? Didn't you see the gold with your own two eyes?"

But it was no use talking. Pay for it he must, and should. There was a meal-sack handy, and into it Hudden and Dudden popped Donald O'Neary, tied him up tight, ran a pole through the knot, and off they started for the Brown Lake of the Bog, each with a pole-end on his shoulder, and Donald O'Neary between.

But the Brown Lake was far, the road was dusty, Hudden and Dudden were sore and weary, and they were parched with thirst. There was an inn by the roadside.

"Let's go in," said Hudden, "I'm dead beat. It's heavy he is for the little he had to eat."

If Hudden was willing, so was Dudden. As for Donald, you may be sure his leave wasn't asked, but he was dumped down at the inn door for all the world as if he had been a sack of potatoes.

"Sit still, you vagabond," said Dudden, "if we don't mind waiting, you needn't."

Donald held his peace, but after a while he heard the glasses clink, and Hudden singing away at the top of his voice.

"I won't have her, I tell you; I won't have her!" said Donald. But nobody heeded what he said.

"I won't have her, I tell you; I won't have her!" said Donald, and this time he said it louder; but nobody heeded what he said.

"I won't have her, I tell you; I won't have her!" said Donald; and this time he said it as loud as he could.

"And who won't you have may I be so bold as to ask?" said a farmer, who had just come up with a drove of cattle and was turning in for a glass.

"It's the King's daughter. They are bothering the life out of me to marry her."

"You're the lucky fellow. I'd give something to be in your shoes."

"Do you see that now! Wouldn't it be a fine thing for a farmer to be marrying a Princess, all dressed in gold and jewels?"

"Jewels, do you say? Ah, now, couldn't you take me with you?"

"Well, you're an honest fellow, and as I don't care for the King's daughter though she's as beautiful as the day, and is covered in jewels from top to toe, you shall have her. Just undo the cord, and let me out, they tied me up tight, as they knew I'd run away from her."

Out crawled Donald, in crept the farmer.

"Now lie still, and don't mind the shaking, it's only rumbling over the palace steps you'll be. And maybe they'll abuse you for a vagabond, who won't have the King's daughter, but you needn't mind that. Ah! it's a deal I'm giving up for you, sure as it is that I don't care for the Princess."

"Take my cattle in exchange," said the farmer; and you may guess it wasn't long before Donald was at their tails driving them homewards.

Out came Hudden and Dudden, and the one took one end of the pole, and the other the other.

"I'm thinking he's heavier," said Hudden.

"Ah, never mind," said Dudden; "it's only a step now to the Brown Lake."

"I'll have her now! I'll have her now!" bawled the farmer, from inside the sack.

"By my faith, and you shall though," said Hudden, and he laid his stick across the sack.

"I'll have her! I'll have her!" bawled the farmer louder than ever.

"Well, here you are," said Dudden for they were now come to the Brown Lake, and, unslinging the sack, they pitched it plump into the lake.

"You'll not be playing your tricks on us any longer," said Hudden.

"True for you," said Dudden. "Ah, Donald, my boy, it was an ill day for you when you borrowed my scales."

Off they went, with a light step and an easy heart, but when they were near home, who should they see but Donald O'Neary, and all around him the cows were grazing, and the calves were kicking up their heels and butting their heads together.

"Is it you, Donald?" said Dudden. "Faith, you've been quicker than we have."

"True for you, Dudden, and let me thank you kindly; the turn was good, if the will was ill. You'll have heard, like me, that the Brown Lake leads to the Land of Promise. I always put it down as lies, but it is just as true as my word. Look at the cattle."

Hudden stared, and Dudden gaped, but they couldn't get over the cattle, fine fat cattle they were too.

"It's only the worst I could bring up with me," said Donald O'Neary, "the others were so fat, there was no driving them. Faith, too, it's little wonder they didn't care to leave, with grass as far as you could see, and as sweet and juicy as fresh butter."

"Ah, now Donald, we haven't always been friends," said Dudden, "but, as I was just saying, you were ever a decent lad, and you'll show us the way, won't you?"

"I don't see that I'm called upon to do that, there is a power more cattle down there. Why shouldn't I have them all to myself?"

"Faith, they may well say, the richer you get, the harder the heart. You always were neighbourly lad, Donald. You wouldn't wish to keep all the luck to yourself?"

"True for you Hudden, though 'tis a bad example you set me. But I'll not be thinking of old times. There is plenty for all there, so come along with me."

Off they trudged, with a light heart and an eager step. When they came to Brown Lake, the sky was full of little white clouds, and, if the sky was full, the lake was just as full.

"Ah! now, look, there they are," cried Donald, as he pointed to the clouds in the lake.

"Where? Where?" cried Hudden, and "Don't be greedy!" cried Dudden, as he jumped his hardest to be up first with the fat cattle. But if he jumped first Hudden wasn't long behind.

They never came back. Maybe they got too fat, like the cattle. As for Donald O'Neary, he had cattle and sheep all his days to his heart's content.

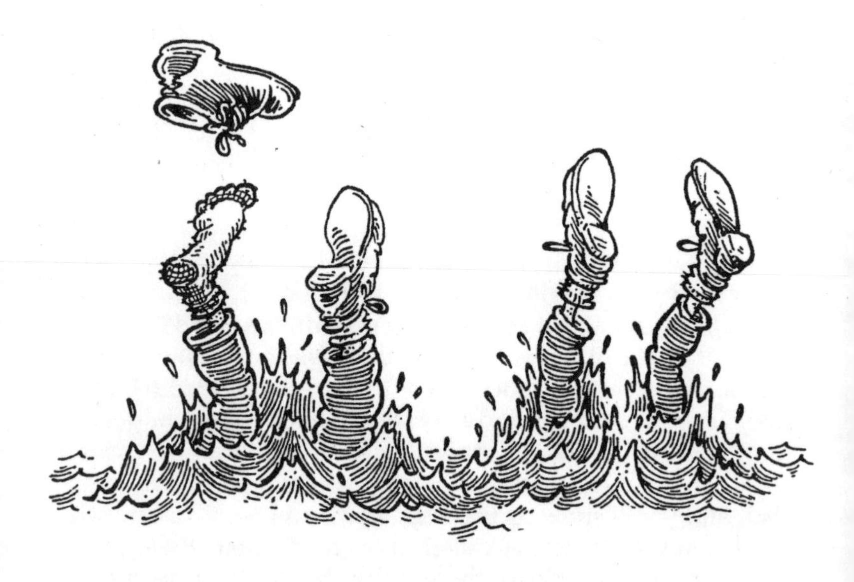

THE GREAT SEA SERPENT

HANS CHRISTIAN ANDERSEN

THERE ONCE WAS a little fish. He was of good family; his name I have forgotten – if you want to know it, you must ask someone learned in these matters. He had one thousand and eight hundred brothers and sisters, all born at the same time. They did not know their parents and had to take care of themselves. They swam around happily in the sea. They had enough water to drink – all the great oceans of the world. They did not speculate upon where their food would come from, that would come by itelf. Each wanted to follow his own inclinations and live his own life; not that they gave much thought to that either.

The sun shone down into the sea and illuminated the water. It was a strange world, filled with the most fantastic creatures; some of them were so big and had such huge jaws that they could have swallowed all eighteen hundred of the little fish at once. But this, too, they did not worry about, for none of them had been eaten yet.

The little fishes swam close together, as herring or mackerel do. They were thinking about nothing except swimming. Suddenly they heard a terrible noise, and from the surface of the sea a great thing was cast among them. There was more and more of it; it was endless and had neither head nor tail. It was heavy and every one of the small fishes that it hit was either stunned and thrown aside or had its back broken.

The fishes – big and small, the ones who lived up near the waves and those who dwelled in the depths – all fled, while this monstrous serpent grew longer and longer as it sank deeper and deeper, until at last it was hundreds of miles long, and lay at the bottom of the sea, crossing the whole ocean.

All the fishes – yes, even the snails and all the other animals that live in the sea – saw or heard about the strange, gigantic, unknown eel that had descended into the sea from the air above.

What was it? We know that it was the telegraph cable, thousands of miles long, that human beings had laid to connect America and Europe.

All the inhabitants of the sea were frightened of this new huge animal that had come to live among them. The flying fishes leaped up from the sea and into the air; and the gurnard since it knew how, shot up out of the water like a bullet. Others went down into the depths of the ocean so fast that they were there before the telegraph cable. They frightened both the cod and the flounder, who were swimming around peacefully, hunting and eating their fellow creatures.

A couple of sea cucumbers were so petrified that they spat out their own stomachs in fright; but they survived, for they knew how to swallow them again. Lots of lobsters and crabs left their shells in the confusion. During all this, the eighteen hundred little fishes were separated; most of them never saw one another again, nor would they have recognized one another if they had. Only a dozen of them stayed in the same spot, and after they had lain still a couple of hours their worst fright was over and curiosity became stronger than fear.

They looked about, both above and below themselves, and there at the bottom of the sea they thought they saw the monster that had frightened them all. It looked thin, but who knew how big it could make itself or how strong it was. It lay very still, but it might be up to something.

The more timid of the small fish said, "Let it lie where it is, it is no concern of ours." But the tiniest of them were determined to find out what it was. Since the monster had come from above, it was better to seek information about it up there. They swam up to the surface of the ocean. The wind was still and the sea was like a mirror.

They met a dolphin. He is a fellow who likes to jump and to turn somersaults in the sea. The dolphin has eyes to see with and ought to have seen what happened, and therefore the little fishes approached him. But a dolphin only thinks about himself and his somersaults; he didn't know what to say, so he didn't say anything, but looked very proud.

A seal came swimming by just at that moment, and even though it eats small fishes, it was more polite than the dolphin. Luckily it happened to be full, and it knew more than the jumping fish. "Many a night have I lain on a wet stone – miles and miles away from here – and looked towards land, where live those treacherous creatures who call themselves, in their own language, men. They are always hunting me and my kind, though usually we manage to escape. That is exactly what happened to the great sea serpent that you are asking about – it got away from them. They had had it in their power for ever so long, and kept it up on land. Now men wanted to transport it to another country, across the sea. – Why? you may ask, but I can't answer. – They had a lot of trouble getting it on board the ship. But they finally succeeded; after all, it was weakened from its stay on land. They rolled it up, round and round into a coil. It wiggled and writhed, and what a lot of noise it made! I heard it. When the ship got out to sea, the great eel slipped overboard. They tried to stop it. I saw them, there were dozens of hands holding on to its body. But they couldn't. Now it is lying down at the bottom of the sea, and I think it will stay there for a while."

"It looks awfully thin," said the tiny fishes.

"They had starved it," explained the seal. "But it will soon get its old figure and strength back. I am sure it is the great sea serpent: the one men are so afraid of that they talk about it all the time. I had not believed it existed, but now I do. And that was it." With a flip of its tail, the seal dived and was gone.

"How much he knew and how well he talked," said one of the little fishes admiringly. "I have never known so much as I do now – I just hope it wasn't all lies."

"We could swim down and look," suggested the tiniest of the tiny fishes. "And on the way down we could hear what the other fishes think."

"We wouldn't move a fin to know anything more," said all the other tiny fishes, turned, and swam away.

"But I will," shouted the tiniest one, and swam down into the depths. But he was far away from where the great sea serpent had sunk. The little fish searched in every direction. Never had he realized that the world was so big. Great shoals of herring glided by like silver boats, and behind them came schools of mackerel that were even more splendid and brilliant. There were fishes of all shapes, with all kinds of markings and colours. Jellyfish, looking like transparent plants, floated by, carried by the currents. Down at the bottom of the sea the strangest things grew: tall grasses and palm-shaped trees whose every leaf was covered with crustaceans.

At last the tiny fish spied a long dark line far below it and swam down to it. It was not the giant serpent but the railing of a sunken ship, whose upper and lower decks had been torn in two by the pressure of the sea. The little fish entered the great cabin, where the terrified passengers had gathered as the ship went down; they had all drowned and the currents of the sea had carried their bodies away, except for two of them: a young woman who lay on a bench with her babe in her arms. The sea rocked them gently; they looked as though they were sleeping. The little fish grew frightened as he looked at them. What if they were to wake? The cabin was so quiet and so lonely that the tiny fish hurried away again, out into the light, where there were other fishes. It had not swum very far when it met a young whale; it was awfully big.

"Please don't swallow me," pleaded the little fish. "I am so little you could hardly taste me, and I find it such a great pleasure to live."

"What are you doing down here?" grunted the whale. "It is much too deep for your kind." Then the tiny fish told the whale about the great eel – or whatever it could be – that had come from the air and descended into the sea, frightening even the most courageous fishes.

"Ha, ha, ha!" laughed the whale, and swallowed so much water that it had to surface in order to breathe and spout the water out. "Ho-ho . . . ha-ha. That must have been the thing that tickled my back when I was turning over. I thought it was the mast of a ship and was just about to use it as a back scratcher; but it must have been that. It lies farther out. I think

I will go and have a look at it; I haven't anything else to do."

The whale swam away and the tiny fish followed it, but not too closely for the great animal left a turbulent wake behind it.

They met a shark and an old sawfish. They, too, had heard about the strange great eel that was so thin and yet longer than any other fish. They hadn't seen it but wanted to.

A catfish joined them. "If that sea serpent is not thicker than an anchor cable, then I will cut it in two, in one bite," he said, and opened his monstrous jaws to show his six rows of teeth. "If I can make a mark in an anchor I guess I can bite a stem like that in two."

"There it is," cried the whale. "Look how it moves, twisting and turning." The whale thought he had better eyesight than the others. As a matter of fact he hadn't; what he had seen was merely an old conger eel, several yards long, that was swimming towards them.

"That fellow has never caused any commotion in the sea before, or frightened any other big fish," said the catfish with disgust. "I have met him often."

They told the conger eel about the new sea serpent and asked him if he wanted to go with them to discover what it was.

"I wonder if it is longer than I am," said the conger eel, and stretched himself. "If it is, then it will be sorry."

"It certainly will," said the rest of the company. "There are enough of us so we don't have to tolerate it if we don't want to!" they exclaimed, and hurried on.

They saw something that looked like a floating island that was having trouble keeping itself from sinking. It was an old whale. His head was overgrown with seaweed, and on his back were so many mussels and oysters that its black skin looked as if it had white spots.

"Come on, old man," the young whale said. "There is a new fish in the ocean and we won't tolerate it!"

"Oh, let me stay where I am!" grumbled the old whale. "Peace is all I ask, to be left in peace. Ow! Ow! . . . I am very sick, it will be the death of me. My only comfort is to let my back emerge above the water, then the sea gulls scratch it: the sweet birds. That helps a lot as long as they don't dig too deep with their bills and get into the blubber. There's the skeleton of one still sitting on my back. It got stuck and couldn't get loose when I had to submerge. The little fishes picked his bones clean. You can see it . . . Look at him, and look at me . . . Oh, I am very sick."

"You are just imagining all that," said the young whale. "I am not sick, no one that lives in the sea is ever sick."

"I am sorry!" said the old whale. "The eels have skin diseases, the carp have smallpox, and we all suffer from worms."

"Nonsense!" shouted the shark, who didn't like to listen to that kind of talk. Neither did the others, so they all swam on.

At last they came to the place where part of the telegraph cable lies, that stretches from Europe to America across sand shoals and high mountains, through endless forests of seaweed and coral. The currents move as the winds do in the heavens above, and through them swim schools of fishes, more numerous than the flocks of migratory birds that fly through the air. There was a noise, a sound, a humming, the ghost of which you hear in the great conch shell when you hold it up to your ear.

"There is the serpent!" shouted the bigger fish and the little fishes too. They had caught sight of some of the telegraph cable but neither the beginning nor the end of it, for they were both lost in the far distance. Sponges, polyps, and gorgonia swayed above it and leaned against it, sometimes hiding it from view. Sea urchins and snails climbed over it; and great crabs, like giant spiders, walked tight-rope along it. Deep-blue sea cucumbers – or whatever those creatures are called who eat with their whole body – lay next to it; one would think that they were trying to smell it. Flounders and cod kept turning from side to side, in order to be able to listen to what everyone was saying. The starfishes had dug themselves down in the mire; only two of their points were sticking up, but they had eyes on them and were staring at the black snake, hoping to see something come out of it.

The telegraph cable lay perfectly still, as if it were lifeless; but inside, it was filled with life: with thoughts, human thoughts.

"That thing is treacherous," said the whale. "It might hit me in the stomach, and that is my weak point."

"Let's feel our way forward," said one of the polyps. "I have long arms and flexible fingers. I've already touched it, but now I'll take a firmer grasp."

And it stuck out its arms and encircled the cable. "I have felt both its stomach and its back. It is not scaly. I don't think it has any skin either. I don't believe it lays eggs and I don't think it gives birth to live children."

The conger eel lay down beside the cable and stretched itself as far as it could. "It is longer than I am," it admitted. "But length isn't everything. One has to have skin, a good stomach and, above all, suppleness."

The whale – the young strong whale! – bowed more deeply than it ever had before. "Are you a fish or a plant?" he asked. "Or are you a surface creation, one of those who can't live down here?"

The telegraph didn't answer, though it was filled with words. Thoughts travelled through it so fast that they took only seconds to move from one end to the other: hundreds of miles away.

"Will you answer or be bitten in two?" asked the ill-mannered shark.

All the other fishes repeated the question: "Answer or be bitten in two?"

The telegraph cable didn't move; it had its own ideas, which isn't surprising for someone so full of thoughts. "Let them bite me in two," it thought. "Then I will be pulled up and repaired. It has happened to lots of my relations, that are not half as long as I am." But it didn't speak, it telegraphed; besides, it found the question impertinent; after all, it was lying there on official business.

Dusk had come. The sun was setting, as men say. It was a fiery red, and the clouds were as brilliant as fire – one more beautiful than the other.

"Now comes the red illumination," said the polyp. "Maybe the thing will be easier to see in that light, though I hardly think it worth looking at."

"Attack it! Attack it!" screamed the catfish, and showed all his teeth.

"Attack it! Attack it!" shouted the whale, the shark, the swordfish, and the conger eel.

They pushed forward. The catfish was first; but just as it was going to bite the cable the swordfish, who was a little too eager, stuck its sword into the behind of the catfish. It was a mistake, but it kept the catfish from using the full strength of its jaw muscles.

There was a great muddle in the mud. The sea cucumbers, the big fishes and the small ones swam around in circles; they pushed and shoved and squashed and ate each other up. The crabs and the lobsters fought, and the snails pulled their heads into their houses. The telegraph cable just minded its own business, which is the proper thing for a telegraph cable to do.

Night came to the sky above, but down in the ocean millions and millions of little animals illuminated the water. Crayfish no larger than the head of a pin gave off light. It is incredible and wonderful; and quite true.

All the animals of the sea looked at the telegraph cable. "If only we knew what it was – or at least what it wasn't," said one of the fishes. And that was a very important question.

An old sea cow – human beings call them mermen and mermaids – came gliding by. This one was a mermaid. She had a tail and short arms for splashing, hanging breasts, and seaweed and parasites on her head – and of these she was very proud. "If you want learning and knowledge," she said, "then I think I am the best equipped to give it to you. But I want free passage on the bottom of the sea for myself and my family. I am a fish like you, and a reptile by training. I am the most intelligent citizen of the ocean. I know about everything under the water and everything above it. The thing that you are worrying about comes from up there; and everything from above is dead and powerless, once it comes down here. So let it lie, it is only a human invention and of no importance."

"I think it may be more than that," said the tiny fish.

"Shut up, mackerel!" said the sea cow.

"Shrimp!" shouted the others, and they meant it as an insult.

The sea cow explained to them that the sea serpent who had frightened them – the cable itself, by the way, didn't make a sound – was not dangerous. It was only an invention of those animals up on dry land called human beings. When she finished talking about the sea serpent, she gave a little lesson in the craftiness and wickedness of men: "They are always trying to catch us. That is the only reason for their existence. They throw down nets, traps, and long fishing lines that have hooks, with bait attached to them, to try and fool us. This is probably another – bigger – fishing line. They are so stupid that they expect us to bite on it. But we aren't as dumb as that. Don't touch that piece of junk. It will unravel, fall apart, and become mud and mire – the whole thing. Let it lie there and rot. Anything that comes from above is worthless; it breaks or creaks; it is no good!"

"No good!" said all the creatures of the sea, accepting the mermaid's opinion in order to have one.

The little tiny fish didn't agree, but it had learned to keep its thoughts to itself. "That enormously long snake may be the most marvellous fish in the sea. I have a feeling that it is."

"Marvellous!" we human beings agree; and we can prove that it is true.

The great sea serpent of the fable has become a fact. It was constructed by human skill, conceived by human intelligence. It stretches from the Eastern Hemisphere to the Western, carrying messages from country to country faster than light travels from the sun down to the earth. Each year the great serpent grows. Soon it will stretch across all the great oceans, under the storm-whipped waves and the glasslike water, through which the skipper can look down as if he were sailing through the air and see the multitude of fish and the fireworks of colour.

In the very depths is a *Midgards-worm*, biting its own tail as it circumscribes the world. Fish and reptiles hit their heads against it: it is impossible to understand what it is by looking at it. Human thoughts expressed in all the languages of the world, and yet silent: the snake of knowledge of good and evil. The most wonderful of the wonders of the sea: our time's great sea serpent!

THE LIZARD LETDOWN

CHRISTINE McDONNELL

On his way home from school Leo often stopped to look in the pet store window. Sometimes there were puppies tumbling over each other or curled up in balls, sleeping. Sometimes there were kittens – striped ones and spotted ones – so little, they looked as if they had just opened their eyes. At Eastertime the window was filled with fat white rabbits. And once there was a parrot who sat on a stand and screamed, "Hello, Mac."

When he stopped to look on Wednesday, the window was filled with guinea pigs: a round brown one, a sleek black one, an orange one, a fluffy white one, and a little one with patches of every colour, mixed up like a crazy quilt. The patchwork pig had an orange spot covering one eye and a brown spot circling the other. His back was a mixture of white, brown, black, and orange. Two feet were black, one was orange, and the other white. Leo laughed when he saw him. When the patchwork pig noticed Leo standing at the window with his nose pressed up against the glass, he began to make noise. "Wink, wink, wink-wink-wink," he said. His nose twitched like a rabbit and his round black eyes shone.

"Wink, wink, wink," Leo said in return. Then he looked around quickly to make sure no one was passing nearby. The sidewalk was empty. "Wink, wink," Leo bleated some more. The guinea pig answered back.

Leo stepped back from the glass to read the signs on the window.

GUINEA PIGS / *$6.00 each*
CHAMELEONS / *$3.75 each*

Six dollars is a lot, Leo thought. Much more than I've got. Maybe a chameleon would be better.

Leo had read about chameleons. They could change colours to match whatever you put them on. Only $3.75. I'd like a chameleon, he thought. I could carry him around and put him on top of different things and watch him change colours. Only $3.75.

Leo put his hand into his pocket and pulled out his change. Only thirty-five cents, and he had been planning to buy a chocolate crunch bar at the drugstore. There was no money left in his bank either.

He started home with his hands in his pockets, looking carefully at the sidewalk in hopes of finding some change. He picked up a penny in front of the barber shop and a nickel by the fire station. He checked every parking meter on Main Street, but there were no stuck coins. He checked the pay phones on the corner, but no one had forgotten any change. When he turned down his own block, after skipping the chocolate bar, he had forty-one cents in his pocket.

Not enough, thought Leo.

He was still thinking of the chameleon when he reached his own yard. I bet that lizard could turn red and yellow just like all these leaves, he thought. Leaves! Leo looked down at the sidewalk. It was covered with leaves. So was the yard. And the yard next door at Mrs Rider's house. I'll rake up the leaves and earn enough to buy that little lizard, Leo decided.

He dropped his knapsack on the back porch and found the rake in a corner of the garage. Mrs Rider was likely to pay more than his parents, who would probably tell him that his allowance was payment enough. He went next door and rang Mrs Rider's bell.

"Hello, Leo," said Mrs Rider, taking her reading glasses off her nose.

"Want me to rake for you, Mrs Rider?"

The old lady looked out at her yard. "Those leaves have fallen down in earnest, haven't they now? It must have been the rain last night. I don't remember there being so many before."

She scrutinized Leo with a frown. "You want to rake for me, do you?" She paused. "Well, Leo, I don't know. Do you remember what happened last year?"

Leo blushed and scratched the back of his knee with his foot. Last year he had agreed to rake for Mrs Rider. He had raked all the leaves into a gigantic pile in the middle of the front yard. But before he could stuff the leaves into the big green plastic garbage bags, Bulldog Nelson, Tony Rosa, and two other older boys had come along.

"Hey, let's jump in those leaves," Bulldog yelled to the others.

"Wait. Wait a minute." Leo tried to stop them. But Tony just pushed him out of the way. "Step aside, short stuff," he said.

The four big boys jumped in the leaf pile again and again until the leaves were scattered all over the yard. Hearing their loud hoots and yells, Mrs Rider came out of her house. She hated to have children playing in her front yard. "They'll ruin my azaleas," she always said.

"Get away from here, you boys. Get away. Right now," she said, walking stiffly down the front path, leaning on her cane. She stopped and pointed the cane at Leo.

"And you, young man. What have you got to say for yourself? Letting those hoodlums run all over this yard. You've done more harm than good."

Leo tried to explain, but he tripped over his words and felt foolish. He didn't want to admit that he was afraid of Bulldog and his friends. So he apologized, raked up the leaves again, and went home without collecting any pay.

"But that was last year, Mrs Rider. I'm older now. You can

trust me. Those big guys can't push me around now." Then an idea popped into Leo's mind. "Besides, this time I'll rake all the leaves into the backyard and nobody will be able to see the pile from the street."

Mrs Rider peered at him closely once more. Then she smiled, and her stern expression thawed. "Very well, Leo. You may have a second chance. Let's say two dollars for the front and back yards, and another dollar if you'll bring in a supply of firewood from the garage and pile it neatly by the wood stove in the den. I like to keep warm when I read."

Leo quickly agreed. Three dollars. That made $3.41. With this week's allowance he'd have enough to buy that chameleon on Saturday.

He raked all the leaves into a pile in the backyard. They were wet and slippery from last night's rain, so he wasn't even tempted to jump into the pile himself. When he bundled the leaves together, they filled six garbage bags. Leo lugged them one at a time to the side of the house where the garbage cans stood.

The wood was heavy too. Leo made at least ten trips from the garage, piling the wood neatly by the wall in the bright-yellow den. Mrs Rider's wing chair stood between the window and the stove. Bookcases filled the opposite wall. It was a cheerful, sunny room, and the wood stove made it cozy. No wonder she likes to read in here, he thought.

Mrs Rider offered Leo a glass of cold cider when he was finished. "Good work," she said as she gave him three dollar bills. Leo thanked her, put the money in his pocket, and headed home.

Only three days until he could buy the chameleon, he thought as he lay in bed that night. Tomorrow he would build a cage. There was leftover screening and wood in the basement. It wouldn't be hard. He would put in a branch for the lizard to climb on and a bed of moss for a soft place to lie. His paint dishes would be good for food and water.

I wonder what a lizard eats, he thought before he fell asleep.

He finished the cage on Thursday afternoon. His sister, Eleanor, got a look at it as Leo carried it up to his room.

"What's that?" she asked.

"A cage."

"I can see that, dopey. What's it for?"

Leo hesitated. He hadn't asked his parents about the lizard. If Eleanor made a fuss, maybe they wouldn't let him buy one.

"It's a cage for an animal."

"I figured *that*. It's too small for you."

Leo knew he couldn't stall any longer. Eleanor was getting irritated.

"It's for the new pet I'm buying on Saturday."

Eleanor eyed the construction. It didn't look very sturdy.

"It's escape-proof," Leo added.

"I've heard that one before. Like the time you brought your class mouse home."

It had taken Leo three weeks to find the mouse after it got loose.

"What kind of nasty little beast are you bringing home this time?"

Leo had to tell her. "It's a chameleon."

"Ugh! One of those creepy lizards? Why do you want to waste your money on something disgusting like that?"

"It's neat," protested Leo. "It turns colours. It won't bother you at all. I promise. So don't make a big deal out of this, okay?"

"You mean, with Mom and Dad?" Eleanor hesitated for a second, calculating her advantage. "I'll help you out if you promise not to tell that I've been keeping my light on late every night."

Leo had seen the light in Eleanor's room when he got up to go to the bathroom at night. He knew she was staying up, reading.

He agreed happily, thinking he had gotten the best of the bargain.

His parents did not protest too much.

"Are you sure that this is what you want?" his mother asked.

Leo was sure he was sure.

On Friday he spent the afternoon finding different-coloured things to test his chameleon on. He made a pile on his bed.

First there was his red-plaid bathrobe. It was a deep red, with lines of green, yellow, and white in it. The chameleon would look like a Scotch lizard when he landed on the bathrobe, Leo thought.

Next he borrowed the pink blotter from Eleanor's desk. She never used it anyway. It had come in a set that Grandma had sent, a pink desk set that said JUNIOR MISS on it in gold letters. Eleanor hated it.

Then he thought of his blue-and-yellow-striped tie, the one he had to wear for Christmas dinner and visits to his grandmother's. At least it will be good for something fun for a change, Leo thought.

In Leo's imagination his chameleon could turn every colour of the rainbow.

On Saturday morning Leo collected his allowance from his father and headed downtown. The sign was still up in the pet shop window. The guinea pigs were still there too. At least three were – the shiny black one, the orange one, and the patchwork one.

Leo didn't stop to say "Wink, wink," this time. He rushed right inside. The chameleons were crawling around in a tank on the counter.

"One chameleon, please," Leo said to the pet store owner.

"Three seventy-five," said the man, assembling a little square white box with a wire handle.

Leo counted out his money and put it on the counter. The man reached inside the tank.

"Is there one in particular that you want?"

They all looked alike. But one blinked his eyes twice and Leo decided that he must be signalling him.

"That one," he said, pointing to the lizard that had blinked.

The pet store man picked up the chameleon and put him in the box. It looked like a container of Chinese food. Boy, wouldn't somebody be surprised if he opened this up expecting egg foo yung, Leo thought.

"Do you know how to take care of this lizard?" asked the man.

Leo shook his head.

"Fresh water, lettuce, and mealy worms. You can grow them yourself. Here are the instructions and a bunch to start with."

They were disgusting! Little white worms crawling in a heap. Ugh! Who ever thought chameleons would eat anything so awful-looking.

"You put these worms on some oatmeal and they'll start reproducing. You'll have a colony in no time," said the man cheerfully.

And my mother will have a fit, Leo thought.

He took the bag with the lizard, the worms, and a care-

and-feeding sheet and thanked the man. Then he stopped by the window on his way out. The patchwork pig seemed to recognize him right away.

"Wink. Wink-wink," he bleated, and raced around in a circle.

"Wink-wink, yourself," Leo answered. "I bet you don't eat worms."

He put the bag in his bike basket and headed home.

Up in his room Leo set the chameleon container on his desk and opened the top of the cage. Then he lifted the flaps of the white box. The lizard was moving around in the bottom, trying to climb the sides. His claws rasped against the cardboard. Leo tentatively reached a finger into the box to feel the lizard's skin. It was cool, dry, and bumpy; not slimy but still a little creepy. The lizard squirmed away, not enjoying the encounter any more than Leo.

Leo decided not to pick the chameleon up just yet. Instead, he upended the box and slid the surprised lizard into his new home. He landed on the moss but quickly scampered up the branch and perched there quivering, his eyes darting around the cage.

Leo dumped a blob of worms into the food dish and watched his chameleon for a while. But the lizard did not move, and finally, feeling slightly disappointed, Leo went down to lunch.

"Wash your hands well if you've been touching that animal," said Leo's mother as she put Leo's sandwich in front of him.

"I only touched him with one finger," Leo said.

"That's enough. Wash up."

Leo decided not to mention the mealy worms during lunch. It was probably not table talk, as his mother always said.

After lunch he went back upstairs. The chameleon had not moved. Maybe it wouldn't be so hard to pick him up after all.

Leo spread his bathrobe on the bed. Next to it he placed the pink blotter. Then, finally, he draped his tie across the bedspread.

"Time to experiment," he announced. "Introducing the rainbow lizard."

The chameleon sat on the branch in his cage, so still that he didn't seem alive. Leo carefully opened the top and reached in. Just as his hand came down on the chameleon, it whisked away to the other side of the cage.

"Oh-ho! Tricky, eh?" Leo reached again and missed.

He finally cornered the lizard between the screen and the branch and picked him up. The chameleon wiggled madly for a second and then was very still. Quick, abrupt moves were his specialty. Leo kept his hand firmly around him even though he didn't like the way he felt.

"Time to see what you can do."

He placed the chameleon on top of the red-plaid bathrobe,

making a fence around him with his legs. The lizard sat there, blinking. He turned his head so one beady little eye was staring straight at Leo. Leo watched and waited. The chameleon was brown. The bathrobe was a bright-red plaid. Leo waited and watched carefully to see the transformation.

Nothing happened.

The chameleon remained brown. He didn't turn even the slightest bit red.

Maybe plaid is too hard to start with, Leo thought, beginning to feel worried about his investment. He probably has to start off on something easier. Leo pushed the lizard farther over until he was standing on the pink blotting paper and watched carefully. The lizard stuck out his tongue, but it was red, not pink. His skin stayed brown. He was definitely not co-operating with the experiment.

After waiting for a few minutes, Leo decided to try the tie.

"Maybe these bright colours are too difficult for you," he said to the chameleon, moving him over onto the tie. "If you can't do the stripe, at least try to turn blue."

The chameleon remained a dull brown.

"What a gyp! What good are you, anyway?"

He picked up the little lizard and put him back in the cage, setting him down on the moss. This time the chameleon stayed there instead of climbing the branch. Gradually he turned from a dull brown to a dull green.

Leo watched the change. "Okay. At least you can do something. Brown and green. Is that all?" He was very disappointed. "I wonder if those are the only colours you turn." Maybe the rainbow lizard existed only in his imagination.

There was a set of encyclopedias in Eleanor's room. Leo found what he was hunting for in volume three. It even had a little drawing that looked exactly like his lizard. The description said that they only turn colours for camouflage, and can become green or brown depending on their surroundings.

"What a gyp," Leo repeated. "Three dollars and seventy-five cents, and he doesn't know any good colours. And I have to grow his disgusting old worms."

He went back into his room to look at his pet. There wasn't really anything he could do with the lizard. He wasn't any fun to play with. He didn't make any noises. He wasn't even good to pet.

The white box was still standing next to the cage. In a flash Leo decided what to do. He trapped the lizard again and lifted him out. Then he dumped him back into the container and folded down the top. He looked at the clock. Three forty-five. Plenty of time to get downtown.

The pet store was still open when Leo pulled up on his bike. And the patchwork pig was still in the window. Leo crossed his toes inside his sneakers for luck as he waited at the counter.

"Back already?" said the pet store man when it was Leo's turn.

Leo put the chameleon container on the counter. "Do you think I could trade this lizard in?"

"Trade it in for what?"

Leo glanced back at the window. "For the guinea pig with all the different colours. I know I need another two twenty-five, but I'll earn that by Monday. Could you take this lizard back and keep my three seventy-five as a down payment on a guinea pig?"

Leo held his breath as he waited for the answer.

The man opened the box and looked at the chameleon. "Looks none the worse for wear," he said.

He dumped the chameleon back into the cage with the others. It darted around until it found a space behind a piece of bark.

"Which guinea pig did you say?"

"The spotted one with all the different colours."

"Oh. The patchwork pig. All right, I'll hold it for you."

Before he left, Leo reached in and gave the patchwork pig a pat. His fur was soft and his nose was cold. His whiskers tickled as he sniffed Leo's hand.

"I'll call you Patches."

Leo spent Sunday raking leaves in three other yards. By dinnertime his arms ached, but he had made five dollars. Enough for the guinea pig, a book on how to care for him, and the water bottle that he needed for drinking.

He went by after school on Monday to pick him up. The man put the guinea pig in a large white box with air holes. Leo carried him home carefully. The pig did not make a sound the whole trip. Not a single "wink".

"Don't be scared," Leo said in a soft voice.

Up in his room Leo set the box softly on his bed. Then he emptied out all of the moss and branches from the cage. He lined the bottom with a thick layer of newspaper and bunched soft pieces of towel in the corner.

"That's for your bed," he said to the guinea pig, who was still in the box.

Next Leo fastened the water bottle to the side of the cage. "All set," he said as he opened the box.

The guinea pig looked up with his shiny round eyes. His nose twitched. Leo gave his soft fur a pat with his finger. Then he reached underneath and picked him up. The guinea pig was surprisingly heavy. Leo could feel his heart beating against his side.

"Hey, don't be scared," he said again.

He set the guinea pig down gently in his new home. The animal waddled around the edges of the cage sniffing the corners. He licked the spout of the water bottle. Then he lay down on the towel.

Leo watched him closely, anxious to make sure he was comfortable. "Welcome home, Patches," he said. "I bet you're hungry."

He raced downstairs and scrounged in the refrigerator vegetable bin. He found two carrots that were starting to shrivel and started back upstairs. When he reached the top step, Patches began to make noise.

"Wink, wink. Wink-wink," he bleated when he heard Leo coming.

"Hold on, Patches. I'm on my way," Leo called. He grinned as he skipped down the hall, a carrot in each hand. I bet he'll call me like this every day when I get home from school, Leo thought. A pet who says hello, now that's something special.

HANDSEL AND GRISTLE

MICHAEL ROSEN

ONCE A PLUM A TIME, in the middle of a forest, there lived a poor woodnutter and his woof. They lived in a little wooden sausage with their two children, Handsel and Gristle. The one was called Handsel because he had huge hands and the other was called Gristle because it was all gristly.

One day the woodnutter came home and he says: "I've been nutting wood all day long but I couldn't sell Lenny."

(No one knew who Lenny was, no one asked him and no one has ever found out.)

Anyway, that night the children went to bed with puffin to eat.

Downstairs, the woodnutter and woof talked. The woodnutter says, "How can we feed the children? They've gone to bed with puffin to eat again."

"Quite," says woof, "that's what I was stinking. There's only one thing we *can* do – take them off to the forest and leave them there."

"But that would be terrible," said the woodnutter. "They might die of gold, they'd sneeze to death out there. Or they might starve and die of Star Station."

"Well," said woof, "they might die of Star Station here. We've got no money because you went nutting wood all day and couldn't sell Lenny."

(There's Lenny again.)

What the woodnutter and woof didn't know, was that Handsel and Gristle were still a cake and they could hear everything the woodnutter and woof were sighing.

Later that night, when everybun was in bed, asweep, Handsel crept downstairs, out into the garden and filled his rockets full of phones and then crept back to bed.

The next day, woof said, "Right, children, today we're all going to the forest to nut wood."

They all left the little wooden sausage and off they went.

As they walked along woof noticed that Handsel kept stopping.

"Keep up, Handsel," woof said. What woof didn't notice was that Handsel was taking the phones out of his rocket and dropping them on the ground.

They walked and walked and walked until in the end they hopped.

"Well," said woof, "you two stay here, we've got to go off and nut some wood." And off they went.

Handsel and Gristle played together for a bit till they felt so tired they lay down and fell asweep.

When they poke up it was bark and they were all abone.

Gristle didn't know where it was, but Handsel said, "Don't worry, leave it to me," and there, shining in the spoon-light were the phones all the way back comb.

When they got back, their father was very pleased to see them but woof was very cross.

"Oh, you wicked children, why did you sweep so wrong in the forest. We thought you'd never get back comb."

That night the woodnutter and woof sat and talked again.

"Well," said woof, "we'll just have to try again. We'll take them a long way, bleep into the forest."

Upstairs Handsel and Gristle were still a cake and they could fear everything their father and woof were sighing.

So later, when everybun was in bed, Handsel staired down crept. But this time the sausage door was locked. He couldn't get out. Sadly he went back to bed.

Curly in the morning, woof got the two children up. "Right, we're all going off to the forest again to nut wood. Here's some bread for you to eat when we get there."

And off they went.

As they walked along, Handsel broke off little boots of bread and dropped them on the ground behind them.

"Handsel," said his father, "Why do you keep shopping?"

"I'm not shopping," said Handsel. "We haven't got any money – you couldn't sell Lenny, remember?"

"Who's Lenny?" said the woodnutter.

"Keep up, Handsel," said woof.

They went bleeper and bleeper into the forest to a place they had never seen before or five.

"We're just going off to nut some wood. We'll come and get you before it gets bark," said woof. And off they went.

Handsel and Gristle played for a pile and then, when they smelt tired, they went to sweep. When they poke up it was bark.

"Don't worry, Gristle," said Handsel, "all we have to do is follow the boots of bread."

"What boots? What bread?" said Gristle.

"I croak up my bread into little boots," said Handsel, "and all we have to do is follow the creadbums."

But when they started to look for the creadbums, there weren't Lenny.

(Hallo, Lenny.)

You see all the birds of the forest had eaten them. So they walked and walked, lay down, walked and walked and walked – but they were lost. They walked some more and suddenly they came upon a little house.

The whales of the house were made of gingerbread, the wind-nose were made of sugar and the tyres on the roof were made of chocolate.

Handsel and Gristle were so hungry that they ran up to the house and started to break off bits of the chocolate tyres and sugar wind-nose.

Then all of a sudden, a little old ladle came out of the house.

"Oh, what dear little children, come in, come in. You look so hungry. I'll give you something to beat."

She took them inside and gave them a huge pile of cancakes.

Handsel and Gristle thought they were very lucky – what they didn't know was that the little old ladle was really a wicked itch – a wicked itch that lay in wait for children. The itch then killed them to eat.

When Handsel and Gristle finished their cancakes, the itch took hold of Handsel's hand (which was very easy considering how big it was) and before he knew what had happened, the itch threw him into a rage in the corner of the room.

"Aha, I'm a wicked itch," said the little old ladle, "and you'll stay in that rage till you're nice and cat. And as for you," said the itch to Gristle, "you can fleep the swore."

"Who swore?" said Gristle. "Not me."

"Shuttup," said the itch, "or I'll eat your eyes."

Now, this itch couldn't see very well. In fact, most itches can't see very well and Gristle noticed this.

Every day, the itch watched Handsel's rage and the itch said,

"Hold out your finger, boy. I want to know if you're getting cat."

"Are we getting a cat?" said Gristle.

"Shuttup," said the itch "or I'll eat your nose."

It was about this time that Gristle told Handsel that the itch couldn't see. (Which Handsel knew all along because all the itches he knew just itched and nothing much else.)

Anyway, because of this, Handsel didn't hold out his finger for the itch, he yelled out a bone instead.

"Not ready yet," the itch said.

Well, four weeks passed by and the itch said, "I can't wait this pong. You're cat enough for me."

"He's nothing like a cat," said Gristle.

"Shuttup," said the itch, "or I'll eat your lips."

Then the itch told Gristle to fill a kettle of water and light the fire in the gloven. When Gristle got back, the itch said,

"Is the fire ready?"

"I don't know," said Gristle.

"Stupiddle thing," said the itch. "I have to do everyping round here."

Then the wicked itch went right up to the gloven door, but Gristle was just behind and Gristle gave the itch one pig push; the itch went flying into the gloven; Gristle slammed the door, and that was the end of the wicked itch.

Then Gristle ran over to Handsel and got him out of his rage.

"Handsel, we're free," said Gristle.

"Three?" said Handsel. "There's only two of us now you've got rid of the itch."

But they were so happy they hugged and missed and danced and sank all round the room.

Then they filled their rockets full of bits of chocolate tyres, gingerbread whales and sugar wind-nose and ran back through the forest to the woodnutter's little sausage.

When he saw Handsel and Gristle, he was overjointed. Woof was dead by now, so Handsel and Gristle and the old woodnutter lived afferly ever harpy.

(And they never did sell Lenny.)

BURGLARS!

NORMAN HUNTER

PROFESSOR BRANESTAWM rang the bell for his Housekeeper, and then, remembering that he'd taken the bell away to invent a new kind of one, he went out into the kitchen to find her.

"Mrs Flittersnoop," he said looking at her through his near-sighted glasses and holding the other four pairs two in each hand, "put your things on and come to the pictures with me. There is a very instructive film on this evening; all about the home life of the brussels sprout."

"Thank you kindly, sir," said Mrs Flittersnoop. "I've just got my ironing to finish, which won't take a minute, and I'll be ready." She didn't care a bent pen-nib about the brussels sprout picture, but she wanted to see the Mickey Mouse one. So while the Professor was putting on his boots and taking them off again because he had them on the wrong feet, and getting some money out of his money-box with a bit of wire, she finished off the ironing, put on her best bonnet, the blue one with the imitation strawberries on it, and off they went.

"Dear, dear," said the Professor when they got back from the pictures, "I don't remember leaving that window open, but I'm glad we did because I forgot my latchkey."

"Goodness gracious, a mussey me, oh deary deary!" cried Mrs Flittersnoop.

The room was all anyhow. The things were all nohow and it was a sight enough to make a tidy housekeeper like Mrs Flittersnoop give notice at once. But she didn't do it.

"The other rooms are the same," called the Professor from the top of the stairs. "Burglars have been."

And so they had. While the Professor and his Housekeeper had been at the pictures thieves had broken in. They'd stolen the Professor's silver teapot that his auntie gave him, and the butter-dish he was going to give his auntie, only he forgot. They'd taken the Housekeeper's picture-postcard album with the views of Brighton in it, and the Professor's best egg-cups that were never used except on Sundays.

"This is all wrong," said the Professor, coming downstairs and running in and out of the rooms and keeping on finding more things that had gone. "I won't have it. I'm going to invent a burglar catcher; that's what I'm going to invent."

"We'd better get a policeman first," said Mrs Flittersnoop.

The Professor had just picked some things up and was wondering where they went. "I'll get a policeman," he said, putting them down again and stopping wondering. So he fetched a policeman, who brought another policeman, and they both went into the kitchen and had a cup of tea while the Professor went into his inventory to invent a burglar catcher and Mrs Flittersnoop went to bed.

Next morning the Professor was still inventing. It was lucky the burglars hadn't stolen his inventory, but they couldn't do that because it was too heavy to take away, being a shed sort of workshop, big enough to get inside. They couldn't even take any of the Professor's inventing tools, because the door was fastened with a special Professor lock that didn't open with a key at all but only when you squeezed some tooth-paste into it and then blew through the keyhole. And, of course, the burglars didn't know about that. They never do know about things of that sort.

"How far have you got with the burglar catcher?" asked Mrs Flittersnoop presently, coming in with breakfast, which the Professor always had in his inventory when he was inventing.

"Not very far yet," he said. In fact, he'd only got as far as nailing two pieces of wood together and starting to think what to do next. So he stopped for a bit and had his breakfast.

Then he went on inventing day and night for ever so long.

"Come and see the burglar catcher," he said one day, and they both went into his study, where a funny-looking sort of thing was all fixed up by the window.

"Bless me!" said Mrs Flittersnoop. "It looks like a mangle with a lot of arms."

"Yes," said the Professor, "it had to look like that because it was too difficult making it look like anything else. Now watch."

He brought out a bolster with his overcoat fastened round it and they went round outside the window.

"This is a dummy burglar," he explained, putting the bolster thing on the window-sill. "In he goes." He opened the window and pushed the dummy inside.

Immediately there were a lot of clicking and whirring noises and the mangle-looking thing twiddled its arms. The wheels began to go round and things began to squeak and whizz. And the window closed itself behind the dummy.

"It's working, it's working," cried the Professor, dancing with joy and treading on three geraniums in the flower-bed.

Suddenly the clicking and whizzing stopped, a trap-door opened in the study floor and something fell through it. Then a bell rang.

"That's the alarm," said the Professor, rushing away. "It means the burglar thing's caught a burglar."

He led the way down into the cellar, and there on the cellar floor was the bolster with the overcoat on. And it was all tied up with ropes and wound round with straps and tapes so that it looked like one of those mummy things out of a museum. You could hardly see any bolster or coat at all, it was so tied up.

"Well I never," said Mrs Flittersnoop.

The Professor undid the bolster and put his overcoat on. Then he went upstairs and wound the burglar catcher up again, put on the Housekeeper's bonnet by mistake and went to the pictures again. He wanted to see the brussels sprout film once more, because he'd missed bits of it before through Mrs Flittersnoop keeping on talking to him about her sister Aggie and how she could never wash up a teacup without breaking the handle off.

Mrs Flittersnoop had finished all her housework and done some mending and got the Professor's supper by the time the pictures were over. But the Professor didn't come in. Quite a long time afterwards he didn't come in. She wondered where he could have got to.

"Forgotten where he lives, I'll be bound," she said. "I never did see such a forgetful man. I'd better get a policeman to look for him."

But just as she was going to do that, "br-r-ring-ing-ing-g-g" went the Professor's burglar catcher.

"There now," cried Mrs Flittersnoop. "A burglar and all. And just when the Professor isn't here to see his machine thing catch him. Tut, tut."

She picked up the rolling-pin and ran down into the cellar. Yes, it was a burglar all right. There he lay on the cellar floor all tied up with rope and wound round with straps and tapes and things till he looked like a mummy out of a museum. And like the bolster dummy, he was so tied up you could hardly see any of him.

"Ha," cried the Housekeeper, "I'll teach you to burgle, that I will," but she didn't teach him that at all. She hit him on the head with the rolling-pin, just to make quite sure he shouldn't get away. Then she ran out and got the policeman she was going to fetch to look for the Professor. And the policeman took the burglar away in a wheelbarrow to the police station, all tied up and hit on the head as he was. And the burglar went very quietly. He couldn't do anything else.

But the Professor didn't come home. Not all night he

didn't come home. But the policeman had caught the other burglars by now and got all the Professor's and the Housekeeper's things back, except the postcards of Brighton, which the burglars had sent to their friends. So they had nothing to do but look for the Professor.

But they didn't find him. They hunted everywhere. They looked under the seat at the pictures, but all they found was Mrs Flittersnoop's bonnet with the imitation strawberries on it, which they took to the police station as evidence, if you know what that is. Anyhow they took it whether you know or not.

"Where can he be?" said the Housekeeper. "Oh! he is a careless man to go losing himself like that!"

Then when they'd hunted a lot more and still hadn't found the Professor, the Judge said it was time to try the new burglar they'd caught. So they put him in the prisoner's place in the court, and the court usher called out " 'Ush" and everybody 'ushed.

"You are charged with being a burglar inside Professor Branestawm's house," said the Judge. "What do you mean by it?"

But the prisoner couldn't speak. He was too tied up and wound round to do more than wriggle.

"Ha," said the Judge, "nothing to say for yourself, and I should think not, too."

Then the policeman undid the ropes and unwound the straps and tapes and things. And there was such a lot of them that they filled the court up, and everyone was struggling about in long snaky sort of tapes and ropes and it was ever so long before they could get all sorted out again.

"Goodness gracious me!" cried Mrs Flittersnoop. "If it isn't the Professor!"

It was the Professor. There he was in the prisoner's place. It was he all the time, only nobody knew it because he was so wound up and hidden.

"What's all this?" said the Judge.

"Please, I'm Professor Branestawm," said the Professor, taking off all his five pairs of glasses, which fortunately hadn't been broken, and bowing to the court.

"Well," snapped the Judge. He was very cross because the mixed-up tangle of tapes and things had pulled his wig crooked and he felt silly. "What has that got to do with anything? Didn't you break into the Professor's house?"

"I left my key at home and got in through the window," said the Professor, "forgetting about the burglar catcher."

"That is neither here nor there," said the Judge, "nor anywhere at all for that matter, and it wouldn't make any difference if it was. You broke into the Professor's house. You can't deny it."

"No," said the Professor, "but it was my own house."

"All the more reason why you shouldn't break into it," said the Judge. "What's the front door for?"

"I forgot the key," said the Professor.

"Don't argue," said the Judge, and he held up Mrs Flittersnoop's bonnet that the Professor had worn by mistake and left under the seat at the pictures. "This bonnet, I understand, belongs to your housekeeper."

Mrs Flittersnoop got up and bowed. "Indeed it does, your Majesty," she said, thinking that was the right way to speak to a judge, "but the Professor's welcome to it, I'm sure, if he wants it."

"There you are," said the Judge, "she says he's welcome to it if he wants it. That means she didn't give it to him, did you?"

"No," said Mrs Flittersnoop, "I thought . . ."

"What you thought isn't evidence," snapped the Judge.

"Well, what is evidence, then?" said Mrs Flittersnoop, beginning to get cross. "I never heard of the stuff. And I'm tired of all this talk that I don't understand. Give me my best bonnet and let me go. I've the dinner to get."

"Oh, give the woman her bonnet," said the Judge, and then he turned to the Professor.

"If it had been anybody else's house you'd broken into," he said, "we'd have put you in prison."

"Of course," said the Professor, trying on all his pairs of spectacles one after the other to see which the Judge looked best through.

"And if it had been anyone else who'd broken into your house, we'd have put him in prison," said the Judge.

"Of course," said the Professor, deciding that the Judge looked best through his blue sun-glasses because he couldn't see his face so well.

"But," thundered the Judge, getting all worked up, "as it was you who broke into the house and as it was your own house you broke into, we can only sentence you to be set free, and a fine waste of good time this trial has been."

At this everyone in the court cheered, for they most of them knew the Professor and liked him and were glad everything was going to be all right. And the twelve jurymen cheered louder than anyone, although the Judge hadn't taken the least bit of notice of them and hadn't even asked them their verdict, which was very dislegal of him, if you see what I mean.

And as for Mrs Flittersnoop, she clapped her bonnet on the Professor's head, and then several people carried him shoulder-high out of the court and home, with the imitation strawberries in Mrs Flittersnoop's hat rattling away and the Professor bowing and smiling and looking through first one pair of glasses and then another.

NO MULES

WILLIAM PAPAS

FAAN LIVED RIGHT next to a water-hole on a deep wide river in South Africa. He lived in a kraal with his mother and father and his mule, called Golo. Golo was a pure white mule, except for his nose, which was pink.

Every morning after breakfast Faan, Dad and Golo set off to work in the forest. As they went along Faan played on his flute, which he had made for himself from a reed. When he was going to work he liked to play the woodmen's favourite song. It went like this:

"The tree is tall
So chop it down.
I hope it will fall
On the boss's crown."

All the woodmen liked this song because the tune had a jolly rhythm and even the boss had to smile when he heard it.

Faan's father was a woodcutter. Every day he and the other woodcutters had to chop down the tall trees that the boss had marked out. Then Golo was harnessed to the great trunks and Faan had to lead him to the road, where a truck was waiting to carry the logs away to the sawmill on Pink River.

Faan liked it best when he had to drag the logs downhill

to the waiting trucks. It was fun rushing down the hill. But sometimes the road was higher up the hillside and then Faan and Golo had to heave and struggle to pull the heavy trunks up to it.

When they got to the road, the men took the harness off Golo and began to load the trunks on to the trucks. They chanted and sang and Faan, when he had got his breath back, joined in on his flute.

> "The boss is in a hurry
> So-get-a-move-on.
> Do not linger,
> Load the timber.
> The boss is in a hurry
> So-get-a-move-on.
> The boss is in a hurry
> So-get-a-move-on."

Then the boss climbed into the driving seat and the truck roared off to Pink River.

The cutting, the dragging and the loading went on all day. But after the last truck had gone roaring off to the sawmill, Faan and Golo went down to the river to wash. While he swam in the clear water, Faan thought with longing of the day when *he* would be old enough to go to Pink River.

At last the great day arrived. Faan's father and mother had decided to make a trip to Pink River and said that Faan could go too. Faan jumped up and down with excitement. Then he remembered that Golo had never seen Pink River either, and he asked Dad whether he could take him too.

Dad agreed and they set off. Mum and Dad rode in front and Faan and Golo came behind.

When they arrived at Pink River, Faan was amazed, and even a little frightened, to see so many people, shops, cars and bicycles – and so was Golo.

Dad sent Faan to look around the town while he and Mum went visiting. Faan led Golo along the busy street, staring all round him, and especially into all the shop windows.

Suddenly, in the window of a general store, he saw a shiny new flute. He knew at once that he wanted that flute more than anything else in the world.

He gripped the money he had saved for his trip tightly in his hand and walked boldly into the shop to buy the flute.

The shopkeeper was very surprised to see Faan coming into his shop, and before Faan could ask for the flute, he took him by the arm and pointed to a sign hanging outside the door.

"Can't you read what it says?" he asked. "It says *'NO BLACKS'*. I only serve whites in here." And he went back inside his shop, leaving Faan in the street.

Faan wanted the flute more than anything in the world and he tried to think of a way to get it. Then he looked at Golo.

"You're white," he said. "Well, except for your pink nose, but I don't think he'll mind that. I'll send *you* into the shop for it."

But Golo was not used to shops – or to being indoors at all, for that matter. He flicked a bottle of sweets over with his tail, his ears got caught up in a coat, and his hooves slithered and clattered on the wooden floor.

Women inside the shop screamed and Golo began to be frightened. But he did remember to drop the money in front of the shopkeeper.

Then some men came after Golo and tried to drive him out. They began to shout, and Golo thought he had better get outside very quickly. He kicked out his hooves and made a dash for the street – straight through the plate-glass window!

Faan was astonished to see Golo coming out of the window. Then he saw the flute flying through the air. As he caught it, people came rushing out of the shop trying to catch Golo. Faan saw that the best thing to do was to run away as fast as possible.

He leaped on to Golo's back and shouted, "Home!" But the mule did not need to be told. He was already streaking down the street as fast as he could gallop.

The shopkeeper ran after them until he was too breathless to run any more, and when Faan saw that he had given up the chase he slowed Golo down to a walk. Then he took out his flute and blew a few notes.

Soon he was playing merrily, and Golo began to trot to the tune of the woodcutters' song:

"The boss is in a hurry
So-get-a-move-on.
Do not linger,
Load the timber.
The boss is in a hurry
So-get-a-move-on.
The boss is in a hurry
So-get-a-move-on."

The shopkeeper returned to his shop. It was in a terrible mess. Slowly he began to clear things up.

He put everything back in its place, swept up the broken glass, and soon his shop was looking almost as it did before.

Except for one thing . . . the sign outside the door.

He changed that to *'NO MULES'*.

THE MUSICIANS OF BREMEN

JANOSCH

A DONKEY HAD WORKED thirty-five years for his master in Bremen and carried everything without grumbling, but he had had no wages, only some grass to eat. Then he had grown old, and now his knees buckled or he fell to the ground under a heavy load.

The master considered having him slaughtered, but that would have cost four pounds, which he didn't want to part with. So he chased him away. There stood the poor old donkey, in his shabby suit, alone in Bremen. He had no friends–how could he? He had only worked. He had no relatives, because he had been born in Naples in Italy, a long way from Bremen. He had nothing to eat and nowhere to sleep.

He went down to the station where the Italians, the foreign workers, always stand because they're homesick.

"Italians are Italians and I am Italian too," thought the donkey. "I shan't feel so lonely there."

But the men only kicked and punched and beat him and chased him out of the station.

Then the donkey went to a green park and would have slept a while. But someone chased him away, because lying around in parks was forbidden even to human beings. There was nowhere he could rest, no wall to lean his head against. He had to walk all night, stop and walk again, until it was day.

The donkey went into the labour exchange and asked for

work, no matter what, without pay, just for some grass to eat and straw to lie on.

"Foreigners!" said the official. "Yes, yes. But it's no good. No permit, no labour transfer, no fixed abode and besides that, too old. You see there's no demand for your age group. I'm sorry, honestly!"

He was not at all sorry. That was just something he said. People say things without considering what they mean.

Outside in the street the donkey met a dog, unkempt and tired of life.

"Friend, what a sight you are," said the donkey, "drooping tail and ears, bowed back, no collar, no licence. Look out, if they catch you they'll kill you."

"That's just what I want," said the dog, "because I don't want to live any more. I've lived with Farmer Afterman for twenty dog years and we were good friends. Now he's dead. So I'm sick of life. I don't want to live any longer."

"But I've seen dogs," said the donkey, "who wear fur coats, felt jackets and clothes to keep them warm. They're allowed a seat to themselves on the bus. They smell of French perfume and their hair is curled like a filmstar's. Comrade, you could have the same."

"Those aren't dogs, those are creatures, lamp-post hounds, sofa-cushion smirchers, poodles. Things like that would make me shudder. I'm a real dog. And I don't want to go on living without my friend Afterman."

"Come on, friend, come with me, two is better than one."

Then they met a cat. Unwashed, uncombed, it looked like a thirty-year-old mop after rain.

"You're not doing too well, friend," said the donkey. "If they find you here, unwashed and uncombed, they'll kill you."

"That's right," said the cat. "They're always killing our sort. They drowned my six little kittens. The children of men are the worst. They tortured a friend of mine to death, tied tin cans on her tail and drove her to her death. It was bad, comrades, it was very bad. The blood ran out of her mouth."

The donkey took her on his shoulder and carried her for a while.

When they reached the edge of the town they met a cock which was half plucked and half skinned.

"They were going to kill me," said the cock. "I wouldn't have minded, because the world's not a good place any more. There are not many free hens left. They get shut up in hen houses, 40,000 at a time, each in a little cage. None of them ever gets out in her life-time. And they're never allowed to see the sun, they get 30 grammes of synthetic food twice a day, and as soon as a hen weighs 750 grammes she's electrocuted. Never in their lives do they get to see a cock! Killed, frozen, sold for eighty pence in the supermarket, grilled and eaten. I'd rather have a free death fighting a fox. The world has become a hell."

"Come on, sit on me," said the donkey. "I'll carry you a while. Four is better than three."

They were very hungry and the nights were very cold, but wherever they went in search of food they were chased away and sticks were thrown at them.

People tried to attract the cock with grain – because they wanted to eat it.

One good woman said that they ought to go to the animal refuge. The week before she had given a pound to an animal protection society.

At the animal refuge the people were friendly, but a man said: "We are very fond of animals, but we have no staff to feed and care for them."

A bird which had escaped told them that his friends had been put to sleep there with chloroform because no one had time to feed them. Put to sleep is a pack of lies anyway, because put to sleep means – killed.

The four went on and when they could go no further for hunger and cold they turned into a farmyard. They lay down together as best they could. The cock warmed the cat, the cat warmed the dog, the dog warmed the donkey, and because it was their last hour they began to howl softly – for hunger, thirst and cold.

But in the house which belonged to the farm was the office of a record company: sound studio, technical department, recording apparatus, and an advertising department on the third floor.

As soon as Mr Jansen, the arranger in the second department, heard the muted twittering and mewing and howling he raised his right hand to his moustache and his forehead fell into wrinkles.

"Hey, Swoboda, c'm'ere a moment! Easy now! Get anything? No? Man, where's your ears? This is gonna hit the jackpot. Man, I'm going crazy. It's gonna be a humdinger, a sky-rocket, Apollo 219! Just listen to it, Swoboda! Think about it: the cock, three times louder, right in front, the cat in stereo to the left of the donkey . . . Call up Hanselmann right away. Tell him to give me all the juice he's got. Man, it's gonna be a sensation! It's the most! We'll swing it on the market as a new gig. Send Klüterbaum down quietly to bolt the gates so that the brutes don't run out on us."

"Hallo, Jansen, Smitz on the blower about Udo Jurgen!"

"So what! Tell him I'm in conference. Call up advertising, give me Linke – that you? Look, Linke, look down on the ground! No, the farmyard, of course. Well, whadda ya say? Right, now listen good! We'll put it in all the cans we've got, and tomorrow Zacharias can back all that yowling with a soft fiddle. Look, it's going to be a bomb, it's out of sight, man! A sleeve by Dufte with a coupla wierdies half stripped on the front and all done 'Indian', or whatever they call the spiel! Whadda ya say? No. We'll have to drop 120, mebbe 150 thousand in the advertising. You know the way it is, nothing for nothing. You do that! Work the thing out and give me the figures down here, but now. Out."

In the next twenty minutes dubbing mixers, assistants, electricians and porters poured in. They brought loudspeakers, walkie-talkies, microphones, linked the cock to the amplifier and hung large microphones over the heads of the donkey, the cat and the dog. The sound men twiddled their metering instruments.

Then Miss Bertram tried to feed the donkey with the remains of an apple and said: "Isn't he sweet?" But Mr Jansen hissed, "Wouldya mind cutting that out, Miss Bertram? If the animals ain't hungry they'll stop howling. That'll cost me three million, man!"

"For God's sake, quieter, don't scare the animals!"

"Get a bit of water so they don't croak so fast, perhaps we can get enough for three LPs. A soft harmonium coming in from behind, I think that'd be class."

"This is gonna be a bomb, friend, the Shadows'll be bees' pees beside them."

"Mr Jansen, Linke on the line!"

"Yes! Jansen here! What's that you say? A name? Oh, let's pick something real groovy! 'Bremen Town Musicians'. Bad cheese? Ah well, you think about it, man! Tell you what, 'Bremen Street Fiddlers'. Yes, not bad. Well, let's leave out the Bremen, then! Look, Linke, I think that's groovy, 'Street Fiddlers'. Yep! That's it! Boy, oh boy! I'll get Zacharias moving right away, we'll have the first test in three hours and then get ready to go! Out."

By nine they had about enough music for three long-playing records, when the donkey died. Then the dog.

"Quick, take the cock to the caretaker. He'd better pop it in the pan before it croaks!"

Finally the cat died.

They had made three long-playing records, two backed with Zacharias and his soft fiddle and one with the harmonium – the papers were full of the 'Street Fiddlers' of Bremen. A year later Mr Jansen received two golden discs and could be seen on television at 8.15 p.m.

THE GIRL WHO DIDN'T BELIEVE IN GHOSTS

DAVID HENRY WILSON

CATHY TUMBLEWEED KNEW everything. She knew that the earth was nearly 25,000 miles round and nearly 8,000 miles across; she knew that it was 238,854 miles away from the moon and nearly 93 million miles away from the sun; she knew that there were about 4,000 million people on the earth, and she knew that none of them was as clever as Cathy Tumbleweed. The other children in Miss Arnold's class knew that Cathy knew all these things, because whenever anybody told her anything she would immediately say: "I know", which meant they were wasting her time and theirs by telling her. It's true that Cathy didn't always put her hand up when Miss Arnold asked a question, and it's also true that she made quite a lot of mistakes in her adds, her take-aways, her stories and her comprehensions, but she would simply say: "I knew it really", or "I couldn't be bothered", and nobody could *prove* that she wasn't telling the truth.

Mr and Mrs Tumbleweed were both teachers, like Miss Arnold, and they were always pleased when Cathy got things right, but not so pleased when she got them wrong. Perhaps if Mr and Mrs Tumbleweed had been a little less anxious about Cathy's getting things right, Cathy might have been a little less anxious about getting them wrong, but there are some parents who worry too much about their children, just as there are some who don't worry enough.

Every so often Miss Arnold would read to the class from a story book, and then there would be a discussion about it. On the day that we're concerned with, she read them a ghost story – all about a creaky old house which was inhabited by a creaky old man who was one day visited by a very creaky, very old ghost who said he was really the creaky old man himself as he would be in a few creaky years' time. The children enjoyed the story – especially all the creaky bits – and afterwards Miss Arnold asked them what they knew about ghosts. Of course Cathy Tumbleweed knew everything about ghosts, and so she put up her hand.

"Yes, Cathy?" said Miss Arnold.

"Ghosts," said Cathy, "don't exist. They are pigments of people's imagination."

"You mean figments," said Miss Arnold.

"I know," said Cathy.

"Well how do you know they don't exist?" asked Miss Arnold.

"Because," said Cathy, "It's a fact, and nobody's ever seen one."

"Some people say they have," said Miss Arnold.

"Well they can't *prove* it," said Cathy. "Nobody's ever *proved* it. If they can't *prove* it, it's not true."

Jonathan Justin James pointed out that nobody had ever *proved* that ghosts *didn't* exist, Melvin Woolaway said he'd seen lots of ghosts on television once, Andrew McAndrew said television was better than real life, Gary Gillbank said he'd seen a ghost once in a circus, Cathy said that was just someone dressed up as a ghost . . . and so they went on and on till the bell rang and put an end to what Miss Arnold could only call a spirited discussion.

But that night the spirited discussion was to continue, for as soon as Cathy Tumbleweed's head came to rest on her pillow . . .

Creak. Crrrrrreak. Her bedroom door slowly grinds open on its hinges, and in the darkness she sees a strange white shape floating towards the bed. The air is cold and clammy, like the hand of an ice-cream salesman, and Cathy shivers beneath her cover.

"Hello, Cathy Tumbleweed," says a thin, whining voice.

"Who . . . who . . . who are you?" asks Cathy.

"Don't you know?" says the voice.

"N . . . n . . . no," says Cathy.

"Ugh, I thought you knew everything," says the ghost, "I'm one of those things you don't believe in. I've come to *prove* I'm here."

"I . . . I can s . . . see you're here," says Cathy.

"I know," says the ghost. "Now listen to me, Cathy Tumbleweed. According to you, ghosts are figments of the imagination, aren't they?"

"Pigments," says Cathy.

"Figments!" howls the ghost. "Don't you know anything?! Now if I'm a figment of your imagination, why are you afraid of me?"

"I don't know!" says Cathy, shivering so hard that even her bed begins to creak.

"According to you nobody's ever seen a ghost. But you're seeing a ghost, aren't you?"

"Y . . . y . . . yes, I am."

"Can you *prove* it?"

"Yes . . . no . . . no . . . yes."

"That," says the ghost, "hardly answers my question. When you go to school tomorrow, will you be able to prove to everyone that you saw a ghost?"

"N . . . no," says Cathy.

"Ha ha, ho ho," says the ghost, with a spine-chilling giggle, "but according to you, if you can't prove it, it's not true. Ha ha, ho ho!"

So saying, the ghost sits down on the bed right in front of Cathy, and puts its hand on Cathy's cheek. Imagine a slug crawling over your face, or someone slapping you with a wet sock, or putting your head through a thick, damp cobweb, and you'll have some idea of the feeling Cathy had when the ghost put its hand on her cheek.

"Are you sure I'm here?" asks the ghost.

"Y . . . y . . . yes," says Cathy. "I can see you and feel you."

"But no one at school has seen me or felt me!" says the ghost.

So saying, the ghost stands up right in front of Cathy, and blows down into her face. Imagine the smell of a cowshed that hasn't been cleaned for a week, or a piece of cheese left in the sun for a month, or the feet of an army after a ten-hour march, and you'll have some idea of the smell Cathy smelt when the ghost blew into her face.

"Are you positive I'm here?" asks the ghost.

"Y . . . y . . . yes," says Cathy. "I can see you and feel you and . . . ugh ugh . . . smell you!"

"But no one at school has seen me or felt me or . . . ugh ugh . . . smelt me," says the ghost. "And so, Cathy Tumbleweed, how can you prove that I was here?"

"But you *are* here!" wails Cathy.

"You know I'm here," says the ghost, "and I know I'm here. But how will *they* know I was here?"

"I don't know!" says Cathy. "I don't know I don't know I don't know!"

"Aha!" says the ghost, in a voice that's just a little bit softer and a little bit friendlier. "Now that's quite a good answer. That really is quite a good answer."

"Is it?" says Cathy, in a voice that's just a little less miserable and a little less frightened.

"Yes, it is," says the ghost. "Now let's see if you can tell me the answers to these questions. If it's half-past seven here, what's the time in New Zealand?"

"I . . . I don't know," says Cathy.

"You don't know," says the ghost. "How tall is Mount Kilimanjaro?"

"I don't know," says Cathy.

"You don't know," says the ghost. "How hot is the sun?"

"I don't know," says Cathy.

"You don't know," says the ghost. "Good. That's what I like to hear. Now shall I tell you something, Cathy Tumbleweed?"

"Y . . . yes, please," says Cathy.

"Well," says the ghost, "I don't know either! Ha ha, ho ho, hi hi, I don't know either!"

And the ghost laughs so loud and so long that Cathy starts laughing herself.

"Then why did you ask me?" giggles Cathy.

"Just to show you," giggles the ghost, "that nobody knows everything."

And now the ghost stops giggling, and Cathy stops, too, because not knowing things is really quite a serious business.

"You see," says the ghost, "none of us can be expected to know everything. And if we don't know something, it's best to admit it straight out. Then if we're lucky, someone might tell us the answer, or if we're clever we might find it out for ourselves. Now here's another question for you. What is tumbleweed?"

"I don't know," says Cathy, confidently.

"Good," says the ghost. "That's a sensible answer. Well, tumbleweed is a plant that curls itself up into a ball and rolls around. And if you're going to get up in time for school tomorrow, I suggest you curl yourself up in a little ball right now, and roll yourself to sleep."

And that's just what Cathy did. When she woke up in the morning, of course, the ghost had gone, but – as she pointed out over breakfast when Mr Tumbleweed told Mrs Tumbleweed he couldn't see much hope for the British economy – you don't have to see things in order to believe in them. In fact, Cathy has really changed a lot since her meeting with the ghost, and she's learnt a lot, too, because she's always asking intelligent questions. Miss Arnold is very pleased with her, and so are Mr and Mrs Tumbleweed, though they're a little puzzled by her sudden passionate interest in ghost stories. Puzzled, but not worried.

"It's just one of these phases," said Mrs Tumbleweed one day. "Children always go through them."

"I know," said Mr Tumbleweed.

Oh no you don't, thought Cathy, but she didn't say it out loud. After all, grown-ups can't know everything, but sometimes it's best not to tell them so.

THE STORY-TELLER

SAKI (H. H. MUNRO)

THE AFTERNOON WAS HOT, and so was the railway carriage. The next stop was at Templecombe, nearly an hour ahead. In the carriage were a small girl, and a smaller girl, and a small boy. An aunt belonging to the children sat in one corner seat, and in the further corner seat on the opposite side was a man who was a stranger to them, but the small girls and the small boy were the ones who filled the compartment. The children chatted on and on to their aunt, like a housefly that refuses to be put off. Most of the aunt's remarks seemed to begin with "Don't", and nearly all of the children's remarks began with "Why?" The man said nothing out loud.

"Don't, Cyril, don't," exclaimed the aunt, as the small boy began smacking the cushions of the seat, producing a cloud of dust at each blow.

"Come and look out of the window," she added.

The child moved reluctantly to the window. "Why are those sheep being driven out of the field?" he asked.

"I expect they're being driven to another field where there is more grass," said the aunt weakly.

"But there is lots of grass in that field," protested the boy; "there's nothing else but grass there. Aunt, there's lots of grass in that field."

"Perhaps the grass in the other field is better," suggested the aunt absurdly.

"Why is it better?" came the swift, inevitable question.

"Oh, look at those cows!" exclaimed the aunt. Nearly every field along the line had contained cows or bullocks, but she spoke as though she were drawing attention to something rare.

"Why is the grass in the other field better?" persisted Cyril.

The frown on the man's face was deepening to a scowl. He was a hard, unsympathetic man, the aunt decided.

She was utterly unable to come up with any satisfactory answer about the grass in the other field.

The smaller girl began to recite a poem: 'On the Road to Mandalay'. She only knew the first line, but she put the little she knew to the fullest possible use. She repeated the line over and over again in a dreamy but determined and very audible voice; it seemed to the man as though some one had had a bet with her that she could not repeat the line aloud two thousand times without stopping. Whoever it was who had made the bet was likely to lose.

"Come over here and listen to a story," said the aunt, when the man had looked at her twice and once at the emergency cord.

The children dragged themselves towards the aunt's end of the carriage. Obviously they did not think much of her as a story-teller.

In a low, confidential voice, interrupted at frequent intervals by loud, whining questions from her listeners, she began an awful, boring story about a little girl who was good, and made friends with everyone all because she was *so* good, and was finally saved from a mad bull by a group of rescuers who admired her moral character.

"Wouldn't they have saved her if she hadn't been good?" demanded the bigger of the small girls. It was exactly the question that the man had wanted to ask.

"Well, yes," admitted the aunt lamely, "but I don't think they would have run quite so fast to her help if they had not liked her so much."

"It's the stupidest story I've ever heard," said the bigger of the small girls.

"I didn't listen after the first bit, it was so stupid," said Cyril.

The smaller girl made no actual comment on the story, but she had long ago started murmuring again, over and over, the first line of the poem.

"You don't seem to be a success as a story-teller," said the man suddenly from his corner.

The aunt bristled in instant defence at this unexpected attack.

"It's a very difficult thing to tell stories that children can both understand and enjoy," she said stiffly.

"I don't agree with you," said the man.

"Perhaps *you* would like to tell them a story," was the aunt's retort.

"Tell us a story," demanded the bigger of the small girls.

"Once upon a time," began the man, "there was a little girl called Bertha, who was extraordinarily good."

The children's interest began at once to fade. All stories seemed dreadfully alike, no matter who told them.

"She did all that she was told, she was always truthful, she kept her clothes clean, ate milk puddings as though they were jam tarts, learned her lessons perfectly, and was polite in her manners."

"Was she pretty?" asked the bigger of the small girls.

"Not as pretty as any of you," said the man, "but she was horribly good."

Suddenly, the children looked as if they were enjoying themselves. The word 'horrible' linked to 'good' sounded really interesting. It seemed to have a ring of truth that was missing from the aunt's tales of infant life.

"She was so good," continued the man, "that she won several medals for goodness, which she always wore, pinned on to her dress. There was a medal for obedience, another medal for punctuality, and a third for good behaviour. They were large metal medals and they clicked against one another as she walked. No other child in the

town where she lived had as many as three medals, so everybody knew that she must be an extra good child."

"Horribly good," quoted Cyril.

"Everybody talked about her goodness, and the Prince of the country got to hear about it, and he said that as she was so very good she might be allowed once a week to walk in his park, which was just outside the town. It was a beautiful park, and no children were ever allowed in it, so it was a great honour for Bertha to be allowed to go there."

"Were there any sheep in the park?" demanded Cyril.

"No," said the man, "there were no sheep."

"Why weren't there any sheep?" came the inevitable question arising out of that answer.

The aunt permitted herself a smile, which might almost have been described as a grin.

"There were no sheep in the park," said the man, "because the Prince's mother had once had a dream that her son would either be killed by a sheep or else by a clock falling on him. For that reason the Prince never kept a sheep in his park or a clock in his palace."

The aunt had to stop herself from gasping with admiration.

"Was the Prince killed by a sheep or by a clock?" asked Cyril.

"He is still alive, so we can't tell whether the dream will come true," said the man unconcernedly; "anyway, there were no sheep in the park, but there were lots of little pigs running all over the place."

"What colour were they?"

"Black with white faces, white with black spots, black all over, grey with white patches, and some were white all over."

The story-teller paused to let a full idea of the park's treasures sink into the children's imaginations; then he carried on:

"Bertha was rather sorry to find that there were no flowers in the park. She had promised her aunts, with tears in her eyes, that she would not pick any of the kind Prince's flowers, and she had meant to keep her promise, so of course it made her feel silly to find that there were no flowers to pick."

"Why weren't there any flowers?"

"Because the pigs had eaten them all," said the man promptly. "The gardeners had told the Prince that you couldn't have pigs and flowers, so he decided to have pigs and no flowers."

There was a murmur of approval at the excellence of the Prince's decision; so many people would have decided the other way.

"There were lots of other delightful things in the park. There were ponds with gold and blue and green fish in them, and trees with beautiful parrots that said clever things at a moment's notice, and humming birds that hummed all the popular tunes of the day. Bertha walked up and down and enjoyed herself immensely, and thought to herself: "If I were not so extraordinarily good I should not have been allowed to come into this beautiful park and enjoy all that there is to be seen in it," and her three medals clinked against one another as she walked and helped to remind her how very good she really was. Just then an enormous wolf came prowling into the park to see if it could catch a fat little pig for its supper."

"What colour was it?" asked the children, amid an immediate quickening of interest.

"Mud-colour all over, with a black tongue and pale grey eyes that gleamed with unspeakable ferocity. The first thing that it saw in the park was Bertha; her pinafore was so spotlessly white and clean that it could be seen from a great distance. Bertha saw the wolf and saw that it was stealing towards her, and she began to wish that she had never been allowed to come into the park. She ran as hard as she could, and the wolf came after her with huge leaps and bounds. She managed to reach a shrubbery of myrtle bushes and she hid herself in one of the thickest of the bushes. The wolf came sniffing among the branches, its black tongue lolling out of its mouth and its pale grey eyes glaring with rage. Bertha was terribly frightened, and thought to herself: "If I had not been so extraordinarily good I should have been safe in the town at this moment." However, the scent of myrtle was so strong that the wolf could not sniff out where Bertha was hiding, and the bushes were so thick that he might have hunted about in them for a long time without catching sight of her, so he thought he might as well go off and catch a little pig instead. Bertha was trembling very much at having the wolf prowling and sniffing so near her, and as she trembled, the medal for obedience clinked against the medals for good conduct and punctuality. The wolf was just moving away when he heard the sound of the medals clinking and stopped to listen; they clinked again in a bush quite near him. He dashed into the bush, his pale grey eyes gleaming with ferocity and triumph, and dragged Bertha out and devoured her to the last morsel. All that was left of her were her shoes, bits of clothing, and the three medals for goodness."

"Were any of the little pigs killed?"

"No, they all escaped."

"The story began badly," said the smaller of the small girls, "but it had a beautiful ending."

"It is the most beautiful story that I ever heard," said the bigger of the small girls.

"It is the *only* beautiful story I have ever heard," said Cyril.

The aunt disagreed.

"A most *improper* story to tell young children! You have ruined the effect of years of careful teaching."

"At any rate," said the man, collecting his belongings before leaving the carriage, "I kept them quiet for ten minutes, which was more than you were able to do."

"Unhappy woman!" he observed to himself as he walked down the platform of Templecombe station; "for the next six months or so those children will be nagging her in public with demands for an '*improper*' story!"

THE HOLIDAY

GEORGE LAYTON

IT WASN'T FAIR. Tony and Barry were going. In fact, nearly all of them in Class Three and Four were going, except me. It wasn't fair. Why wouldn't my mum let me go?

"I've told you. You're not going camping. You're far too young."

Huh! She said that last year.

"You said that last year!"

"You can go next year when you're a bit older."

She'd said that last year, too.

"You said that last year an' all."

"Do you want a clout?"

"Well you did, Mum, didn't you?"

"Go and wash your hands for tea."

"Aw, Mum, everybody else is going to school camp. Why can't I?"

Because you're coming to Bridlington with me and your Aunt Doreen like you do every year.

"Because you're coming to Bridlington with me and your Auntie Doreen like you do every year!"

I told you. Oh, every year the same thing; my mum, me, and my Auntie Doreen at Mrs Sharkey's boarding house. I suppose we'll have that room next door to the lavatory: a double bed for my mum and my Auntie Doreen, and me on a camp bed behind a screen.

"I suppose we'll have that rotten room again."

"Don't be cheeky! Mrs Sharkey saves that room for me every year – last week in July and first week in August. It's the best room in the house, facing the sea like that, and nice and handy for the toilets. You know how important that is for your Auntie Doreen."

"Aw, Mum, I never get any sleep – the sea splashing on one side and Auntie Doreen on the . . . aw!"

My mum gave me a great clout right across my head. She just caught my ear an' all.

"Aw, bloomin' heck. What was that for?"

"You know very well. Now stop being so cheeky and go and wash your hands."

"Well, you've done it now. You've dislocated my jaw – that's it now. I'll report you to that RSPCC thing, and they'll sue you. You've really had it now . . . ow!"

She clouted me again, right in the same place.

"It's not fair. Tony's mum and dad are letting him go to school camp, and Barry's. Why won't you let me go?"

She suddenly bent down and put her face right next to mine, right close. She made me jump. Blimey, that moustache was getting longer. I wish she'd do something about it – it's embarrassing to have a mum with a moustache.

"Now, listen to me, my lad. What Tony's mum and dad do, and what Barry's mum and dad do, is their lookout. You will come with me and your Auntie Doreen to Bridlington and enjoy yourself like you do every year!"

Huh! Enjoy myself – that's a laugh for a start. How can you enjoy yourself walking round Bridlington town centre all day looking at shops? You can do that at home. Or else it was bingo. 'Key-of-the-door, old-age pension, legs-eleven, clickety-click' and all that rubbish. You could do that at home as well. And when we did get to the beach, I had to spend all day rubbing that oily sun stuff on my Auntie Doreen's back. It was horrible. Then the rain would come down and it was back to bingo. Honest, what's the point of going on holiday if you do everything that you can do at home? You want to do something different. Now camping, that's different. Tony's dad had bought him a special sleeping bag, just for going camping. Huh! I wish I had a dad.

"I bet if I had a dad, he'd let me go to school camp."

I thought Mum was going to get her mad up when I said that, but she didn't at all.

"Go and wash your hands for tea, love. Your spam fritters will be ready in a minute."

Ugh. Bloomin' spam fritters! Not worth washing your hands for!

"Yeh. All right."

I started to go upstairs. Ooh, I was in a right mess now. I'd told all the other lads I was going. Our names had to be in by tomorrow. We had to give Mr Garnett our pound deposit. Well, I was going to go. I didn't care what Mum said, I was going to go – somehow! When I got to the top of the stairs, I kicked a tin wastepaper bin on the landing. It fell right downstairs. It didn't half make a clatter.

"What on earth are you doing?"

She would have to hear, wouldn't she?

"Eh. It's all right, Mum. I just tripped over the wastepaper bin. It's all right."

"Oh, stop playing the goat and come downstairs. Your tea's ready."

What was she talking about, playing the goat? I couldn't help tripping over a wastepaper bin. Well, I couldn't have helped it if I had tripped over it, an' well, I might have done for all she knew. Well, I wasn't going to wash my hands just for spam fritters. Oh, bet we have macaroni cheese as well. I went straight downstairs.

"Are your hands clean?"

"Yeh."

"Here we are then. I've made some macaroni cheese as well."

"Lovely."

"C'mon. Eat it up quickly, then we'll have a nice bit of telly."

I didn't say anything else about the school camp that night. I knew it was no good. But I was going to go. I'd told Tony and Barry I was going, I'd told all the lads I was going. Somehow, I'd get my own way. When I got to school next morning, I saw Tony and Barry with Norbert Lightowler over by the Black Hole. That's a tiny snicket, only open at one end, where we shove all the new lads on the first day of term. There's room for about twenty kids. We usually get about a hundred in. It's supposed to be good fun, but the new kids don't enjoy it very much. They get to enjoy it the next year.

"Hello, Tony. Hello, Barry."

Norbert Lightowler spat out some chewing-gum. It just missed me.

"Oh, don't say 'hello' to me then, will ya?"

"No. And watch where you're spitting your rotten chewing-gum – or you'll get thumped."

Barry asked us all if we'd brought our pound deposit for school camp. Tony and Norbert had got theirs, of course. Nobody was stopping them going. I made out I'd forgotten mine.

"Oh heck. I must have left mine on the kitchen table."

"Oh. I see. Well, maybe Garnett'll let you bring it tomorrow."

I didn't say anything, but Norbert did.

"Oh, no. He said yesterday today's the last day. He said anybody not bringing their deposit today wouldn't be able to go. He did, you know."

"Aw, shurrup, or I'll do you."

"I'm only telling you."

"Well, don't bother."

Tony asked me if I'd learnt that poem for Miss Taylor. I didn't know what he was talking about.

"What poem?"

Norbert knew of course. He brought a book out of his pocket.

"*Drake's Drum*. Haven't you learnt it?"

Oh crikey! *Drake's Drum.* With all this worry about trying to get to school camp, I'd forgotten all about it. Miss Taylor had told us to learn it for this morning.

"We're supposed to know it this morning, you know."

"I know, Norbert, I know."

Honest, Norbert just loved to see you in a mess, I suppose because he's usually in trouble himself.

"*I* know it. I spent all last night learning it. Listen:

> "'Drake he's in his hammock an' a
> thousand mile away.
> Captain, art thou sleeping there below?
> Slung a'tween the round shot in
> Nombres Dios bay . . .'"

I snatched the book out of his hands.

"Come 'ere. Let's have a look at it."

"You'll never learn it in time. Bell'll be going in a minute."

"You were reading it, anyway."

"I was not. It took me all last night to learn that."

Barry laughed at him.

"What, all last night to learn three lines?"

"No, clever clogs. I mean the whole poem."

Just then, the bell started going for assembly. Norbert snatched his book back.

"C'mon, we'd better get into line. Garnett's on playground duty."

Norbert went over to where our class was lining up. Barry's in Class Four, so he went over to their column.

"See you at playtime."

"Yeh. Tarah."

While we were lining up, we were all talking. Mr Garnett just stood there with his hands on his hips, staring at us, waiting for us to stop.

"Thank you."

Some of us heard his voice and stopped talking. Those that didn't carried on.

"Thank you."

A few more stopped, and then a few more, till the only voice you could hear was Norbert Lightowler's, and as soon as he realized nobody else was talking, he shut up quickly.

"Thank you. If I have to wait as long as that for silence at the end of this morning's break, then we shall spend the whole break this afternoon learning how to file up in silence. Do you understand?"

We all just stood there, hardly daring to breathe.

"Am I talking to myself? Do you understand?"

Everybody mumbled "Yes, sir", except Norbert Lightowler. He had to turn round and start talking to me and Tony.

"Huh! If he thinks I'm going to spend my playtime filing up in silence, he's got another think coming."

"Lightowler!"

Norbert nearly jumped out of his skin.

"Are you talking to those boys behind you?"

"No, sir. I was just telling 'em summat . . ."

"Really?"

"Yes, sir . . . er . . . I was just . . . er . . . telling them that we have to give our pound in today, sir, for school camp, sir."

"I want a hundred lines by tomorrow morning: 'I must not talk whilst waiting to go into assembly.'"

"Aw, sir."

"Two hundred."

He nearly did it again, but stopped just in time, or he'd have got three hundred.

"Right. When I give the word, I want you to go quietly into assembly. And no talking. Right – wait for it. Walk!"

Everybody walked in not daring to say a word. When we got into the main hall, I asked Tony for the book with *Drake's Drum* in, and during assembly, I tried to snatch a look at the poem but, of course, it was a waste of time. Anyway, I was more worried about my pound deposit for Mr Garnett. After prayers, the Headmaster made an announcement about it.

"This concerns only the boys in Classes Three and Four. Today is the final day for handing in your school camp deposits. Those of you not in Three B must see Mr Garnett during morning break. Those of you in Three B will be able to hand in your money when Mr Garnett takes you after Miss Taylor's class. Right, School turn to the right. From the front, dismiss! No talking."

I had another look at the poem while we were waiting for our turn to go.

> "'Drake he's in his hammock an' a
>   thousand mile away.
> Captain, art thou sleeping there below?'"

Well, I knew the first two lines. Tony wasn't too bothered. He probably knew it.

"Don't worry. She can't ask everybody to recite it. Most likely she'll ask one of the girls. Anyway, what are you going to do about Garnett? Do you think he'll let you bring your pound deposit tomorrow?"

"Yeh, sure to."

If only Tony knew that it'd be just as bad tomorrow. I had to get a pound from somewhere. Then I'd have about four weeks to get my mum to let me go. But I had to get my name down today or I'd . . . I'd had it. Miss Taylor was already waiting for us when we got into our classroom.

"Come along, children. Settle down."

Miss Taylor took us for English and Religious Instruction.

"Now today, we're going to deal with some parts of the Old Testament."

Tony and me looked at each other. She'd got mixed up. Today was English and tomorrow was Religious Instruction.

"Now you've all heard of the Ten Commandments . . ."

Bloomin' hummer. What a let-off. Tony was grinning at me.

"Do you know the first of these Ten Commandments?"

Jennifer Greenwood put her hand up. She was top of the class every year. Everyone reckoned she was Miss Taylor's favourite.

"Yes, Jennifer."

Jennifer Greenwood wriggled about a bit in her seat and went red. She's always going red.

"Please, Miss, it's English this morning, Miss; it's Religious Instruction tomorrow, Miss."

Honest, I could've thumped her. Then Norbert put his hand up.

"Yes, Miss. You told us to learn *Drake's Drum* for this morning, Miss."

I leaned across to Tony.

"I'll do him at playtime."

"Quite right, Norbert. Thank you for reminding me. Now, who will recite it for me?"

Everybody shoved their hands up shouting, "Miss, Miss, me Miss, Miss", so I thought I'd better look as keen as the rest of them.

"Miss! Miss! Miss!"

I stretched my hand up high. I got a bit carried away. I was sure she'd pick one of the girls.

"Me, Miss. Please, Miss. Me, Miss!"

She only went and pointed at me. I couldn't believe it.

"Me, Miss?"

"Yes. You seem very keen for once. Stand up and speak clearly."

I stood up as slowly as I could. My chair scraped on the floor and made a noise like chalk on the blackboard.

"Hurry up, and lift your chair up. Don't push it like that."

Everybody was looking at me. Norbert, who sits in the front row, had turned round and was grinning.

"Er . . . um *Drake's Drum* . . . by Henry Newbolt . . ."

Miss Taylor lifted up her finger.

"*Sir* Henry Newbolt!"

"Yes, Miss."

I was glad she stopped me. Anything to give me more time.

"Carry on."

I took a deep breath. I could feel Norbert still grinning at me.

"Ahem. *Drake's Drum* . . . by Sir Henry Newbolt."

I stopped: then I took another deep breath . . .

"'Drake is in his cabin and a thousand mile away . . .'"

I stopped again. I knew after the next line, I'd be in trouble.

"'Cap'n, art thou sleeping down below . . .'"

The whole class was listening. I didn't know what I was going to say next. I took another breath and I was just about to tell Miss Taylor I couldn't remember any more, when Norbert burst out laughing. Miss Taylor went over to him:

"What are you laughing at, Norbert?"

"Nothing, Miss."

"You think you can do better – is that it?"

"No, Miss."

"Stand up!"

Norbert stood up. Miss Taylor looked at me. "Well done. That was a very dramatic opening. Sit down, and we'll see if Norbert Lightowler can do as well."

I couldn't believe it. Tony could hardly keep his face straight.

Norbert went right through the poem. Miss Taylor had to help him once or twice, but he just about got through. Miss Taylor told him he hadn't done badly, but not quite as well as me. After that a few of the others recited it, and then we went on to do some English grammar.

After Miss Taylor, we had Mr Garnett. He gave the girls some arithmetic to do, while he sorted out the deposits for school camp. He went through the register, and everybody that was going gave him their pound deposit – until he got to me.

"I've forgotten it, sir."

"You know today is the last day, don't you?"

"Yes, sir."

"And all the names have to be in this morning? I told you all that yesterday, didn't I?"

"Yes, sir. Yes, sir – I'll bring my pound tomorrow, sir."

Mr Garnett tapped his pencil.

"I'll put the pound in for you, and I want you to repay me first thing tomorrow morning. All right?"

"Er . . . um . . . yes, sir. I think so, sir."

"You do want to go to school camp?"

"Yes, sir."

"Right then. Don't forget to give me your pound tomorrow."

"No, sir."

I didn't know what I was going to do now. I reckoned the best thing was to tell Mr Garnett the truth, so when the bell went for playtime, I stayed behind in the classroom, and I told him about my mum wanting me to go to Bridlington with her and my Auntie Doreen. He told me not to worry, and gave me a letter to give to my mum that night. I don't know what it said, but after my mum had read it, she put it in her pocket and said she'd give me a pound for Mr Garnett in the morning.

"Can I go to camp, then?"

"Yes, if that's what you want."

"I don't mind coming to Bridlington with you and Auntie Doreen, if you'd rather . . ."

My mum just got hold of my face with both her hands.

"No, love, you go to school camp and enjoy yourself."

So I did – go to school camp, that is – but I didn't enjoy myself. It was horrible. They put me in a tent with Gordon

Barraclough: he's a right bully and he gets everybody on to his side because they're all scared of him. I wanted to go in Tony's and Barry's tent, but Mr Garnett said it would upset all his schedules, so I was stuck with Gordon Barraclough and his gang. They made me sleep right next to the opening, so when it rained, my sleeping-bag got soaked. And they thought it was dead funny to pull my clothes out of my suitcase (my mum couldn't afford a rucksack) and throw them all over the place.

"Huh! Fancy going camping with a suitcase!"

"Mind your own business, Barraclough! My mum couldn't afford a proper rucksack. Anyway, I'm off to Bridlington on Sunday."

And I meant it. Sunday was parents' visiting day, and my mum and Auntie Doreen were coming to see me on their way to Bridlington. So I was going to pack up all my stuff and go with them. Huh . . . I couldn't stand another week with Gordon Barraclough. I wished I'd never come.

So on Sunday morning, after breakfast in the big marquee, I packed everything into my suitcase and waited for my mum and my Auntie Doreen to come. They arrived at quarter to eleven.

"Hello, love. Well, isn't it grand here? You are having a nice time, aren't you?"

"Yeh, it's not bad, but I want to tell you summat."

My mum wasn't listening. She was looking round the camp site.

"Well, it's all bigger than I thought. Is this your tent here?"

She poked her head through the flap. I could hear her talking to Gordon Barraclough and the others.

"No! No! No! Don't move, boys. Well, haven't you got a lot of room in here? It's quite deceiving from the outside."

Her head came out again.

"Here, Doreen, you have a look in here. It's ever so roomy."

She turned back to Gordon Barraclough.

"Well, bye-bye boys. Enjoy the rest of your holiday. And thank you for keeping an eye on my little lad."

I could hear them all laughing inside the tent. I felt sick.

"Mum, I want to ask you something."

"In a minute, love, in a minute. Let's just see round the camp, and then we'll have a little natter before your Auntie Doreen and I go. Oh, and I want to say hello to Mr Garnett while I'm here. You know, on the way here today, I kept saying wouldn't it be lovely if I could take you on to Bridlington with us. Wasn't I, Doreen? But now I'm here, I can see you're all having a real good time together. You were right, love, it's much better to be with your friends than with two fuddy-duddies like us, eh, Doreen? Well, c'mon, love, aren't you going to show us round? We've got to get our bus for Bridlington soon."

I showed them both round the camp site, and they went off just before dinner. I didn't feel like anything to eat myself. I just went to the tent and unpacked my suitcase.

THE ENCHANTED TOAD

JUDY CORBALIS

THERE WAS ONCE A KING who had a daughter called Princess Grizelda. Princess Grizelda was rather quiet and didn't say very much but she was very very stubborn and determined once she had decided on something.

The Queen, her mother, had left their home at the palace many years before, when Grizelda was a small girl, to seek her fortune as a racing driver, so the king had had to bring up his daughter himself.

"Grizelda," he said to her one day, "I have a serious problem to discuss with you. Come into the blue drawing room."

The Princess sighed, put down her bow and arrows and followed him.

"What is it, Papa?"

"Grizelda," said the king, "it's time you were married."

"But I'm only fourteen, Papa," protested the princess.

"What do you mean – 'only fourteen'?" said the king crossly. "Fourteen's quite old enough to be married."

"But I don't *want* to be married, Papa."

"Well, sooner or later you'll have to be," said the king, "so why not now?"

"I don't know if I ever want to be married, Papa."

"What nonsense!" shouted the king. "Everyone wants to

be married. Why I was married at twenty and your mother was married at fifteen."

"I know, Papa," said the princess, "and when she was eighteen she went off to race cars and we haven't seen her since."

"Well, she always sends you a birthday present," said the king defensively.

"Yes, I know, but I'd rather *see* her sometimes."

"Grizelda," said the king, "you are not to talk about Mama. You know it only upsets me. I'm not going to listen if you do. And I want you, in fact, I'm ordering you, to start thinking about who you want to marry. Because if you don't come up with some good suggestions yourself, I shall have to choose for you."

And he stormed out of the blue drawing room.

"Oh dear," said Grizelda to herself. "Now I really *do* have a problem."

She thought about all the neighbouring princes but she really couldn't face the thought of marrying any of them.

"Well," asked the king at dinner, "have you decided, Grizelda?"

"Really, Papa, you only asked me to think about it five hours ago."

The king stamped his foot and his soup plate rattled.

"Five hours is long enough for anyone," he thundered.

"Not for me, Papa," said the princess calmly. "And you've spilt your soup."

"Oh, be quiet!" shouted the king and he slammed out of the royal dining room.

The princess ate the rest of her dinner in thoughtful silence.

Next day she had breakfast in her room, got dressed in her best golden dress and slipped outdoors in her blue silk cloak.

"Your Highness," said the Court Usher as she passed him on the stairs, "have you remembered that His Majesty has asked several kings and queens from neighbouring kingdoms to lunch with him today? He particularly wanted Your Highness to be present."

The princess nodded.

"Thank you for reminding me," she said, and to herself she thought, "He's asked them because he thinks they might be interested in marrying me off to one of their sons."

And she carried on downstairs even faster.

She stayed in the gardens for an hour or two, then slipped back into the palace and up to her bedroom unnoticed. She had just enough time to sort out one or two things before lunch.

There was a blast of trumpets from downstairs.

"That'll be the heralds announcing the arrival of the other monarchs," said Princess Grizelda aloud and she smoothed her golden dress, picked up something in her hand and set off for the main staircase and the royal reception room.

"The Princess Grizelda," announced the Court Usher.

"My dear!" cried the king and he walked up and embraced her warmly. "Behave yourself, please," he muttered in her ear.

"I always do, Papa," said the princess.

"And this," announced the king, leading her forward, "is my daughter, Grizelda, my only child, who will, naturally, inherit the kingdom in due course and who, I really feel, is just of an age to be married."

The royal guests smiled at her. The princess smiled back. She took a deep breath.

"Papa," she said loudly, taking a step forward, "I've found a husband for myself."

"Really, Grizelda?" said the king. "I am surprised. And who is the lucky young man going to be?"

"It isn't a *young man*, Papa," said the princess. "I met him in the garden this morning and brought him in to lunch with me."

The king was curious.

"Let him come in!" he commanded, "so we can all see this mysterious fellow. Met him in the garden, indeed! These young girls are so fanciful."

The princess went out to the hallway, picked up a small box she had deposited there and carried it in.

"Well?" demanded the king. "Where is he then?"

The princess lifted the lid of the box.

"Here, Papa."

The king looked in the box.

"It's a toad!!"

"Yes, I know, Papa. I've fallen in love with it and I'm going to marry it."

"GRIZELDA!" thundered the king.

"Lunch is served, Sire," announced the footman appearing at the door.

One of the visiting kings leaned over to Grizelda's father and whispered in his ear, "I shouldn't discourage her too hard if I were you. It will almost certainly be a prince under enchantment."

The king was doubtful.

"Are you sure?"

"They always are," said the visiting king. "Let her have him on the table at lunch and have your Court Wizard change him back later on."

"What a splendid idea," said the king. "Thank you. I hadn't thought of that."

"There have been dozens of cases exactly like it," pointed out the visiting king.

So the Princess Grizelda took her toad in to lunch and it sat by her golden plate as she fed it with tiny scraps of her own food.

The visitors left in the early afternoon. Grizelda shook hands with them all and smiled prettily. The toad looked at them with its unblinking eyes.

The king felt a light touch on his shoulder.

"Don't forget. Get the enchanter in right away," murmured his friend.

The king nodded.

"And many thanks," he said gratefully.

"Don't mention it," said the visiting king.

The princess took her toad into the library. She was examining its warts when the herald arrived with a message that she and the toad were wanted in the throne room.

"The throne room!" The princess was impressed. "Something special must be happening."

"His Majesty is in full regalia," announced the herald importantly.

"Really? It must be something vital then. I wonder what it can be?" said the princess, and picking up her toad she set off along the palace corridor.

The throne room door was opened by the Chief Usher. Inside the room were the King, the Lord Chamberlain, the Court Jester, the Chief Judge and the Court Enchanter. The Court Enchanter was considered to be one of the best wizards in the world. He was always going off to perform difficult spells or to change people back into their normal shapes or to magic someone or something somewhere. People said he could conjure up all sorts of wonderful things and nobody wanted to get on the wrong side of him because it was reputed that he had once put a bad spell on someone who had offended him and caused lizards to jump out of her mouth every time she opened it.

Grizelda went into the room.

"Good afternoon, Papa," she greeted him, and she smiled and nodded at his retinue.

"Good afternoon, my dear," said the king and, looking at the toad, he said, obviously making a great effort, "and how is my future son-in-law this afternoon?"

"Oh, very well, thank you, Papa."

"Good," said the king.

"Would you like to stroke him, Papa?"

"No, no thanks!" said the king hastily. "Ah, I'm sure he's, ah, very, ah, friendly, yes, I'm sure he's got a wonderful nature and so on, but, ah, I don't think I'll stroke him just yet, thank you, Grizelda."

"Now," he went on, "the reason I've brought you down here is because I happen to believe your toad, that is, my son-in-law to be, is really a prince under enchantment."

The Princess Grizelda was very disappointed.

"Oh no, Papa, I hope not!"

"Now look here," said the king. "Don't be ridiculous, Grizelda. I mean you can get toads anywhere but princes are another thing altogether. I'll get you another toad as a wedding present if you want. And that's a promise. Now bring that toad over here and put him on the small table."

Grizelda put her toad down in front of the enchanter.

The enchanter looked at her with his piercing green eyes.

"Stand back, Your Highness," he ordered. Then, taking a huge red silk handkerchief from one pocket of his robe, and a wand from the other, he dropped the handkerchief over the toad, threw a powder from another pocket into a glass of water, poured the water over the handkerchief, then waved his wand over it muttering strangely to himself all the time.

There was a sudden flash of pink smoke and a dull boom, the handkerchief and the toad disappeared, and in its place stood a white rabbit.

The princess was overjoyed.

"A rabbit! Oh, Papa, how wonderful! I've always wanted a rabbit."

"Not for a *husband*!" bellowed the king, enraged.

And to the enchanter he said nastily, "You'll have to do something considerably better than that!"

The enchanter turned his piercing green eyes towards the king.

"Patience, Your Highness. These things are very skilled and take time."

"I can see that," said the king bitterly.

The enchanter pulled out another handkerchief, a blue one this time, and laid it over the rabbit.

"Oh no, please don't, please don't." The princess was distressed.

The enchanter put his hand deep in his robe, pulled out a tiny top hat, and presented it to her.

"Here you are," he said gravely. "Put your hand in there."

Grizelda could only get two fingers into the hat because it was so small. Feeling something soft and furry, she pulled at it.

Out popped the tiniest baby rabbit she had ever seen.

"For you," said the enchanter. "A present to make up for losing this one."

"Oh thank you!" cried Princess Grizelda and she put the baby rabbit back in the hat for safe keeping and put the hat in her pocket.

The enchanter was busy with his spell. He had taken out a large book from behind the throne, a book Grizelda was sure had never been there before, and was studying it intently.

Suddenly he leaned forward towards the king.

"Excuse me, Your Majesty," he said, reached behind the king's ear and pulled out a large lemon.

"Oh dear," he said, and reaching behind the king's other ear, pulled out an enormous black spider.

"Stop it *at once!*" commanded the king. "And that's an order."

"Sorry, Your Majesty," murmured the enchanter. "I just thought you'd like to know they were there."

"Thank you for that consideration," said the king. "Now get on with the job."

The enchanter plucked a star from out of the air above his head, laid it on the blue handkerchief, twirled three times round on his toes, and shouted "Abracadabra!"

There was a blinding flash of green light and, lo and behold, a beautiful red sportscar appeared before them.

"My gosh!" breathed Grizelda.

The Lord Chancellor leaned forward enviously. "I'd like that," he sighed.

The king looked very hard at the enchanter. "I see: a sportscar."

"Well, yes," said the enchanter. "I told Your Majesty these things take time."

"Look," said the king through clenched teeth, "I cannot have a sportscar as a son-in-law. The princess cannot marry a *sportscar*."

His voice rose to a shriek. "WHOEVER HEARD OF A KINGDOM RULED BY A SPORTSCAR?"

"A passing bagatelle, Your Majesty," said the enchanter hastily. "We're almost there now."

"It's a very beautiful sportscar," pointed out the princess.

"Grizelda . . .," said the king warningly.

The Lord Chamberlain broke in. "Your Majesty, the enchanter is about to try again."

"He'd better," said the king.

The enchanter took out a checked tablecloth from the back pocket of his robe and flung it over the sportscar.

The Lord Chamberlain sighed. "What a pity."

The king shot him a furious look.

The enchanter lifted three lizards out of a banqueting dish on the regalia table and laid them on the cloth. He took a vial of red liquid from his sleeve, shook it over the lizards and waved his wand low over them.

A tongue of flame shot into the air. Everybody screamed and jumped back.

The smoke cleared and there before them lay – a fish finger.

"NO, NO, NO, NO," groaned the king. "THERE IS NO SUCH THING AS A KINGDOM RULED BY A FISH FINGER! I'm *not* having a fish finger as a son-in-law. I'd rather have a toad. Take him away!" he shouted, pointing at the enchanter. "Off with his head and bring it to me on a plate! It'll be a pleasure, I can tell you."

"Papa!" The princess was deeply shocked. "What a *terrible* thing to say."

The enchanter burst into tears. He reached into his other sleeve and brought out a placard saying,

"WIFE AND SIX CHILDREN TO SUPPORT".

"You won't get my sympathy *that* way," said the king. "My mind is made up. Take him away!"

The Princess Grizelda jumped to her feet and stood in front of her father.

"I won't have it, Papa," she cried sternly. "This was all your idea in the first place and it wasn't even your toad. It was mine. Of course you're not going to chop off his head. You're going to give him one last chance to succeed and, if he doesn't, you're going to send him on a month's holiday."

"That's just encouraging him to fail," said the king.

"Honestly, Sire," said the enchanter, "it was just a temporary setback. I've prepared my next and final spell now. I *am* in the entertainment business, Sire, after all."

"Entertainment!" exploded the king. "You call this entertainment?"

"Stop it, at once, both of you," ordered the princess. And turning to the enchanter she said, "Would you please try again now?"

"And you'd better get it right this time," snorted the king.

"I will," the enchanter assured them.

He pulled a purple silken cloth with golden stars on it from the Chief Judge's trouser leg and laid it over the fish finger. Then he reached inside his own mouth, pulled out a tonsil and laid that on the cloth.

"Yuk!" said the king. "How disgusting!"

"But effective, Sire," replied the enchanter. "And now, please, absolute silence."

He bent down on his knees, crossed his fingers, his toes, and his eyes and breathed on the tonsil.

The tonsil quivered and grew and grew. The purple cloth with golden stars rose and flapped and shook until it seemed to fill the room. There was a boom of thunder and a light like the sun dazzled them all.

"How beautiful!" murmured the princess to herself.

Suddenly there was a jolt and a bang and without warning they all flew up to the ceiling and fell to the ground again. The room grew dark.

"Sorry about this," came the enchanter's voice through the gloom. "We're nearly there."

A misty cloud was gathering in the middle of the room. A dim human shape was forming inside it.

The enchanter sighed inaudibly with relief, the king muttered aloud, "At last!"

And the Princess Grizelda said to herself, "I do hope he's nice and he likes having fun."

The cloud began to dispel, the light slowly returned to normal and the figure emerged more clearly until it stood visible to them all.

"GOOD HEAVENS!" bellowed the king. "It's Marguerite!"

"Hello, darling," said the figure.

"Mother!" shouted Grizelda and threw herself into the stranger's arms.

"And where have *you* been for the last eleven years then, if it's not a rude question?" asked the king.

"Oh, Arthur," said the queen, holding Grizelda tightly, "don't go on and on, please. I thought you'd be so pleased to see me again. I've been away seeking my fortune, of course. I'm an extremely famous racing driver."

"Well, I've never heard of you," announced the king, "and I've checked the racing lists every time there's been a Grand Prix."

"Oh, Arthur. Did you!" The queen was touched. "That is romantic of you."

The king blushed.

"But," went on the queen, "I raced under an assumed name of course, otherwise people might have thought my winning was favouritism. And, Grizelda," she continued, "it's so wonderful to see you at last, my darling. I've wanted and wanted to come back, but I knew I couldn't until I'd proved myself. And I've finally done it."

The Princess Grizelda clung tighter to her mother's neck.

"Oh, Mama, I'm so glad you're back at last."

"What I don't understand," said the king, "is if you've reached the peak of your career, what on earth you were doing in the palace garden disguised as a toad. And then to put me through that dreadful business of the rabbit and the sportscar and the fish finger! It's a wonder I'm not grey with worry and strain."

"Well, I couldn't help it," explained the queen. She turned to the enchanter. "It was a terribly strong spell. You did marvellously well to break it at all."

The enchanter looked modest.

"It was nothing, Your Highness."

"It was everything to *me*," the queen assured him. "I could have just about coped with spending the rest of my life as a pet rabbit or a sportscar and at least I would have been at the palace. But a fish finger! I ask you? Here one day and gobbled up the next. I was quite terrified. I was shaking in my breadcrumbs."

"Oh, Mama," breathed Grizelda, "just imagine if the enchanter had failed and we'd eaten you up for tea."

Her eyes filled with tears at the thought.

"Well, we didn't," said the king cheerfully, "so stop crying, Grizelda."

He came and put his arm round the queen and kissed her cheek.

"I'm so glad you've come back."

"I shall never go off again now, I can tell you," promised the queen, "though I had some fun while I was racing."

"Will you tell me all about it?" asked Grizelda eagerly.

"Later," promised the queen.

"We must have a banquet and a party to celebrate your return," said the king, "but there's still one thing I don't understand. How did you come to be a toad?"

"Well," explained the queen, "I was racing very well indeed and clearly I was going to win the major prize. The only person who was anywhere near as good as I was, was a driver who had been a wizard and had given it up for racing, but he was still not up to my standard. And when I had won the competition and it came to the presentation of the prizes, he was so jealous that he cast a spell over me and changed me into a toad, and it took me seven months to hop back here to the palace and then it wasn't till this morning, when Grizelda found me, that anyone noticed me at all, and, of course, you know the rest of the story."

"Amazing," said the king.

"That wizard should be punished," said the Chief Judge.

"He will be," promised the king. "I shall make a point of it."

"Well, if everyone is happy now," put in the enchanter, "I'd quite like to be getting home to my family . . ."

"Just a moment," said the king sternly. "You promised me a husband for the princess and I haven't got one. She can't marry her mother."

"With respect, Sire," said the enchanter, "*you* asked me if I could change a toad into a prince and I said I'd do my best. I rather thought," he went on huffily, "that I'd done better than my best, but of course if Your Majesty disagrees . . ."

"Absolutely. You've done *marvellously*," cried the queen, "and I shall personally see about a reward in due course."

The enchanter smiled gratefully.

"I still don't know how I'm going to get Grizelda a husband though," muttered the king.

"A husband!" The queen was incredulous. "What on

earth does she want a *husband* for? She's only fourteen."

"I don't," put in Grizelda hastily.

"I should think *not*," said the queen. "I've never heard such nonsense. I married young, and look what happened to me. You're surely not encouraging her, Arthur?"

"Well, what else is she going to do?" asked the king defensively.

"What do you want to do, Grizelda?" asked her mother.

Grizelda thought for a bit.

"Well, Mama," she said finally, "what I'd like to do first is to stay here with you for a while and play with my rabbit, and the toad Papa has promised me, and then there is something I'd really like to do."

"And what is that?"

"I hope you won't think it's silly," said the princess, "but I'd simply *love* to be an astronaut. I've always wanted to be one."

"I've never heard of anything so ridiculous," said the king.

"I think it's a wonderfully exciting idea," said the queen, "and you should certainly be allowed to try it. And now, Arthur," she continued, turning to the king, "if it's possible, and I'm sure it should be, I'd love something to eat. I'm so sick of slugs and snails and worms."

"Oh, my dear," cried the king remorsefully, "of course, of course. I'm so sorry. I completely forgot about it in the shock of the moment. Yes. At once. Let's all three of us have a special celebration meal together tonight. I'm so delighted to have you back again."

"And so am I, Mama," murmured the Princess Grizelda, snuggling up to her mother.

"It seems to me," said the enchanter to himself, "that this time I've made an entirely satisfactory job of things."

And wrapping his cloak tightly round himself, he waved a hasty goodbye to everyone and slipped out of the palace off home to his own supper.

THE LITTLE HATCHET STORY

ANON (USA)

I HAVE AN ENORMOUS ability for pleasing children, and when Mrs Caruthers requested me one day to amuse her little son while she went shopping, I graciously agreed. Taking the child upon my knee, I began –

"George Washington was the greatest man that ever lived."

And so, smiling, I went on.

"Well, one day, George's father –"

"George who?" asked Clarence.

"George Washington. He was a little boy then, just like you. One day his father –"

"Whose father?" demanded Clarence.

"George Washington's – this great man I am telling you of. One day George Washington's father gave him a little hatchet for a –"

"Gave who a little hatchet?" the dear child interrupted, with a gleam of bewitching intelligence. Most people would have got mad; but I didn't. I know how to talk to children. So I went on –

"George Washington. His –"

"Who gave him the little hatchet?"

"His father. And his father –"

"Whose father?"

"George Washington's."

"Oh!"

"Yes, George Washington. And his father told him –"

"Told who?"

"Told George."

"Oh yes – George."

I took up the story right where the boy interrupted, for I could see he was just crazy to hear the end of it.

"And he was told –"

"George told him?" queried Clarence.

"No; his father told George."

"Oh!"

"Yes; told him he must be careful with the hatchet –"

"Who must be careful?"

"George must."

"Oh!"

"Yes; must be careful with his hatchet –"

"What hatchet?"

"Why, George's."

"Oh!"

"With the hatchet, and not cut himself with it, or drop it in the water tank or leave it out in the grass all night. So George went round cutting everything he could reach with his hatchet. And at last he came to a splendid apple tree, his father's favourite, and cut it down, and –"

"Who cut it down?"

"George did."

"Oh!"

"But his father came home and saw it the first thing, and –"

"Saw the hatchet?"

"No; saw the apple tree. And he said, 'Who has cut down my favourite apple tree?' "

"What apple tree?"

"George's father's. And everybody said they didn't know anything about it, and –"

"Anything about what?"

"The apple tree."

"Oh!"

"And George came up and heard them talking about it –"

"Heard who talking about it?"

"Heard his father and the men."

"What were they talking about?"

"About this apple tree."

"What apple tree?"

"The favourite tree that George cut down."

"George who?"

"George Washington."

"Oh!"

"So George came up and heard them talking about it, and he –"

"What did he cut it down for?"

"Just to try his little hatchet."

"Whose little hatchet?"

"Why, his own – the one his father gave him."

"Gave who?"

"Why, George Washington."

"Oh!"

"So George came up, and he said, 'Father, I cannot tell a lie. I –' "

"Who couldn't tell a lie?"

"Why, George Washington. He said, 'Father, I cannot tell a lie. It was –' "

"His father couldn't?"

"Why, no; George couldn't."

"Oh! George! Oh yes!"

" 'It was I cut down your apple tree; I did –' "

"His father did!"

"No, no; it was George said this."

"Said he cut his father?"

"No, no, no; said he cut down his apple tree."

"George's apple tree?"

"No, no; his father's."

"Oh!"

"He said –"

"His father said?"

"No, no, no; George said, 'Father, I cannot tell a lie; I did it with my little hatchet.' And his father said, 'Noble boy, I would rather lose a thousand trees than have you tell a lie.' "

"George did?"

"No; his father said that."

"Said he'd rather have a thousand apple trees?"

"No, no, no; said he'd rather lose a thousand apple trees than –"

"Said he'd rather George would?"

"No; said he'd rather he would than have him lie."

"Oh! George would rather have his father lie?"

I am patient, and I love children; but if Mrs Caruthers hadn't come for her little genius at that critical moment, I do not know what would have happened. As Clarence Alençon de Marchemont Caruthers pattered down the stairs I heard him telling his ma about a boy who had a father named George, and he told him to cut down an apple tree, and he said he'd rather tell a thousand lies than cut down one apple tree.

THE PRIVATE LIFE OF MR BIDWELL

JAMES THURBER

FROM WHERE SHE WAS sitting, Mrs Bidwell could not see her husband, but she had a curious feeling of tension: she knew he was up to something.

"What are you doing, George?" she demanded, her eyes still on her book.

"Mm?"

"What's the matter with you?"

"Pahhhhh-h-h," said Mr Bidwell, in a long, pleasurable exhale. "I was holding my breath."

Mrs Bidwell twisted creakingly in her chair and looked at him; he was sitting behind her in his favourite place under the parchment lamp with the street scene of old New York on it. "I was just holding my breath," he said again.

"Well, please don't do it," said Mrs Bidwell, and went back to her book. There was silence for five minutes.

"George!" said Mrs Bidwell.

"Bwaaaaaa," said Mr Bidwell. "What?"

"Will you please *stop* that?" she said. "It makes me nervous."

"I don't see how that bothers you," he said. "Can't I breathe?"

"You can breathe without holding your breath like a

goop," said Mrs Bidwell. "Goop" was a word that she was fond of using; she rather lazily applied it to everything. It annoyed Mr Bidwell.

"Deep breathing," said Mr Bidwell, in the impatient tone he used when explaining anything to his wife, "is good exercise. You ought to take more exercise."

"Well, please don't do it around me," said Mrs Bidwell, turning again to the pages of Mr Galsworthy.

At the Cowan's party, a week later, the room was full of chattering people when Mrs Bidwell, who was talking to Lida Carroll, suddenly turned around as if she had been summoned. In a chair in a far corner of the room, Mr Bidwell was holding his breath. His chest was expanded, his chin drawn in; there was a strange stare in his eyes, and his face was slightly empurpled. Mrs Bidwell moved into the line of his vision and gave him a sharp, penetrating look. He deflated slowly and looked away.

Later, in the car, after they had driven in silence a mile or more on the way home, Mrs Bidwell said, "It seems to me you might at least have the kindness not to hold your breath in other people's houses."

"I wasn't hurting anybody," said Mr Bidwell.

"You looked silly!" said his wife. "You looked perfectly crazy!" She was driving and she began to speed up, as she always did when excited or angry. "What do you suppose people thought – you sitting there all swelled up, with your eyes popping out?"

"I wasn't all swelled up," he said, angrily.

"You looked like a goop," she said. The car slowed down, sighed, and came to a complete, despondent stop.

"We're out of gas," said Mrs Bidwell. It was bitterly cold and nastily sleeting. Mr Bidwell took a long, deep breath.

The breathing situation in the Bidwell family reached a critical point when Mr Bidwell began to inhale in his sleep, slowly, and exhale with a protracted, growling, "woooooooo". Mrs Bidwell, ordinarily a sound sleeper (except on nights when she was sure burglars were getting in), would wake up and reach over and shake her husband. "George!" she would say.

"Hawwwwww," Mr Bidwell would say, thickly. "Wahs maa nah, hm?"

After he had turned over and gone back to sleep, Mrs Bidwell would lie awake, thinking.

One morning at breakfast she said, "George, I'm not going to put up with this another day. If you can't stop blowing up like a grampus, I'm going to leave you." There was a slight, quick lift in Mr Bidwell's heart, but he tried to look surprised and hurt.

"All right," he said. "Let's not talk about it."

Mrs Bidwell buttered another piece of toast. She described to him the way he sounded in his sleep. He read the paper.

With considerable effort, Mr Bidwell kept from inflating his chest for about a week, but one night at the McNally's he hit on the idea of seeing how many seconds he could hold his breath. He was rather bored by the McNally's party, anyway. He began timing himself with his wrist-watch in a remote corner of the living-room. Mrs Bidwell, who was in the kitchen talking children and clothes with Bea McNally, left her abruptly and slipped back into the living-room. She stood quietly behind her husband's chair. He knew she was there, and tried to let out his breath imperceptibly.

"I see you," she said, in a low, cold tone. Mr Bidwell jumped up.

"Why don't you let me alone?" he demanded.

"Will you please lower your voice?" she said, smiling so that if anyone were looking he wouldn't think the Bidwells were arguing.

"I'm getting pretty damned tired of this," said Bidwell in a low voice.

"You've ruined my evening!" she whispered.

"You've ruined mine, too!" he whispered back. They knifed each other, from head to stomach, with their eyes.

"Sitting here like a goop, holding your breath," said Mrs Bidwell. "People will think you are an idiot." She laughed, turning to greet a lady who was approaching them.

Mr Bidwell sat in his office the next afternoon, a black, moist afternoon, tapping a pencil on his desk, and scowling. "All right, then, get out, get out!" he muttered. "What do I care?" He was visualizing the scene when Mrs Bidwell would walk out on him. After going through it several times, he returned to his work, feeling vaguely contented. He made up his mind to breathe any way he wanted to, no matter what she did. And, having come to this decision, he oddly enough, and quite without effort, lost interest in holding his breath.

Everything went rather smoothly at the Bidwells' for a month or so. Mr Bidwell didn't do anything to annoy his wife beyond leaving his razor on her dressing-table and forgetting to turn out the hall light when he went to bed. Then there came the night of the Bentons' party.

Mr Bidwell, bored as usual, was sitting in a far corner of the room, breathing normally. His wife was talking animatedly with Beth Williamson about negligees. Suddenly her voice slowed and an uneasy look came into her eyes: George was up to something. She turned around and sought him out. To anyone but Mrs Bidwell he must have seemed like any husband sitting in a chair. But his wife's lips set tightly. She walked casually over to him.

"What are you doing?" she demanded.

"Hm?" he said, looking at her vacantly.

"What are you *doing*?" she demanded, again. He gave her a harsh, venomous look, which she returned.

"I'm multiplying numbers in my head," he said, slowly and evenly, "if you must know." In the prolonged, probing examination that they silently, without moving any muscles save those of their eyes, gave each other, it became solidly, frozenly apparent to both of them that the end of their endurance had arrived. The curious bond that held them together snapped – rather more easily than either had supposed was possible. That night, while undressing for bed, Mr Bidwell calmly multiplied numbers in his head. Mrs Bidwell stared coldly at him for a few moments, holding a stocking in her hand; she didn't bother to berate him. He paid no attention to her. The thing was simply over.

George Bidwell lives alone now (his wife remarried). He never goes to parties any more, and his old circle of friends rarely sees him. The last time that any of them did see him, he was walking along a country road with the halting, uncertain gait of a blind man: he was trying to see how many steps he could take without opening his eyes.

CRICK, CROCK AND HOOKHANDLE

ITALO CALVINO

THERE WERE ONCE THREE scoundrels, Crick, Crock and Hookhandle. One day, they made a bet with each other to see which of them was the cleverest rogue. So they set off together; Crick went ahead of the other two and noticed a magpie sitting on her eggs in a nest at the top of a tree.

"Would you like to see me take that magpie's eggs from underneath her, without her noticing that anything is happening?" he asked his friends.

"Yes. Let's see you do it!"

As Crick was climbing the tree to steal the eggs, Crock cut off the heels of his friend's shoes and hid them in his own hat. But before Crock had time to put his hat back on his head, Hookhandle sneaked the heels out of it without either of the others seeing.

Crick came down the tree and said, "I'm the cleverest for I've stolen the magpie's eggs while she was sitting on them."

But Crock said, "No, I'm the cleverest for I've cut the heels off your shoes without you even noticing," and he took off his hat to show Crick the pair of heels that he had put inside but, of course, they were not there.

Then Hookhandle said, "I'm the cleverest for I took the

heels out of your hat. As I'm so much sharper than either of you, I'm going to leave you both and make my own way in the world."

He went off on his own and did so well for himself that he became rich. He moved to a city where he was not known, got married and opened a little shop which sold cheeses, salami, pickles and all sorts of good things to eat.

The other two, who went from place to place seeing what they could pick up, arrived in the city where Hookhandle had set up in business.

When they saw the shop full of delicious food, they said to each other, "Let's go in and see what good we can do ourselves!"

So they went in and said to Hookhandle's wife, who was alone behind the counter, "Would a lovely lady like you give us something to eat?"

"What would you like?"

"A slice of strong cheese," they replied.

While she was cutting the cheese, the two men were looking all round to see what they could take. They noticed a great piece of salt pork hanging from the ceiling and they made signs to each other that they would come back at night and steal it.

Hookhandle's wife, who understood what they had in mind, said nothing, but when her husband came home she told him what had happened.

Hookhandle realized who it might be and said, "That sounds to me like Crick and Crock! So they want to steal our pork, do they! All right! I'll soon deal with them!"

He took the pork down from the ceiling, hid it in the oven and went to bed as usual.

In the middle of the night, when Crick and Crock came back to steal the pork, they looked high and low but could not find it. So what did Crock do then? Without making a sound, he went up close to the bed, on the side where Hookhandle's wife was lying, and said, "I can't find that piece of pork. Where have you put it?"

Believing it was her husband's voice, she replied, "Don't

you remember you put it in the oven? Come to bed now," and went back to sleep.

The two villains went to the oven, took the pork out and made off with it. Crock went out first and Crick followed him with the piece of pork slung over his shoulder. As they were crossing the garden at the back of the shop, Crick noticed some vegetables growing there which would make a good soup. He caught up with Crock and said, "Go back to Hookhandle's garden and pick some of those vegetables. We can cook them with a leg of this pork when we get home."

Crock turned back to the garden and Crick went on walking.

Meanwhile Hookhandle had got up. He went to the oven and, not finding the pork there, looked out into the garden and saw Crock stealing the vegetables.

"I'll soon fix those two ruffians," said Hookhandle to himself. Taking a large bunch of greenstuff from the kitchen, he ran out of the house without letting Crock see him.

Crick was hurrying along, bent nearly double under the weight of the pork. When Hookhandle caught him up, he said nothing but signed to Crick that he wanted to take his turn at carrying the pork. Crick, believing it was Crock, willingly exchanged the heavy pork for the vegetables that Hookhandle was holding out to him.

As soon as the pork was on his back, Hookhandle turned round and went home as fast as he could.

Quite soon, Crock joined up with Crick again, his hands full of vegetables, and said, "What has happened to the pork? Where have you put it?"

"You've got it!" said Crick.

"Me? I haven't got it!" said Crock.

"But only a few minutes ago we exchanged the pork and the vegetables," said Crick.

"When?" asked Crock. "You sent me back to get some vegetables to make soup."

At last they realized they had been outwitted by Hookhandle, their old companion, who had certainly turned out to be the cleverest rogue of all.

BRER RABBIT TRICKS BRER BEAR

JULIUS LESTER

Brer Rabbit decided gardening was too much hard work. So he went back to his old ways – eating from everybody else's garden. He made a tour through the community to see what everybody was planting and his eye was caught by Brer Fox's peanut patch.

Soon as the peanuts were ready, Brer Rabbit decided to make his acquaintance with them. Every night he ate his fill and started bringing his family, including some second and third cousins of his great-aunt on his daddy's uncle's side of the house.

Brer Fox had a good idea who was eating his peanuts, but he couldn't catch him. He inspected his fence and finally found a small hole on the north side. Brer Fox tied a rope with a loop knot and put it inside the hole. If anybody stepped in it, the rope would grab his leg and hoist'im right up in the air.

That night Brer Rabbit came down to the peanut patch. He climbed through the hole and WHOOSH! Next thing he knew he was hanging in the air upside down.

There wasn't a thing he could do, so he tried to make himself comfortable and catch a little sleep. He'd worry about Brer Fox when Brer Fox showed up the next morning.

Long about daybreak Brer Rabbit woke up, because he heard somebody coming. It was Brer Bear.

"Good morning, Brer Bear," he sang out, merry as Santa Claus.

Brear Bear looked all around.

"Up here!"

Brer Bear looked up and saw Brer Rabbit hanging upside down. "Brer Rabbit. How you do this morning?"

"Just fine, Brer Bear. Couldn't be better."

"Don't look like it to me. What you doing up there?"

"Making a dollar a minute," said Brer Rabbit.

"How?"

"I'm keeping the crows out of Brer Fox's peanut patch."

Brer Bear was overjoyed. He'd been on his way down to the welfare office, 'cause his family had gotten too big for him to support. "Say, Brer Rabbit. Could you let me take over for a while? I need the work and I promise I won't work too long, but it sure would be a help to me and my family."

Brer Rabbit didn't want to appear too anxious, so he hemmed and hawed before agreeing. Brer Bear let Brer Rabbit down, and Brer Rabbit helped Brer Bear get the rope around his foot and swung him up in the air.

No sooner was Brer Bear swinging in the breeze than Brer Rabbit ran to Brer Fox's house. "Brer Fox! Brer Fox! Come quick! Come quick if you want to see who's been stealing your peanuts."

Brer Fox ran down to the garden and there was Brer Bear. Before Brer Bear could thank Brer Fox for the chance to make a little money, Brer Fox grabbed a stick and was beating on Brer Bear like he was a drum in a marching band.

Brer Rabbit got away from there as quick as he could.

BRER WOLF, BRER FOX, AND THE LITTLE RABBITS

JULIUS LESTER

BRER WOLF AND Brer Fox went to see Brer Rabbit one day. Wasn't nobody home except the little Rabbits playing in the yard. Brer Wolf looked at them. They looked so plump and fat he was licking his chops without knowing he was doing it. Brer Wolf looked at Brer Fox and licked his chops again. Brer Fox looked at Brer Wolf and licked his.

"They mighty fat, ain't they?" said Brer Wolf.

Brer Fox grinned. "Man, hush your mouth!"

The little Rabbits kept on playing but began easing out of the yard. They kept their ears sharp, though.

"Ain't they slick and pretty?" said Brer Wolf.

Brer Fox started drooling. "I wish you'd shut up," he grinned.

The little Rabbits kept playing and inching their way out of the yard and they kept listening.

Brer Wolf smacked his mouth. "Ain't they juicy and tender?"

Brer Fox's eyes started to roll around in his head. "Man, if you don't hush up, I'm going to start twitching, and when I start twitching, I can't help myself."

The little Rabbits kept playing and easing out of the yard and they kept listening.

"Let's eat'em!" Brer Wolf said suddenly!

"Let's eat'em!" exclaimed Brer Fox, twitching all over.

The little Rabbits were still playing, but they knew everything that was going on.

Brer Wolf and Brer Fox decided that when Brer Rabbit got home, one of them would get him in a dispute about something or other and the other one would catch the little Rabbits.

"You best at talking, Brer Wolf. I'll coax the little Rabbits. I got a way with children, you know."

Brer Wolf snorted. "You can't make a gourd out of a pumpkin. You know I ain't never been too good at talking, but your tongue's as slick as glass. I can bite a whole lot better than I can talk. Them little Rabbits don't need coaxing; they need grabbing, and I'm the man for that. You keep Brer Rabbit busy. *I'll* grab the little Rabbits."

They knew that whichever one grabbed the little Rabbits first wasn't gon' leave even a shadow for the other one. While they were arguing back and forth, the little Rabbits took off down the road – *blickety-blickety* – looking for their daddy.

They hadn't gone far when they ran into him coming from town with a jug over his shoulder.

"What you got, Daddy?" they cried.

"A jug of molasses."

"Can we have some?" they wanted to know.

Brer Rabbit pulled the stopper out and let them lick the molasses off the bottom of it. After they'd gotten their breath, they told him all about Brer Fox and Brer Wolf. Brer Rabbit chuckled to himself.

He picked up the jug and he and the little Rabbits started home. When they were almost there, Brer Rabbit said, "Now y'all stay out of sight until I call you."

The little rabbits were happy to get out of sight, because they had seen Brer Wolf's sharp teeth and Brer Fox's red red tongue. They got down in the weeds and were as still as a mouse in a barrel of flour.

Brer Rabbit sauntered on home. Brer Fox and Brer Wolf

were sitting on his front-porch step, smiling smiley smiles. They how-do'd with Brer Rabbit and he how-do'd with them.

"What you got in that jug there, Brer Rabbit?" Brer Wolf wanted to know.

Brer Rabbit hemmed and hawed and made like he didn't want to tell. That made Brer Wolf more curious.

"What you got in that jug, Brer Rabbit?"

Brer Rabbit shook his head and looked real serious. He started talking to Brer Wolf about the weather or whatever and Brer Fox took this chance to sneak off and grab the little Rabbits.

Brer Rabbit unstoppered the jug and handed it to Brer Wolf. "Take a little taste of this."

Brer Wolf took a hit on the jug and smacked his lips. "That's all right, Brer Rabbit! What is it?"

Brer Rabbit leaned close to Brer Wolf. "Don't tell nobody. It's Fox blood."

Brer Wolf's eyes got big. "How you know?"

"I knows what I knows."

"Let me have another hit on that, Brer Rabbit."

Brer Rabbit shook his head. "Don't know how come you want to drink up what little I got when you can get some more for yourself. And the fresher it is, the better."

"How you knows?"

"I knows what I knows."

Brer Wolf jumped up and started off after Brer Fox. When he got close, he made a grab for him. Brer Fox ducked and dodged and headed for the woods with Brer Wolf's hot breath on his tail.

When Brer Rabbit got through laughing, he called his young'uns out of the weeds.

Now don't come asking me if Brer Wolf caught Brer Fox. It's all I can do to follow the tale when it's on the big road. Ain't no way I can keep up with them animals when they get to running through the woods. I don't know about you, but when I go in the woods, I got to know where I'm going.

THE LOADED DOG

HENRY LAWSON

DAVE REGAN, Jim Bently and Andy Page were sinking a shaft at Stony Creek in search of a rich gold quartz reef which was supposed to exist in the vicinity. They used old-fashioned blasting-powder and time-fuse. The result of the blasting was usually an ugly pot-hole in the bottom of the shaft and half a barrow-load of broken rock.

There were plenty of fish in the creek; freshwater bream, cod, cat-fish, and tailers. Andy would fish for three hours at a stretch if encouraged by a nibble or a bite now and then – say once in twenty minutes. The butcher was always willing to give meat in exchange for fish when they caught more than they could eat; but now it was winter, and these fish wouldn't bite.

Dave got an idea. "Why not blow up the fish in the big waterhole with a cartridge?" he said. "I'll try it."

Andy usually put Dave's theories into practice and bore the blame for the failure and the chaffing of his mates if they didn't work.

He made a cartridge about three times the size of those they used in the rock. The inner skin was of stout calico; Andy stuck the end of a two-metre piece of fuse well down in the powder and bound the mouth of the bag firmly to it with whipcord. The idea was to sink the cartridge in the water with the open end of the fuse attached to a float on the surface, ready for lighting. Andy dipped the cartridge in melted beeswax to make it watertight. "We'll have to leave it some time before we light it," said Dave, "to give the fish time to get over their scare when we put it in, and come nosing round again; so we'll want it well watertight."

Round the cartridge Andy, at Dave's suggestion, bound a strip of sail canvas – that they used for making water-bags – to increase the force of the explosion, and round that he pasted layers of stiff brown paper – on the plan of the sort of fireworks we called 'gun-crackers'. He let the paper dry in the sun, then he sewed a covering of two thicknesses of canvas over it, and bound the thing from end to end with stout fishing-line. The cartridge was rigid and solid enough now – a formidable bomb; but Andy and Dave wanted to be sure. Andy sewed on another layer of canvas, dipped the cartridge in melted tallow, twisted a length of fencing wire round it as an afterthought, dipped it in tallow again, and stood it carefully against a tent peg, where he'd know where to find it, and wound the fuse loosely round it. Then he went to the camp-fire to try some potatoes which were boiling in their jackets in a billy, and to see about frying some chops for dinner. Dave and Jim were at work in the claim that morning.

They had a big, black, young retriever dog – or rather an over-grown pup, a foolish, four-footed mate, who was always slobbering round them and lashing their legs with his heavy tail that swung round like a stockwhip. His name was Tommy. When they went in swimming, Tommy would jump in after them, and take their hands in his mouth, and try to swim out with them, and scratch their naked bodies with his paws. They loved him for his good-heartedness and his foolishness, but when they wished to enjoy a swim they had to tie him up in camp.

Tommy watched Andy with great interest all the morning, making the cartridge and hindered him considerably trying to help; but about noon he went off to the claim to see how Dave and Jim were getting on, and to come home to dinner with them. Andy was cook today; Dave and Jim stood with their backs to the fire, as bushmen do in all weathers, waiting till dinner should be ready. The retriever went nosing round after something he seemed to have missed.

Andy's brain still worked on the cartridge; his eye was caught by the glare of an empty kerosene tin lying in the bushes, and it struck him that it wouldn't be a bad idea to sink the cartridge packed with clay, sand, or stones in the tin, to increase the force of the explosion. He may have been all out, from a scientific point of view, but the notion looked right to him. He was turning to suggest this to Dave, when Dave glanced over his shoulder to see how the chops were doing – and bolted. He explained afterwards that he thought he heard the pan spluttering extra, and looked to see if the chops were burning. Jim Bently looked behind and bolted after Dave. Andy stood stock-still, staring after them.

"Run, Andy! Run!" they shouted back at him. "Run! Look behind you, you fool!" Andy turned slowly and looked, and there, close behind him, was the retriever with the cartridge in his mouth – wedged into his broadest and silliest grin. And that wasn't all. Tommy had come round the fire to Andy, and the loose end of the fuse had trailed over the burning sticks into the blaze; now it was hissing and spitting properly.

Andy's legs started with a jolt; his legs started before his brain did, and he made after Dave and Jim. And the dog followed Andy.

Dave and Jim were good runners – Jim the best – for a short distance; Andy was slow and heavy, but he had the strength and the wind and could last. Tommy capered round him, delighted as a dog could be to find his mates, as he thought, on for a frolic. Dave and Jim kept shouting back, "Don't foller us! Don't foller us, you fool!" But Andy kept on, with the dog circling round him and the live fuse swishing in all directions. Jim yelling to Dave not to follow him, Dave shouting to Andy to go in another direction – to "spread out", and Andy roaring at the dog to go home. Then Andy's brain began to work; he tried to get a running kick at the dog, but the dog dodged; he snatched up sticks and stones and threw them at the dog and ran on again.

Tommy saw that he'd made a mistake about Andy, and left him and bounded after Dave. Dave, who had the presence of mind to think that the fuse's time wasn't up yet, made a dive and a grab for the dog, caught him by the tail, and as he swung round snatched the cartridge out of his mouth and flung it as far as he could; the dog immediately bounded after it and retrieved it. Dave roared and cursed at Tommy, who, seeing that Dave was offended, left him and went after Jim, who was well ahead.

Jim swung to a sapling and went up it like a native bear; it was a young sapling, and Jim couldn't safely get more than about three metres from the ground. Thinking it was all part of the lark, Tommy laid the cartridge, as carefully as if it were a kitten, at the foot of the sapling, and capered and leaped and whooped joyously round under Jim. The fuse sounded as if it were going a mile a minute. Jim tried to climb higher and the sapling bent and cracked and he fell on his feet and ran.

The dog swooped on the cartridge and followed. It all took but a very few moments. Jim ran to a digger's hole, about three metres deep, and dropped down into it – landing on soft mud – and was safe. The dog grinned sardonically down on him, as if he thought it would be a good lark to drop the cartridge down on Jim.

"Go away, Tommy," said Jim feebly, "go away."

The dog bounded off after Dave, who was the only one in sight now. Andy had dropped behind a log, where he lay flat on his face, having suddenly remembered a picture of the Russo-Turkish war with a circle of Turks lying flat on their faces (as if they were ashamed) round a newly-arrived shell.

There was a small hotel or shanty on the main road, not far from the claim. Dave was desperate; the time flew much faster in his stimulated imagination than it did in reality, so he made for the shanty. There were several bushmen on the veranda and in the bar; Dave rushed in, banging the door behind him. "My dog!" he gasped, in reply to the astonished stare of the publican, "the blanky retriever – he's got a live cartridge in his mouth . . ."

The retriever, finding the front door shut against him, had bounded round and in by the back way, and now stood smiling in the doorway leading from the passage, the cartridge still in his mouth and the fuse spluttering. They burst out of that bar; Tommy bounded first after one and then after another, for, being a young dog, he tried to make friends with everybody.

The bushmen ran round corners, and some shut themselves in the stable. There was a new weatherboard and corrugated-iron kitchen and wash-house on piles in the backyard, with some women washing clothes inside. Dave and the publican bundled in there and shut the door – the publican cursing Dave and calling him a crimson fool, in hurried tones, and wanting to know why he had come to the hotel.

The retriever went in under the kitchen, amongst the piles, but luckily for those inside, there was a vicious yellow mongrel cattle-dog sulking and nursing his nastiness under there – a sneaking, thieving canine, whom neighbours had tried for years to shoot or poison. Tommy saw his danger – he'd had experience from this dog – and started out across the yard, still sticking to the cartridge. Half-way across the yard the yellow dog caught him and nipped him. Tommy dropped the cartridge, gave one terrified yell, and took to the bush. The yellow dog followed him to the fence and then ran back to see what he had dropped.

Nearly a dozen other dogs came – cold-blooded kangaroo-dogs, mongrel sheep- and cattle-dogs, vicious black and yellow dogs. They kept at a respectable distance round the nasty yellow dog, for it was dangerous to go near him when he thought he had found something which might be good for a dog or cat. He sniffed at the cartridge twice, and was just taking a third cautious sniff when . . .

It was very good blasting powder and the cartridge had been well made.

Bushmen say that the kitchen jumped off its piles and on again. When the smoke and dust cleared away, the remains of the nasty yellow dog were lying against the paling fence. Saddle-horses, which had been 'hanging-up' round the veranda, were galloping wildly down the road in clouds of dust. From the scrub, came the yelping of dogs. Two of them went home, 65 kilometres away and stayed there. Towards evening the rest came back cautiously to make enquiries.

For half an hour or so after the explosion there were several bushmen doubled up or rolling gently on the dust, trying to laugh without shrieking. There were two women in hysterics at the house. The publican was holding his sides with laughter.

Dave decided to apologize later on, "when things had settled a bit", and went back to camp. And the dog that had done it all, Tommy, came slobbering round Dave smiling his broadest smile of amiability, and apparently satisfied for one afternoon with the fun he'd had.

Andy chained the dog up securely, and cooked some more chops, while Dave went to help Jim out of the hole.

And most of this is why, for years afterwards, bushmen, riding lazily past Dave's camp, would cry, "Ello, Da-a-ve! How's the fishin' getting on, Da-a-ve?"

SNOW-WHITE AND THE SEVEN DWARFS

ROALD DAHL

When little Snow-White's mother died,
The king, her father, up and cried,
"Oh, what a nuisance! What a life!
"Now I must find another wife!"
(It's never easy for a king
To find himself that sort of thing.)
He wrote to every magazine
And said, "I'm looking for a Queen."
At least ten thousand girls replied
And begged to be the royal bride.
The king said with a shifty smile,
"I'd like to give each one a trial."
However, in the end he chose
A lady called Miss Maclahose,
Who brought along a curious toy
That seemed to give her endless joy –
This was a mirror framed in brass,
A MAGIC TALKING LOOKING-GLASS.
Ask it something day or night,
It always got the answer right.
For instance, if you were to say,
"Oh Mirror, what's for lunch today?"

The thing would answer in a trice,
"Today it's scrambled eggs and rice."
Now every day, week in week out,
The spoiled and stupid Queen would shout,
"Oh Mirror Mirror on the wall,
"Who is the fairest of them all?"
The Mirror answered every time,
"Oh Madam, you're the Queen sublime.
"You are the only one to charm us,
"Queen, you are the cat's pyjamas."
For ten whole years the silly Queen
Repeated this absurd routine.

Then suddenly, one awful day,
She heard the Magic Mirror say,
"From now on, Queen, you're *Number Two*.
"*Snow-White* is prettier than you!"
The Queen went absolutely wild.
She yelled, "I'm going to scrag that child!
"I'll cook her flaming goose! I'll skin 'er!
"I'll have her rotten guts for dinner!"
She called the Huntsman to her study.
She shouted at him, "Listen buddy!
"You drag that filthy girl outside,
"And see you take her for a ride!
"Thereafter slit her ribs apart
"And bring me back her bleeding heart!"
The Huntsman dragged the lovely child
Deep deep into the forest wild.
Fearing the worst, poor Snow-White spake.
She cried, "Oh please give me a break!"
The knife was poised, the arm was strong,
She cried again, "I've done no *wrong*!"
The Huntsman's heart began to flutter.
It melted like a pound of butter.
He murmured, "Okay, beat it, kid,"
And you can bet your life she did.

Later, the Huntsman made a stop
Within the local butcher's shop,
And there he bought, for safetys sake,
A bullock's heart and one nice steak.

"Oh Majesty! Oh Queen!" he cried,
"That rotten little girl has died!
"And just to prove I didn't cheat,
"I've brought along these bits of meat."
The Queen cried out, "Bravissimo!
"I trust you killed her nice and slow."
Then (this is the disgusting part)
The Queen sat down and ate the heart!
(I only hope she cooked it well.
Boiled heart can be as tough as hell.)

While all of this was going on,
Oh where, oh where had Snow-White gone?
She'd found it easy, being pretty,
To hitch a ride in to the city,
And there she'd got a job, unpaid,
As general cook and parlour-maid
With seven funny little men,
Each one not more than three foot ten,
Ex horse-race jockeys, all of them.
These Seven Dwarfs, though awfully nice,
Were guilty of one shocking vice –
They squandered all of their resources
At the race-track backing horses.
(When they hadn't backed a winner,
None of them got any dinner.)
One evening, Snow-White said, "Look here,
"I think I've got a great idea.
"Just leave it all to me, okay?
"And no more gambling till I say."

That very night, at eventide,

Young Snow-White hitched another ride,
And then, when it was very late,
She slipped in through the Palace gate.
The King was in his counting house
Counting out his money,
The Queen was in the parlour
Eating bread and honey,
The footmen and the servants slept
So no one saw her as she crept
On tip-toe through the mighty hall
And grabbed THE MIRROR off the wall.
As soon as she had got it home,
She told the Senior Dwarf (or Gnome)
To ask it what he wished to know.
"Go on!" she shouted. "Have a go!"
He said, "Oh Mirror, please don't joke!
"Each one of us is stony broke!
"Which horse will win tomorrow's race,
"The Ascot Gold Cup Steeplechase?"
The Mirror whispered sweet and low,
"The horse's name is Mistletoe."
The Dwarfs went absolutely daft,
They kissed young Snow-White fore and aft,
Then rushed away to raise some dough
With which to back old Mistletoe.
They pawned their watches, sold the car,
They borrowed money near and far,
(For much of it they had to thank
The manager of Barclays Bank.)
They went to Ascot and of course
For once they backed the winning horse.
Thereafter, every single day,
The Mirror made the bookies pay.
Each Dwarf and Snow-White got a share,
And each was soon a millionaire,
Which shows that gambling's not a sin
Provided that you always win.

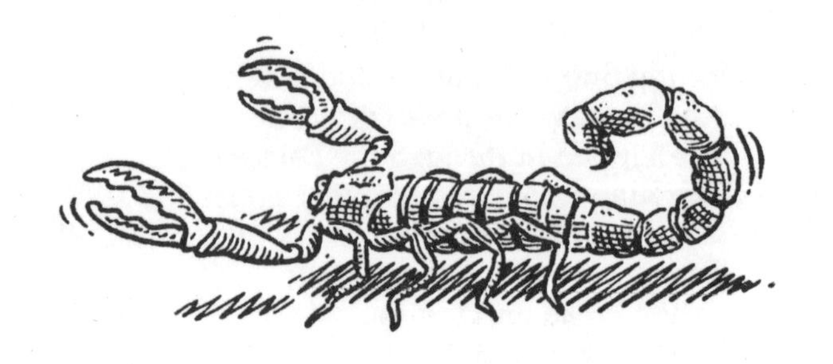

THE WORLD IN A WALL

GERALD DURRELL

THE CRUMBLING WALL that surrounded the sunken garden alongside our house in Corfu was a rich hunting ground for me. It was an ancient brick wall that had been plastered over, but now this outer skin was green with moss, bulging and sagging with the damp of many winters.

The inhabitants of the wall were a mixed lot, and they were divided into day and night workers, the hunters and the hunted. At night the hunters were the toads that lived among the brambles, and the geckos, pale, translucent with bulging eyes, that lived in the cracks higher up the wall. Their prey was the population of stupid, absent-minded crane-flies that zoomed and barged their way among the leaves; moths of all sizes and shapes, moths striped, tessellated, checked, spotted and blotched, that fluttered in soft clouds along the withered plaster; the beetles, rotund and neatly clad as business men, hurrying with portly efficiency about their night's work. When the last glow-worm had dragged his frosty emerald lantern to bed over the hills of moss, and the sun rose, the wall was taken over by the next set of inhabitants. Here it was more difficult to differentiate between the prey and the predators, for everything seemed to feed indiscriminately off everything else. Thus the hunting wasps searched out caterpillars and spiders; the spiders hunted for flies; the dragon-flies, big, brittle and hunting-pink, fed off the spiders and the flies; and the swift, lithe and multi-coloured wall lizards fed off everything.

But the shyest and most self-effacing of the wall community were the most dangerous; you hardly ever saw one unless you looked for it, and yet there must have been several hundred living in the cracks of the wall. Slide a knife-blade carefully under a piece of the loose plaster and lever it gently away from the brick, and there, crouching beneath it, would be a little black scorpion an inch long, looking as though he were made out of polished chocolate. They were weird-looking things, with their flattened, oval bodies, their neat, crooked legs, the enormous crab-like claws, bulbous and neatly jointed as armour, and the tail like a string of brown beads ending in a sting like a rose-thorn. The scorpion would lie there quite quietly as you examined him, only raising his tail in an almost apologetic gesture of warning if you breathed too hard on him. If you kept him in the sun too long he would simply turn his back on you and walk away, and then slide slowly but firmly under another section of plaster.

I grew very fond of these scorpions. I found them to be pleasant, unassuming creatures with, on the whole, the most charming habits. Provided you did nothing silly or clumsy (like putting your hand on one) the scorpions treated you with respect, their one desire being to get away and hide as quickly as possible. They must have found me rather a trial, for I was always ripping sections of the plaster away so that I could watch them, or capturing them and making them walk about in jam-jars so that I could see the way their feet moved. By means of my sudden and unexpected assaults on the wall I discovered quite a bit about the scorpions. I found that they would eat bluebottles (though how they caught them was a mystery I never solved), grass-hoppers, moths, and lacewing flies. Several times I found them eating each other, a habit I found most distressing in a creature otherwise so impeccable.

By crouching under the wall at night with a torch, I managed to catch some brief glimpses of the scorpions' wonderful courtship dances. I saw them standing, claws clasped, their bodies raised to the skies, their tails lovingly entwined; I saw them waltzing slowly in circles among the moss cushions, claw in claw. But my view of these performances was all too short, for almost as soon as I switched on the torch the partners would stop, pause for a moment, and then, seeing that I was not going to extinguish the light, they would turn round and walk firmly away, claw in claw, side by side. They were definitely beasts that believed in keeping themselves *to* themselves. If I could have kept a colony in captivity I would probably have been able to see the whole of the courtship, but the family had forbidden scorpions in the house, despite my arguments in favour of them.

Then one day I found a fat female scorpion in the wall, wearing what at first glance appeared to be a pale fawn fur coat. Closer inspection proved that this strange garment was made up of a mass of tiny babies clinging to the mother's back. I was enraptured by this family, and I made up my mind to smuggle them into the house and up to my bedroom so that I might keep them and watch them grow up. With infinite care I manoeuvred the mother and family into a matchbox, and then hurried to the villa. It was rather unfortunate that just as I entered the door lunch should be served; however, I placed the matchbox carefully on the mantelpiece in the drawing-room, so that the scorpions should get plenty of air, and made my way to the dining-room and joined the family for the meal. Dawdling over my food, feeding Roger, our dog, surreptitiously under the table and listening to the family arguing, I completely forgot about my exciting new captures. At last Larry, my older brother, having finished, fetched the cigarettes from the drawing-room, and lying back in his chair he put one in his mouth and picked up the matchbox he had brought. Oblivious of my impending doom I watched him interestedly as, still talking glibly, he opened the matchbox.

Now I maintain to this day that the female scorpion meant no harm. She was agitated and a trifle annoyed at being shut up in a matchbox for so long, and so she seized the first opportunity to escape. She hoisted herself out of the box with great rapidity, her babies clinging on desperately, and scuttled on to the back of Larry's hand. There, not quite certain what to do next, she paused, her sting curved up at the ready. Larry, feeling the movement of her claws, glanced

down to see what it was, and from that moment things got increasingly confused.

He uttered a roar of fright that made Lugaretzia, the maid, drop a plate and brought Roger out from beneath the table, barking wildly. With a flick of his hand he sent the unfortunate scorpion flying down the table, and she landed midway between my sister, Margo, and my other brother, Leslie, scattering babies like confetti as she thumped on the cloth. Thoroughly enraged at this treatment, the creature sped towards Leslie, her sting quivering with emotion. Leslie leapt to his feet, overturning his chair, and flicked out desperately with his napkin, sending the scorpion rolling across the cloth towards Margo, who promptly let out a scream that any railway engine would have been proud to produce. Mother, completely bewildered by this sudden and rapid change from peace to chaos, put on her glasses and peered down the table to see what was causing the pandemonium, and at that moment Margo, in a vain attempt to stop the scorpion's advance, hurled a glass of water at it. The shower missed the animal completely, but successfully drenched Mother, who not being able to stand cold water, promptly lost her breath and sat gasping at the end of the table, unable even to protest. The scorpion had now gone to ground under Leslie's plate, while her babies swarmed wildly all over the table. Roger, mystified by the panic, but determined to do his share, ran round and round the room, barking hysterically.

"It's that bloody boy again . . ." bellowed Larry.

"Look out! Look out! They're coming!" screamed Margo.

"All we need is a book," roared Leslie; "don't panic, hit 'em with a book."

"What on earth's the *matter* with you all?" Mother kept imploring, mopping her glasses.

"It's that bloody boy . . . he'll kill the lot of us. . . . Look at the table . . . knee-deep in scorpions. . . ."

"Quick . . . quick . . . do something. . . . Look out, look out!"

"Stop screeching and get a book, for God's sake. . . . You're worse than the dog. . . . Shut *up*, Roger. . . ."

"By the Grace of God I wasn't bitten. . . ."

"Look out . . . there's another one. . . . Quick . . . quick. . . ."

"Oh, shut up and get me a book or something. . . ."

"But *how* did the scorpions get on the table, dear?"

"That bloody boy. . . . Every matchbox in the house is a deathtrap. . . ."

"Look out, it's coming towards me. . . . Quick, quick, do something. . . ."

"Hit it with your knife . . . *your knife*. . . . Go on, hit it . . ."

Since no one had bothered to explain things to him, Roger was under the mistaken impression that the family were being attacked, and that it was his duty to defend them. As Lugaretzia was the only stranger in the room, he came to the logical conclusion that she must be the responsible party, so he bit her in the ankle. This did not help matters very much.

By the time a certain amount of order had been restored, all the baby scorpions had hidden themselves under various plates and bits of cutlery. Eventually, after impassioned pleas on my part, backed up by Mother, Leslie's suggestion that the whole lot be slaughtered was quashed. While the family, still simmering with rage and fright, retired to the drawing-room, I spent half an hour rounding up the babies, picking them up in a teaspoon, and returning them to their mother's back. Then I carried them outside on a saucer and, with the utmost reluctance, released them on the garden wall. Roger and I went and spent the afternoon on the hillside, for I felt it would be prudent to allow the family to have a siesta before seeing them again.

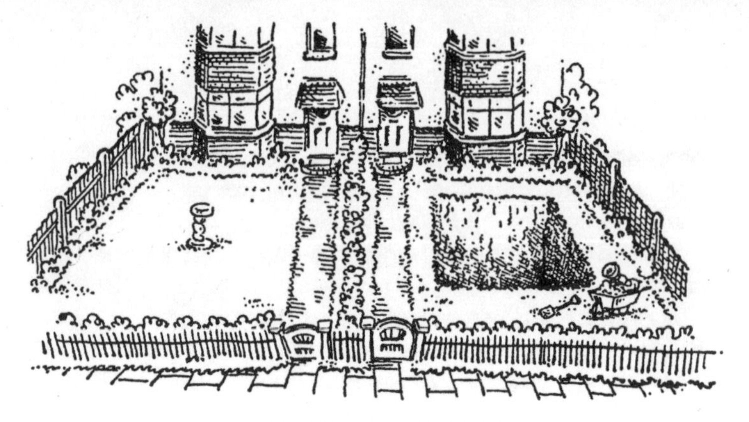

THE HOLE

ERIC PARTRIDGE

IN AN OUTER SUBURB of London – or, as it might be, Liverpool or Birmingham or Glasgow or Belfast – two friends had adjoining houses. The wives became friends. They were, in short, all friends together.

They were also rivals, the Smiths and the Robinsons. Oh! in the nicest, most harmless way. They were gardeners, keen and industrious and well-informed. If the Smiths succeeded with roses, the Robinsons promptly ascertained whether they could do the same; naturally, they did. If the Robinsons proved that with the most niggling and delicate plants they had the greenest of green thumbs, the Smiths immediately showed that their thumbs were no less green.

This happy and prosperous rivalry extended to what is quaintly known as 'garden furniture'. Chairs rivalled chairs, rural bench vied with rural bench; gnomes and elves, rabbits and squirrels, urns and sundials, strove in stone to attain an improbable supremacy.

And then, one glowing day, Mrs Smith had a "marvellous" idea. At the week-end, she and her husband dug a very large hole in the middle of the front lawn. The Robinsons waited to see what their neighbours were going to do with this hole. "Lily pond, do you think? or perhaps a tiny sunken garden?" But the Smiths did nothing with the hole, except to prevent it from silting up. The Robinsons, after several agonizing weeks, decided that this hole must represent something emblematic "or do we mean symbolic?"

There was nothing for it, the Robinsons thought, but to have, in their front lawn, a hole that should resemble, as nearly as possible, that in the Smiths' lawn. But Mr and Mrs Robinson shared an aversion to digging as strenuous as this. So they, or rather Mrs Robinson, wrote to a well-known firm of landscape gardeners and ordered a hole, so many feet in diameter and so many in depth.

Two days later, she received a letter.

> DEAR MADAM,
>
> We regret to say that, at the moment, we have not in stock a hole of the dimensions you require. But, if you wish us to do so, we will advise you when one becomes available.
>
> Yours faithfully,

The Robinsons waited, not very patiently. Sooner than they had expected, they received a second letter:

> DEAR MADAM,
>
> We count ourselves fortunate in being able to offer you, not exactly what you required but something we hope will serve equally well and perhaps better: a hole one foot deeper and eighteen inches more in diameter. The client who had ordered it has had to cancel his order, for he is emigrating to Kenya and selling his house.
>
> To accommodate you, we are prepared to charge for this larger hole the same price we should have charged for one of the size you specified.
>
> Awaiting your esteemed instructions,
>
> Yours faithfully,

The Robinsons were so excited that they wired their

acceptance. The same day, the reply came: "Delivery tomorrow afternoon."

The hole was being transported in a huge truck, driven by Alf, accompanied by Bert, who would keep his eye on the valuable load. They took their work very seriously, these two, and Alf constantly asked Bert whether the hole was safe. For instance, when they approached a railway bridge, "Height twelve feet", they anxiously debated whether the clearance was sufficient. Bert, having measured the total

height of truck and load, said "Six inches to spare", and Alf replied, "I'll have to drive very smoothly, or I'll knock the head off that blinking hole."

He did, and all was well. All continued to go well until, only two and a quarter miles from their destination, they came to a very steep hill.

"Watch it, Bert. We don't want the thing slipping from its moorings."

"All right."

Just before they reached the crest and while, in fact, they were congratulating each other on having "done it", they heard a very odd noise, as of something plopping on to the road behind them.

"Strike a light, Alf, that [unmentionable] hole has fallen off. You'll have to pull up at the top, and I'll go and see what's the matter."

"Cor! What a thing to happen, Bert!" The boss won't half be wild if we've lost that [equally unmentionable] hole."

At the top of the rise, Alf pulled up. Bert hastily descended and ran back to where they had heard that queer plopping noise.

Bert did not return. Alf became anxious and then more and more alarmed. Finally he walked back to find out what had happened; but his pal was never seen again.

Bert had fallen down the hole.

Acknowledgements

For permission to reproduce copyright material, acknowledgement and thanks are due to the following:

Harper and Row Publishers and Penguin Books Ltd for 'Nothing to be Afraid Of' by Jan Mark from *Nothing to be Afraid Of* (Kestrel Books, 1980), copyright © Jan Mark, 1977, 1980, pp. 9–17; Penguin Books Ltd and Random House, Inc. for 'The Guest Who Ran Away' from *Arab Folktales* translated by Inea Bushnaq (Penguin Books, 1987), copyright © Inea Bushnaq, 1986, p. 33; Scholastic, Inc. and The Bodley Head for 'Stupid Marco' by Jay Williams from *The Practical Princess and Other Liberating Fairy Tales*; Century Hutchinson Publishing Group Ltd for 'The Squire's Bride' by James Riordan from *The Woman in the Moon*; Walker Books Ltd and Philomel Books for 'The Baron Rides Out' by Adrian Mitchell from *The Adventures of Baron Munchausen*, text copyright © Adrian Mitchell 1985; JM Dent & Sons Ltd for 'Elephant Milk, Hippopotamus Cheese' by Margaret Mahy from *The Downhill Crocodile Whizz and Other Stories*; Curtis Brown Ltd for 'The Tortoises' Picnic' by Katharine Briggs from *Folktales of England*, copyright © 1965 University of Chicago; Laurence Pollinger Ltd for 'The First Schlemiel' by Isaac Bashevis Singer from *When Schlemiel Went to Warsaw*; Richard Scott Simon Ltd and Macmillan, London and Basingstoke for 'Sing Song Time' by Joyce Grenfell from *George Don't Do That* published by Macmillan and Ventura; AD Peters & Co Ltd for 'The Stowaways' by Roger McGough, published by Viking Kestrel; Victor Gollancz Ltd for 'The Pudding Like A Night on the Sea' (pp. 9–23) from *The Stories Julian Tells* by Ann Cameron, copyright © 1981 by Ann Cameron; Pavilion Books for 'A Fish of the World' by Terry Jones from *Fairy Tales*, first published by Pavilion Books in 1981; Thomas Nelson and Sons Ltd for 'A Good Sixpenn'orth' by Bill Naughton from *The Goalkeeper's Revenge*; William Collins Sons & Co Ltd for 'Harold and Bella, Jammy and Me' by Robert Leeson, copyright © Robert Leeson 1980; Unwin Hyman Ltd for 'Times Aren't What They Were' by Karel Capek, translated by Dora Round from *Apocryphal Stories*; Faber and Faber Ltd for 'The Enchanted Polly' by Catherine Storr from *Tales of Polly and the Hungry Wolf*; Victor Gollancz Ltd and Doubleday Publishing, a division of Bantam, Doubleday, Dell Publishing Group, Inc. for 'The Great Sea Serpent' from *The Complete Fairy Tales and Stories* by Hans Christian Andersen, translated by Erik Christian Haugaard. Translation copyright © 1974 by Erik Haugaard; Andre Deutsch Ltd for 'The Enchanted Toad' by Judy Corbalis from *The Wrestling Princess* and for 'Handsel and Gristle' by Michael Rosen from *Hairy Tales and Nursery Crimes*; The Bodley Head for 'Burglars!' by Norman Hunter from *The Incredible Adventures of Professor Branestawm*; William Papas for 'No Mules'; Blackie and Son Ltd for 'The Musicians of Bremen' by Janosch from *Not Quite As Grimm*, translated by Patricia Crampton; The Bodley Head for 'The Girl Who Didn't Believe in Ghosts' from *The Fastest Gun Alive* by David Henry Wilson; Longman Ltd for 'The Holiday' by George Layton from *A Northern Childhood: The Balaclava Story and Other Stories*, in Knockouts Longman 1978; Hamish Hamilton Ltd and Harper and Row Publishers for 'The Private Life of Mr Bidwell' by James Thurber from *The Middle-Aged Man on The Flying Trapeze*, copyright © 1935 James Thurber, copyright © 1963 Helen W. Thurber and Rosemary A. Thurber; JM Dent & Sons Ltd for 'Crick, Crock and Hookhandle' by Italo Calvino from *Italian Folktales*; The Bodley Head and Dial Books for Young Readers for 'Brer Rabbit Tricks Brer Bear' (pp. 71–74) and 'Brer Wolf, Brer Fox, and the Little Rabbits' (pp. 141–144) by Julius Lester from *The Tales of Uncle Remus: The Adventures of Brer Rabbit*. Text copyright © 1987 Julius Lester; Jonathan Cape Ltd and Alfred A. Knopf Inc., a division of Random House, Inc. for 'Snow White and the Seven Dwarfs' by Roald Dahl from *Revolting Rhymes*; Grafton Books, a division of Collins Publishing Group and Curtis Brown Ltd for part of Chapter 9 from *My Family and Other Animals* by Gerald Durrell, copyright © Gerald M. Durrell 1956; Eric Partridge for 'The Hole' © The Estate of Eric Partridge.

While every effort has been made to obtain permission, there may still be cases in which we have failed to trace a copyright holder, and we would like to apologize for any apparent negligence.